W9-BNO-381

"It seems the games are about to begin."

"What games?" I knew the answer before I'd asked the question though. My dream, my vision—it was the autumnal equinox, and finally Henry knew I was missing.

A sharp pain shot from my back to my abdomen, and I gasped. Cronus was at my side in an instant, exactly the way Henry would've been if he were here. I turned away.

"Calliope has decided it will happen today," he murmured, and his voice would have been comforting if it hadn't come from him.

"Decided what would happen today?" I struggled to stand and make it to the bathroom, but my legs gave out. Cronus's cool hands were there to steady me, but as soon as I was back on the bed, I jerked away from him.

"That your child would be born."

* * *

Select Praise for
Aimée Carter's
THE GODDESS TEST series

"The narrative is well executed, and Kate is a heroine better equipped than most to confront and cope with the inexplicable."
—*Publishers Weekly* on *The Goddess Test*

"*The Goddess Test* puts a fresh twist on the YA paranormal genre by infusing it with back-to-the-basics Greek mythology."
—Renee C. Fountain, *New York Journal of Books*

"Carter's writing is a delight to read—succinct, clean, descriptive. *Goddess Interrupted* is definitely a page-turner, one full of suspense, heartbreak, confusion, frustration and yes, romance."
—*YA Reads*

**Also by
Aimée Carter**

The Goddess Test Novels

THE GODDESS TEST

"The Goddess Hunt" (ebook)

GODDESS INTERRUPTED

THE GODDESS LEGACY

THE GODDESS INHERITANCE

THE
GODDESS
INHERITANCE

AIMÉE CARTER

HARLEQUIN®TEEN

If you purchased this book without a cover you should be aware that this book is stolen property. It was reported as "unsold and destroyed" to the publisher, and neither the author nor the publisher has received any payment for this "stripped book."

Recycling programs
for this product may
not exist in your area.

ISBN-13: 978-0-373-21067-1

THE GODDESS INHERITANCE

Copyright © 2013 by Aimée Carter

All rights reserved. Except for use in any review, the reproduction or utilization of this work in whole or in part in any form by any electronic, mechanical or other means, now known or hereafter invented, including xerography, photocopying and recording, or in any information storage or retrieval system, is forbidden without the written permission of the publisher, Harlequin Enterprises Limited, 225 Duncan Mill Road, Don Mills, Ontario M3B 3K9, Canada.

This is a work of fiction. Names, characters, places and incidents are either the product of the author's imagination or are used fictitiously, and any resemblance to actual persons, living or dead, business establishments, events or locales is entirely coincidental.

This edition published by arrangement with Harlequin Books S.A.

For questions and comments about the quality of this book, please contact us at CustomerService@Harlequin.com.

® and TM are trademarks of Harlequin Enterprises Limited or its corporate affiliates. Trademarks indicated with ® are registered in the United States Patent and Trademark Office, the Canadian Trade Marks Office and in other countries.

Printed in U.S.A.

T 17236

To Sarah Reck, whose patience and insight are true superpowers.

PROLOGUE

Throughout his eternal life, Walter had witnessed countless summers, but never one as endless as this.

He sat behind his glass desk, his head bowed as he read the petition before him, signed by nearly all of the minor gods and goddesses scattered throughout the world. Each vowed to stand aside and allow Cronus supremacy so long as it meant there would be no war. None of them seemed to understand that they were already in the middle of one.

Why would they? He and the remaining members of the council had done their jobs in shielding the world from Cronus's destruction, but they would not last much longer. When Cronus finally broke free from his island prison in the Aegean Sea, the petition would be what it was: a meaningless piece of parchment full of names of those who would be the first to die.

"Daddy?"

He exhaled and straightened, prepared to scold whoever dared to disturb him, but he stopped short. His daughter stood in the doorway, her hair golden as the perpetual sunset poured in through the windows behind Walter. She was the one person he would not turn away.

He set the petition aside. "Ava, my darling. I was not expecting you until morning. Is there news?"

The light gave her skin the illusion of color, but her eyes were dull and her face drawn. Watching her deteriorate since the winter solstice had been the most difficult thing Walter had ever done, but he had no choice. It was for the greater good, and for now the greater good trumped all, even his daughter's health.

"Iris is dead," she said, and Walter stilled. A great sorrow he had not felt in centuries filled him, and the perpetual sunlight seemed to darken.

"How?" he said, struggling to keep his voice steady. He had known sending his messenger to try to broker a cease-fire with Cronus was dangerous, as had Iris. It was war, and there would be casualties. But she had been willing to take that risk, and he had not imagined Cronus would go to such lengths against an ambassador.

"Nicholas finished the weapon an hour ago," she said. "Calliope wanted to test it."

Walter pressed his lips together. He hadn't thought it possible, but his son's skills were greater than even he had estimated. "Is there a body?"

"Calliope tossed her into the ocean," said Ava. "I brought her back for a proper wake."

Swallowing tightly, he forced himself to nod. "Very well. Thank you, my dear. I know how much of a risk that was for you. And because of that, I must insist you do no such thing in the future."

Ava hesitated, but after all their planning, after all their gambles, he knew she could not deny him now. Finally she nodded. "I'm sorry."

Walter opened his arms, and Ava crossed the room to curl up in his lap. He enveloped her, a shell of the daughter he knew, and buried his nose in her hair. "I am the one who is sorry, my darling, but we will do what we must to win. Is there any news of Kate?"

"Calliope says it will happen tomorrow."

At last, something was going right. "Then our wait is over."

"Doesn't matter," she mumbled into his shoulder. "It's been too long. She lost hope ages ago."

Nine months. That was how long Walter had been locked in a game of strategy and deception with the most powerful being on Earth. From the winter solstice to the autumnal equinox, he carried the weight of the world on his shoulders while hiding his burden from the remaining members of the council. With Henry's defection, they were all aware that their chances of winning against Cronus had gone from slim to none at all. Ava was their last hope of bringing Henry to their side.

"And you, my darling?" He brushed a lock of hair out of her eyes. Not even the weariness of the past year could diminish her beauty.

When Ava didn't answer right away, she confirmed his suspicions. He had seen her wilt before him, but never had she willingly shown her despair. She knew the stakes. She knew why they could not fail.

"I'm going to tell him."

At first he thought he had misheard her, but as she pulled away, her blue eyes steely, he knew he had not. "You know you mustn't," he said with both the gentle admonishment of a father and the command of a king. "We have worked too long to risk everything now."

"I thought it was just Kate." Her face became blotchy as it did when she was about to cry, and something tugged inside him. The paternal desire to stop her from hurting. But what could he do when his actions were wholly necessary to prevent pain even worse than what he was causing her? "I would've never agreed if I'd known she was pregnant. You know that."

"Yes, I know." He ran his fingers through her hair to soothe her, but she let out a choking sob. "I am sorry."

She pulled away from him and stumbled to her feet. "The moment Kate gives birth, Calliope's going to kill her—you know that. And you're going to let it happen anyway."

"Perhaps not," he countered. "You yourself have said that Cronus has taken a liking to her. Perhaps that will be enough."

"Perhaps?" said Ava, half-wild with frustration. "You're risking everything on a maybe, Daddy. You don't know for sure what's going to happen, and that poor baby—"

"We must do everything we can to ensure we win this war, no matter what we each must sacrifice." No matter how many had to die. "Now is not the time for holding back."

"It's not the time for unnecessary risks and careless mistakes either." She stormed toward the door. "I'm telling Henry everything."

"Ava."

His voice reverberated through the walls of the palace, shaking the very foundation of Olympus. Any trace of paternal affection was gone. It was the command of a king.

Ava stopped short. She had no choice, not after eons of obedience, and Walter felt a pang of guilt at speaking to her in such a way after all he had put her through. It was necessary, though. The fate of the world depended on it.

"You will not tell," he said. "Not until Kate gives birth."

"What's the difference between telling him now and telling him tomorrow?" said Ava shakily, but she held her ground. From anyone else, talking back would have only angered Walter, but he was simply glad to see she had some fight left.

"He will not stop until he has Kate back," said Walter. "But when he does, he will return to the Underworld and protect her with all his might, and he will continue not to involve himself in our war."

Her eyes widened. "Wait—you're using the baby as bait?"

"I will do what I must to bring Henry into the war," said Walter. "One life is not worth losing it all."

Ava stared at him as if she didn't recognize him. Though Walter rarely experienced fear, it coursed uncomfortably through him, like sludge in his veins instead of immortal blood. "It's a baby," she said. "You can't just— It's a *child*."

"If Henry does not participate in the war, then millions of children will die," said Walter. She had to understand; this was not a matter of obedience and pride. "I realize how difficult it is for you, my darling—"

"You do?" The venom in her voice made him fall short. He had never heard her speak to anyone that way before, least of all him, her father. Her protector. Her king. "It's my fault Kate's there in the first place. That baby might *die* because of me."

"I will do everything I can to ensure that does not happen," said Walter. "Once this is over—"

"You think this is ever going to be over?" hissed Ava. "When the council finds out we're risking Henry's child to get him involved, who are they going to blame, Daddy? Me or you?"

"I will inform the council of my role," said Walter.

"The only role the council's going to see is the one I played, and I'm going to fix it before that baby dies and I really do lose everyone I love."

Walter drew himself up to his full height. He may have looked like an old man, but next to the Titans, he was the most powerful being in the world, and he never let anyone forget it. Even his daughter. "I forbid it."

Ava laughed, but it was not the laugh of someone who found any joy in life; instead it was full of self-loathing and hopelessness. "Too late."

Before Walter could say a word, a heart-wrenching scream full of agony ripped from deep within the earth and rang throughout Olympus.

"He knows," said Ava, and without another word, she slipped through the door and closed it behind her.

CHAPTER 1
BIRTH

Henry.

I bolted upright in the darkness. My forehead was damp with sweat as the dream faded, but his scream enveloped me, imprinting itself on my memory.

Another vision, one of dozens I'd had since leaving the Underworld an eternity ago. This time, however, I wasn't watching Henry go about his life as ruler of the dead as he waited for me to return. I wasn't standing by helplessly as Ava gave Henry false updates about where in Africa we were supposedly searching for Rhea.

Finally Henry knew what had really happened, and in the minutes before dawn broke through the night, I clung to the hope that it wasn't too late.

"A nightmare, my dear?"

I shivered, and the candles scattered throughout my prison lit up. Cronus sat beside my bed, in the same chair he'd oc-cupied every night since late December, when I'd woken up with a pounding headache and memories I wished were nightmares.

This wasn't a nightmare, though. Cronus was here, working side by side with the Queen of the Gods, who would stop at nothing to hurt me as much as she possibly could.

The baby stirred inside me, undoubtedly unhappy about its rude awakening. I didn't dare speculate over whether it was a boy or a girl. If Calliope had her way, I might never know, and that heartache was already more than I could take. I set a hand on my swollen belly, so big that the simplest movements were difficult now, and mentally tried to soothe it. "You didn't hear that?" I said hoarsely.

"My son? Of course," said Cronus, reaching for my stomach. I slapped his hand away, and he chuckled. "It seems the games are about to begin."

"What games?" I knew the answer before I'd asked the question, though. My dream, my vision—it was the autumnal equinox, and finally Henry knew I was missing.

A sharp pain shot from my back to my abdomen, and I gasped. Cronus was at my side in an instant, exactly the way Henry would've been if he were here. I turned away.

"Calliope has decided it will happen today," he murmured, and his voice would have been comforting if it hadn't come from him.

"Decided what would happen today?" I struggled to stand and make it to the bathroom, but my legs gave out. Cronus's cool hands were there to steady me, but as soon as I was back on the bed, I jerked away from him.

"That your child would be born."

All the air left my lungs, and this time it had nothing to do with physical pain. He was bluffing. They were trying to scare me into labor before Henry rescued me, or—or something.

But as I leaned back, my hand found a wet spot on the mattress, and my damp nightgown clung to the back of my thighs. My water had broken sometime in the night. It was really happening.

Nine months of waiting. Nine months of fear. Nine months of time being the only thing standing between Calliope and the baby I was carrying, and now it was over.

I wasn't ready to be a mother. Never in a million years had I imagined having kids before I turned thirty, let alone twenty. But Calliope hadn't given me a choice, and with each day that passed, the sick dread inside me grew thicker until it nearly choked me. Calliope would take the baby from me, and there was nothing I could do about it. In a matter of hours, I would lose my child—Henry's child—to someone who wanted nothing more than to see me suffer.

But now he knew. Now there was a chance, if only I could hold on a little longer until Henry came.

Cronus must have seen the look on my face, because he chuckled and fluffed a pillow for me. "Do not worry, my dear. Calliope cannot kill you unless I allow her, and I assure you I would never hurt you."

It wasn't me I was worried about. "You're not going to hurt me, but you're going to let Calliope do it," I spat. "You're going to let her take the baby the moment it's born, and I'm never going to see it again."

Cronus stared at me blankly. These were the moments I remembered that in spite of his human form, he was anything but. He didn't understand why I loved the baby so much. Or, when I'd given Calliope too much attitude and she'd hit me in the mouth, why I'd instinctively covered my belly. He didn't get how badly the thought of being separated from the baby hurt me before I'd even met him or her.

Then again, Cronus was also the monster who'd tried to

destroy his own children, so I suspected empathy was too much to hope for.

"If you would like to keep the child, all you need to do is say the word," he said, as if it were that simple. Maybe to him it was. "I will ensure that Calliope does not get in the way. In return, all I ask is that you rule by my side."

It wasn't the first time he'd made that offer, and it wasn't the first time that, for a single moment, I entertained the possibility. As the baby's birth loomed, saying no grew more and more difficult.

Cronus had made no secret of the fact that he wanted me as his queen while he ruled over the entire world, destroying everyone who dared to get in his way. I had no idea why—the small bit of compassion I'd shown him in the Underworld, maybe, or because I hadn't fought him in the first war—but it didn't matter. I would be safe from the destruction, and so would the baby. Henry, however, would be the first person Cronus ripped apart, and the entire world would follow.

As much as I loved this baby, as much as I would have done anything to keep it safe, I couldn't stand by Cronus's side as he wiped out humanity. I couldn't do nothing as he killed every last person I loved, and if I agreed, he would keep me alive until the end of all things. I wouldn't have the choice to die like Persephone had, and I couldn't live with that guilt no matter how happy and safe my baby was.

But time was running out. The game had changed now that the council knew I was gone, and if I could keep Cronus guessing long enough not to hurt anyone, then maybe that would give the council a chance to find Rhea. So I lied.

"Promise not to kill anyone, and I'll think about it."

He grinned, showing off a full set of pearly teeth. Cronus had the smile of an airbrushed movie star, and it only made him more unnerving. "Is that so? Very well. Agree and I will leave humanity alone. My quarrels are not with them, and one must have subjects when one rules."

"I said *anyone*," I countered. "Not just humanity. You can't kill the council either."

Cronus eyed me, and I held my breath, hoping against hope I was worth this to him. I had to buy the council more time. "Surely you understand why my children must be contained, but I would be willing to…consider it, depending on the nature of our relationship. On how much you are willing to give." He ran his fingers through my hair, and I suppressed a shudder. "You and I, together for all eternity. Imagine, my dear, the beauty we would create. And of course your child will know your love, and you will never have to say goodbye."

I closed my eyes and pictured the moment I finally got to hold him or her. The baby would have dark hair, I was sure of it, and light eyes like me and Henry. Pink cheeks, ten fingers, ten toes, and I would love it instantly. I already did.

"You would be a mother," he murmured, his voice like a siren's call. "Forever there to love it, to nurture it, to raise it in your image. And I would be a father."

The spell he had over me shattered, and my eyes flew open. "You are *not* this baby's father," I said as another wave of pain washed over me. This was too fast. Contractions were supposed to come on slow and last for hours—my mother had been in labor for over a day when I was born.

Cronus leaned in until his lips were an inch from mine. I wrinkled my nose even though his breath smelled like a cool autumn breeze. "No, I am not. I am so much more."

The door burst open, and Calliope stormed inside. She had aged progressively over the past nine months until the angles on her face had become sharper, and she'd grown several inches to tower over me. As Cronus looked like Henry, with his long dark hair and gray eyes that crackled with lightning and fog, Calliope now looked like my mother. Like an older blond version of me. And I hated her even more for it.

"What's going on?" she said, and I managed a faint smirk. Apparently she'd overheard something she didn't like.

"Nothing for you to worry yourself about," said Cronus as he straightened, though his eyes didn't leave mine.

"Cronus was making me an interesting offer," I said, sounding braver than I felt. "Turns out he isn't going to feed me to the fish like you want."

Her lips twisted into a snarl, but before she could say a word, Ava hurried past her carrying a large basket full of blankets and other things I couldn't make out in the candlelight. "I'm sorry," she said, her face flushed.

"It's about time," snapped Calliope, and she focused on me again. "I'd be careful if I were you, Kate. I have a new toy, and I've been itching to try it out on you."

"What new toy?" I said through gritted teeth.

Calliope glided to the side of my bed. "Haven't I told you? Nicholas generously donated his time and expertise to forge a weapon that will let me kill a god. His timing couldn't be better."

My blood ran cold. Nicholas, Ava's husband, had been kidnapped on the winter solstice during battle. Up until now, no one had said a word to me about him.

"That's impossible," I blurted. Nothing but Cronus could kill an immortal.

"Is it?" said Calliope with a wicked smile. "Are you willing to bet your sweet little darling's life on that?"

My heart dropped. She was going to kill my baby? "Ava?" I said, my tongue heavy in my mouth.

Biting her lip, Ava set her basket down at the foot of the bed. "I'm sorry."

The room spun around me. This was just another game. Calliope was trying to scare me by using the people I loved most against me, and this time my supposed best friend was playing along.

What if it wasn't a game, though? Calliope had sworn she would take away the thing I loved the most, and at the time I thought she'd meant Henry and the rest of my family. But she'd meant the baby. She was about to get everything she wanted from me—there was no reason for her to lie. And the way Ava couldn't so much as look at me...

My throat swelled until I could barely breathe. "Get out."

Ava blinked. "But someone needs to be with you—"

"I'd rather have Calliope here than you, you traitorous bitch," I spat. "Get *out*."

Her eyes watered, and to my satisfaction, she fled, leaving me alone with Cronus and Calliope. Ava deserved this. She'd known what this would mean, that Calliope had every intention of slaughtering my baby. And if Calliope really had forced Nicholas to forge a weapon—if Ava had distracted the council for the past nine months to give him enough time—

I didn't care how much danger Nicholas was in. He was Calliope's son, and no matter how terrible a person she was, I couldn't imagine her killing her own child. But she was going to kill my baby without a second thought, and Ava had known the entire time.

Even if our positions had been reversed, even if Henry was the one Calliope held hostage, I would have never, ever done this to Ava. I would have never betrayed her and allowed Calliope to kill her child.

"That wasn't very nice," said Calliope in a singsong

voice, and my stomach churned. She couldn't kill the baby. I wouldn't let her.

"I need to pee," I said, pushing myself up.

Calliope made a vague gesture and busied herself with unpacking the basket. Cronus offered me his hand, but I brushed it off.

"I think I can make it to the bathroom on my own," I said.

Crossing the room hadn't been easy since August, and my body strained with each step I took, but I made it. My prison wasn't exactly plush, although it wasn't a concrete cell with a thin mattress and grungy toilet either. It was a simple bedroom with a bathroom attached, and it was several stories up, making a window escape impossible. I might've been immortal, but I didn't have a clue whether or not the baby was. And if Calliope really did have a weapon that could kill a god, it didn't matter anyway.

I'd tried to get away several times when I'd still been mobile enough to have a chance, but between Cronus, Calliope and Ava, someone had always been there to stop me. I'd made it as far as the beach once, but I couldn't swim and they knew it. The council may have intended this island to be Cronus's prison, but it was mine now, too.

Closing the door behind me, I eased down onto the edge of the bathtub and cradled my head in my hands. Frustration rose inside me, threatening to spill out in a great sob, but I swallowed it. I needed a moment, and crying would only make Calliope come in after me.

"Henry." I squeezed my eyes shut and tried to picture him. "Please. Help us."

At last I sank into my vision. After nearly a year in this hellhole, I'd learned how to control them, but I still struggled to make it far enough to see him. Three golden walls formed around me, and the fourth became a long pane of windows much like the room in Henry's palace. But instead of black rock, I saw endless blue sky through the glass, and sunlight poured in, illuminating everything.

"You did this." The sound of Henry's voice caught my attention, and I turned. He had Walter by the lapels, and his eyes burned with anger and power I'd never seen before.

"It had to be done," said Walter unsteadily. Even he looked afraid. "We need you, brother, and if this is what it takes to get you to see that—"

Henry threw Walter against the wall so hard that it fractured, leaving a web of cracks behind. "I will see you pay for this if it is the last thing I do," he growled.

"Enough." My mother's voice rang out, and both brothers turned toward her. She looked pale, and she folded her hands in front of her the way she did when she was trying to keep herself under control. "We will rescue Kate. There is still time, and the more we waste—"

"We cannot risk our efforts for the life of one," said Walter.

"Then I will," snarled Henry.

Walter shook his head. "It is far too dangerous for you to go alone."

"He won't be alone," said my mother. "And if you value your hold over the council—"

The muscles in my back and belly contracted, and the pain pulled me from my vision. Back in the bathroom, I let out a soft sob. My mother was wrong—we were out of time. The baby was coming no matter how hard I tried to wait. Calliope would kill it, and there was no one here to stop her. Whether or not anyone came, there was no way out of this. Even if Henry and my mother did attack the island, there was no guarantee they would break through Cronus's defenses, and by then it would be too late anyway.

The baby nudged me from the inside, and I forced myself

to pull it together. I had to do this. I couldn't break down. The baby's life depended on it.

"I'm sorry," I whispered, gently pressing against the spot where it had kicked me. "I love you, okay? I'm not going to stop fighting until you're safe, I promise."

Someone rapped on the door, and I jumped. "Don't think you're going to give birth in the bathtub," said Calliope. "You're not having that baby until I say you are."

"Just a minute," I called, and I stood long enough to turn on the faucet and drown out my whispers in case she was eavesdropping. It wouldn't do much good, but the illusion of privacy would have to be enough for now.

Easing back down onto the edge of the bathtub, I rubbed my belly. "Your dad's really great, and you'll get to see him soon, okay? He's not going to let Calliope do this to you either, and he's way more powerful than me. The whole family is. Today is probably going to be scary, and it'll hurt—well, it'll hurt me, I won't let them hurt you—but in the end, it'll be okay. I promise."

It wasn't an empty promise. Even if I had to die in the process, Calliope would not touch my baby. No matter what it took, I would make sure of it.

Labor progressed so quickly that I barely made it out of the bathroom. Calliope gave me nothing to help, no medication or words of encouragement, and though Cronus remained by my side, he said nothing as my contractions grew closer and closer together. They had to know the others were coming. There was no other reason to force the baby out like this, and I couldn't imagine Calliope giving up the chance to make me hurt as long as possible, not unless it was dire.

I refused to scream. Even in the final moments of labor, as the baby ripped through my body, I clenched my jaw and pushed through the pain. Since I'd become immortal, the only thing that had hurt me was Cronus, and apparently giving birth was another exception. My body was doing this to itself, and immortality wasn't going to stop it.

The moment the baby left me, I felt as if my heart had been ripped from my chest and now rested in Calliope's arms. She straightened, and a lump formed in my throat as I saw the wrinkled, bloody infant she held. "It's a boy," she said, and she smiled. "Perfect."

Somehow, despite the words I'd whispered to him, the hours I'd spent feeling him kick, and the months I'd carried him, he had never felt completely real. But now—

That was my son.

That was my *son,* and Calliope was going to kill him.

She didn't need any tools to cut the cord or finish the rest of the messy birth; in the blink of an eye, everything was clean, and the baby was wrapped in a white blanket. As if she'd done it a thousand times before, she cradled him and stood, leaving me alone on the bed.

"Wait," I said in a choked voice. I was exhausted and drenched in sweat, and despite the pain, I struggled to get up. "You can't—please, I'll do anything, just don't hurt my son."

His wails, so tiny and helpless, filled the room, and my heart crumbled. Every bone in my body demanded that I stand, that I go to him and save him from the pain that awaited him, but I couldn't move. The harder I struggled, the more I froze, and the more my body ached.

Calliope looked at me, her eyes bright and full of malice. She was enjoying this. She was reveling in my pain. "That's not for you to decide, dear Kate."

At the edge of my vision, I saw Cronus shift. "You will not hurt the child," he said, his voice low and full of thunder. "That is not a request."

Her eyes narrowed. She was going to challenge him. Use my son to prove her dominance—that she was the one in control. But she wasn't, and she knew it. And for the first time since I'd heard of the King of the Titans, I was grateful for him.

"Fine," she said in an annoyed voice, as if she were only letting him win because she wanted to. We both knew the truth. "I won't kill him."

Relief swept through me like a drug, and I released the breath I'd been holding. Because of Cronus, he would live. "Please, can I—can I hold my son?"

"Your son?" Her arms tightened around the baby, and a mockery of a smile curled across her lips. "You must be mistaken. The only child in this room belongs to me."

Without another word, she walked through the door in a cloud of victory, leaving me empty and utterly alone.

She wouldn't take his life—that meant there was still time. But how long would it take before she got tired of obeying Cronus and killed the baby just to watch me bleed?

I had to get to him. I had to save him. Even if Calliope didn't touch a hair on his head, the thought of him being raised by that monster, twisted into something black and beyond recognition—if my time in the Underworld had taught me anything, that kind of life was infinitely worse than the peace of death.

Desperation clawed at me, tearing me up from the inside out, and I slowly turned toward Cronus.

His queen. My life, my choices, my freedom for my son's.

"Please," I said, hiccupping. "I'll do anything."

He brushed his cold fingers against my tearstained cheek, and this time I didn't move away. "Anything?"

The words were like knives on my tongue, but I said

them anyway. "Anything," I whispered. "Save him and—and I'm yours."

Cronus leaned toward me, stopping when his lips were only inches from mine. "As you wish, my queen."

Fire spread through my body, burning heat replacing the aches of giving birth as Cronus healed me. It was worth it. Henry would understand, and somehow, someway, I would unite him with the baby.

Dizzy with hope, I sat up and touched my flat stomach. Somehow Cronus had returned my body to the way it had been before I'd become pregnant, and the missing swell of my belly and chest was disorienting. Why not leave me with the ability to feed the baby? Because he knew it wouldn't matter? But before I could say a word, the world began to shake.

"What—" I began, gripping the edge of the mattress, but something in the corner caught my attention. The sky through my window was bathed in an unnatural golden light, and around us the entire island quaked violently.

"I will return, my dear, and then we shall be together," said Cronus. He pressed his cold lips to my cheek, and in an instant he was gone, but I didn't care.

In the distance, a black cloud approached, sizzling with lightning. Though Cronus himself couldn't escape the island, it passed through the barrier the council had created as if it were nothing, and I spotted the silhouette of a man on top of it. Hope swelled within me, and I didn't have to see his face to know who the dark figure was.

Henry.

CHAPTER 2

BLOOD AND STONE

For nine months, I'd dreamed of this moment. In my visions I'd watched Henry go about his day-to-day duties, oblivious to what was happening as he waited for me to come home, and I'd wished with every fiber of my being for him to realize something was wrong and come storming through the doors of my prison. I'd wanted it so badly that I'd ached with the need to leave the island, to leave Calliope and Cronus and all of my greatest fears behind.

Now I might finally have the chance, and I couldn't go. No matter what was waiting out there for me—Henry, my mother, a family, a war to win—I couldn't leave my son.

Henry flew toward the palace, and I searched the skies behind him for the other members of the council. Nothing but that unnatural gold. My chest tightened. He couldn't be alone. He wasn't that careless. He didn't have the power to hold off Cronus in the Underworld, let alone outside his realm.

Where was my mother? Even if the others had no interest in helping me, surely she would have come to protect Henry. Had he insisted she not, that it was too dangerous?

When he was close enough for me to see the rage on his face, it hit me. He was alone.

We were alone.

I expected him to turn the outside wall to rubble, but instead he flew over my room toward another part of the castle, as if he didn't know I was there. Maybe he didn't. Maybe Calliope was trying to lure him away and—

The weapon.

Oh, god.

"Henry!" I screamed. *"Henry!"*

"Kate," said a voice from the hallway. "Kate, it's me."

I hurried to the door, crouching down beside it to peer through the keyhole. "Henry? Is that—"

A blue eye with long lashes stared back at me, and my heart sank. Ava.

"Move away from the door," she whispered, glancing over her shoulder. What was she so afraid of? Henry storming down the hall and blasting her to pieces? If only I were so lucky.

"Why should I trust you?" I said. "You knew Calliope was going to kill my son, and you did everything you could to make that happen."

She blinked rapidly, and her eyes turned red and watery. Once upon a time I'd thought Ava had been one of the few who looked pretty when she cried, but now all I could see was the ugliness underneath.

For months I'd learned about the antics of the Greek gods, the history that was the foundation of their mythology. Not

all of it was right—so much of it had been twisted and corrupted throughout history as mortals passed the stories down.
And because of that, I'd wanted to believe that the gods
were basically good. That they really were looking out for
humankind, that their lives hadn't been full of mischief and
betrayal and selfishness.

Regardless of what Calliope and Cronus had done, Ava
could've proven me right. A single word to the council, and
this could've been over months ago. Instead she'd turned all
of those hopes to dust.

"I'm sorry," she whispered. "You're my best friend, Kate.
Please—I never meant for any of this to happen. I didn't
know."

"You knew enough."

She checked over her shoulder again. "Once this is over,
you can rip me to shreds as much as you want. But right now
I have to get you out of here."

I scoffed. Now Ava wanted to rescue me, after Calliope
had exactly what she wanted? "Like hell I'm going anywhere
with you."

"I can take you to your son."

My heart pounded. In an instant, my disgust turned to
desperation, and it took everything I had not to claw the
door open with my fingernails. "You know where he is?"

Ava nodded. "And if you let me, I can help both of you
get out of here."

That was all I needed to hear. Forget the past nine months.
Forget her betrayal. Forget the very real possibility that this
was just another trap to make sure Henry couldn't find me.
If there was a chance she was telling the truth, if there was
a chance I could save my son, I didn't care.

I stepped back, and a breeze filled the room. The lock
clicked, and the door swung open, revealing Ava. Now that

it was light outside, I could see her properly. Her blond hair hung in limp curls, and the shadows made the dark circles underneath her eyes look hideous. I'd never seen her like this before, not even the night I'd met Henry by the river in Eden—the same night she'd taken a swan dive into the raging waters and crushed her skull against a rock.

Would I have saved her if I'd known less than a year and a half later, she would steal me away from everyone I love? That she would stand by Calliope as she manipulated me into a pregnancy only so she could hurt me as badly as humanly possible?

Would I have saved her if I'd known Ava had been fully aware of Calliope's plan to kill my son the whole time?

I didn't know. I didn't care. If Ava helped save him, if she helped us escape, the past nine months wouldn't matter anymore. I would never forget, but in time I might forgive.

I hurried out the door. Ava offered me her arm, but I pulled away. The thought of touching her made my stomach lurch. "Don't bother. Cronus healed me. Which way?"

Ava wilted and dropped her hand, and a pang of guilt ran through me before I pushed it aside. She didn't deserve my sympathy. We moved at an agonizingly slow pace, all but tiptoeing down the slate-paved corridor. Was I right? Was she just hiding me away so Henry couldn't find me?

Didn't matter. I had to try.

Crack.

The walls around us shook, and Ava flung herself at me, covering my body with hers as the ceiling came crashing down around us. The back of my head slammed against the wall, but even though I expected pain, it never came. I was immortal now. Even if the entire world buried us, we would never die.

"Are you all right?" said Ava, gasping. The air had turned to thick dust, and as I sucked in a breath, the grit choked me.

"Need to keep going," I said, coughing. Henry wouldn't ask any questions—the moment he got his hands on me, he would take me back down to the Underworld. We had to find the baby before Henry found me.

I climbed over the rubble, groping my way through the dust as sharp edges tried to cut my impermeable skin. My foot caught on a rock I couldn't see, and I stumbled, throwing my arms out to catch my fall. But instead a pair of strong hands caught me, and I looked up.

Dark hair, handsome face, broad shoulders. Henry.

I blinked rapidly, my eyes tearing up to flush out the dust, and his face swam into focus.

No, not Henry.

Cronus.

"Come, my dear," he murmured, pulling me to my feet. His palms were hot coals against my skin, and bile rose in my throat. Where was Henry? Why wasn't Cronus trying to stop him?

Because he didn't need to. One god versus the King of the Titans—there was no question. And with Calliope's weapon, it wouldn't be a fair fight between siblings either. Henry wouldn't know what was coming, and then—

I clenched my fists. I had to find the baby before Henry found me, and I had to find Henry before it was too late. No other option was acceptable.

"I want to see my son," I said, jerking my arm away from Cronus and struggling to keep my voice steady. To my left, a gaping hole in the stone wall opened up to a golden sky and the sound of waves crashing against the shore. "Take me to him."

"All in good time." He led me through the wrecked corridor, and the rubble swept aside to make a path for us. For him. Ava trailed after us, dragging her feet and scattering the pebbles as if she were trying to make as much noise as possible. A warning to Calliope that we were coming? A signal to Henry to tell him where we were?

Suddenly the air changed as the dust vanished, and the salt-tinged wind blowing off the sea gave way to the thin wails of a newborn. I blinked. It'd been a long time since I'd slipped into a vision without meaning to.

I was surrounded by walls painted to resemble a sunset, and the room was empty except for a white cradle in the center. A lump formed in my throat, and I peered over the edge, barely daring to hope.

There, wrapped in a knit blanket, was my son.

His sobs paused, and he cracked open his eyes as if he were staring directly at me. But that was impossible—he couldn't see me. No one could see me in my visions. I was an observer. Less than a ghost; I was nothing.

The lure of his blue eyes was irresistible, and I reached out to touch him. For a split second I imagined the warmth of his smooth skin and tiny fingers, and a smile crept onto my face.

"Hi," I whispered. "You're such a handsome little man."

He stared up into the space I occupied, and I could hardly breathe. He was perfection.

"Milo." The name left my mouth before I could think about it, but once it was out, it seemed to wrap around the baby, becoming as much a part of him as his dark hair or how much I loved him.

Yes. Milo.

An enraged cry broke the spell between us, and Milo's sobs returned, even louder than before. I tried to touch him again, to offer whatever small measure of comfort I could if he really could sense I was there, but my hand passed through him. His screams only grew shriller.

"Calliope!"

I froze. Henry.

Torn between leaving Milo or finding Henry, I lingered near the cradle. As much as it killed me to leave the baby, I had to know where Henry was. If he was outside the nursery—if he knew about Milo and was going to save him—

Please, please, please let him know.

I dashed through the open door and into a part of the palace I'd never seen before. The walls were a rich gold, not stone like the ones inside my prison, and the indigo rug matched the silk curtains that hung every ten feet on the outside wall. The hallway stretched nearly the entire length of the palace, and Calliope stood in the middle, only a few feet away from Henry.

He'd saved me from the clutches of death on the banks of the river in Eden. He'd fought for all our lives as Calliope choked me with chains in Tartarus. He was Lord of the Underworld, King of the Dead, and one of the most powerful gods in history.

But never had I seen him look so terrible in his power. It rolled off of him in black waves, shaking the very foundation of the palace, and even though I wasn't really there, for the first time in my life I was genuinely afraid of him.

Satisfaction mingled with that fear though, and disdain ripped through me as I approached Calliope. Henry would end her. Whatever this weapon was she claimed to have, it couldn't possibly match up to the pure rage that surrounded him, fueling his power. Only a Titan could kill a god, and Calliope was exactly like me: immortal. Nothing more.

A blast shook the walls, and panic shot through me. Milo. Henry had no idea he was here, that Calliope stood between him and his son. He might not even know he existed. And if he brought down the entire castle—

All it would take was a single thought, and our son would die.

I dashed into the nursery, but before I could spot Milo's face over the edge of the cradle, the sunset walls disappeared.

It took me several seconds to regain my bearings. Cronus held my arm, his hands still fire against my skin, and Ava lingered on my other side. We stood in a gold-and-indigo corridor, but it was empty.

Was it over? Had we missed it?

No, impossible. My visions were always in the present. I couldn't go into the past or see the future. Henry and Calliope were somewhere nearby. They had to be. Above us, below—

"Kate, my dear." Cronus's voice cut through me like a dagger made of ice. "Are you mine?"

Never. Not in a million years, not if we were the last two beings in the universe. Not if the only other choice I had was to live out eternity buried under boulders.

But only moments stood between now and the entire castle ripping apart at the seams, and I had to save Milo. If that meant making a promise I couldn't keep, then I would deal with the consequences later. "Give me my son, and I'm yours."

My feet left the ground as Cronus floated us upward, leaving Ava behind. Together we passed through the ceiling as if it weren't even there, rising into the hallway above us, and I held my breath.

We stood only a few feet behind Calliope, and beyond her, surrounded by dark power—

Henry.

He and I stared at each other across the hallway, and

my knees nearly buckled with relief. At last, someone who loved me.

He took an involuntary step toward me, but even though it was the first time I'd seen him since the winter solstice, my body pulled me in the direction of Milo's room. Only a few feet away, two doors behind Calliope, and I'd be able to hold my son. I'd have a chance at saving us all.

Cronus gripped my arm, his fingers a cuff of flesh and bone, and no amount of subtle tugging and twisting loosened them. I was as trapped as I'd been in my prison, but this time both pieces of my heart dangled in front of me, taunting me. Begging me to do something.

I was powerless.

In my mind, hours passed, but in reality it took Calliope only seconds to realize what was going on. She turned and grinned, her eyes sparkling with malice, and something slid from the loose sleeve of her gown into her hand. A dagger.

The blade glowed with the same essence that had infused the chains she'd wrapped around my neck, the same opaque power that had threaded through the rock she'd used to knock me unconscious the day she'd kidnapped me. She hadn't been lying, after all. Somehow, even though Cronus stood beside me whole and solid, she'd managed to separate a piece of him from the rest. And now she had the power to kill every last one of us until she was free to rule the universe at Cronus's side.

"Perfect timing," she said, her voice as girly as ever, but regality saturated each syllable.

"Kate?" Henry's voice broke, and the waves of dark power around him faltered. No, no, no, he couldn't stop now. She'd attack the first chance he gave her.

I took a step back. Forget subtlety. Like hell I was letting Cronus keep me from my family. "Don't let them follow me,"

I said to Henry, and without warning, I wrenched my arm from Cronus as hard as I could, pulling against his thumb. The weakest part of his grip—if he had any weak spots at all.

Maybe I managed to take him by surprise, or maybe he was simply amused and wanted to see what I would do, but Cronus didn't fight me. He let go, and before anyone could say a word, I tore down the hallway and into the nursery.

Milo lay in the cradle, crying softly, and I ached to finally touch him. How was it possible that minutes before, we'd been connected? How had I ever allowed my body to let him go?

"It's all right," I whispered, reaching for him. He calmed, and this time when his blue eyes met mine, I knew he saw me. "I won't let anything happen to you."

The moment my fingers brushed his downy cheek, someone cleared their throat behind me, and I turned. Calliope stood framed in the doorway, and she held the dagger to Henry's throat.

All of the air escaped my lungs. This was it. He was going to die. I was going to lose my husband, my baby, my entire family to a crazy goddess who didn't care who she hurt, so long as she got her way. So long as she got to torture me.

"Don't hurt him—you can't, please," I whispered, clutching the edge of the cradle. Henry's eyes were open, and he stared at me—no, not at me. Beyond me. He stared at Milo. It was a small comfort, knowing that he would die with the knowledge he had a son. That at least he would have this moment.

"*Please,*" spat Calliope, a mockery of my desperation. "Always please, as if that's enough. You know it isn't, Kate. Why bother?"

It didn't matter if nothing I ever did was enough; I had to try. I couldn't live with myself if I surrendered and let her have everything that mattered to me. "You love him. If you kill him, you'll never have him. You'll lose."

She scoffed, but a hint of doubt flashed across her face. "I'll be the queen of the world. I'll never lose again."

"Being queen won't make you happy." I studied the way she held Henry. He could break her grip if she lowered the knife. All we needed was that split second, and I could distract her long enough for Henry to take the baby and disappear. "You'll still be alone. You'll still be miserable."

Calliope's eyes narrowed. "Whatever it is you think you're doing, it won't work. I don't need him anymore."

"Then what do you want?"

"I already have exactly what I want." Behind her, Cronus loomed, somehow taller than he had been moments before. The power radiating from Henry was gone now. "First I'm going to kill Henry, and then I'm going to kill your mother and every single member of the council. Once I'm done, when the world kneels at my feet, I will hold your son, and he will call me mother and you a traitor. And together, we will watch you die."

Henry roared and struggled against her, coming to life at last, but whatever chained him held strong. She pressed the blade to his throat. This wasn't about winning anymore—she knew she had me, and I knew this was the end. Now it was about causing me as much pain as possible.

The joke was on her, though. Without Henry, without my mother, without my son, I would welcome death.

Focus. This couldn't be it. There had to be something I could do—some magical combination of words I could say to get her to lower that dagger. Anything.

Behind me, Milo's cries grew louder, and I groped around until I touched his hand. This was it. These were the only few moments I would have with him. Despite the dagger to

Henry's throat, I would have given anything to make them last forever.

"Then kill me," I blurted. "Right now, in front of Henry, in front of the baby—just do it. Because I promise if you hurt either of them, I will make sure you spend eternity burning in Tartarus."

Calliope tilted her head, and I held my breath. She had to agree. Anything to get her to lower that knife, to give Henry that split-second advantage—anything.

But before she could say a word, Cronus exhaled, and fog crept across the floor of the nursery. "No." The word was barely a whisper, but it burrowed inside me, refusing to be ignored. "You will not harm Kate, my daughter. If she dies, so will you."

Behind the flush of her excitement, Calliope paled. "You can either keep Kate or her spawn alive. Not both. Choose."

"I have already told you what you will do," said Cronus. "You will obey me, or you will be the one to die. That is your choice to make, not mine."

Clenching her jaw, she dug the blade deeper into Henry's skin, and he winced. *Forget me.* His voice echoed through my mind as clearly as if he'd spoken. *Do whatever you must to escape before it's too late.*

"No," I whispered, and Henry narrowed his eyes. He could glare at me all he wanted. I wasn't leaving, not without him. Not without the baby.

Though she was still pale, Calliope's lips twisted into a smirk. "How cute. You can try all you want, but she isn't getting out of here ali—" She stopped. "What's that?"

Cronus's expression went blank, and I twisted around, searching for whatever it was that had caught her attention. What was what?

Calliope's gaze unfocused, and her smirk faltered. "Father, do something," she hissed, and at last I heard it.

The distant rumble of thunder, growing louder with each passing second.

The crack of lightning that lit up the sky beyond the indigo curtains in the hallway.

A burst of wind so strong that it howled through the corridors.

And a dozen war cries blending together, forming a fearsome harmony.

The council had arrived.

Calliope's face went from pale to ashen, and her grip on Henry slipped. I didn't think. In that moment, I memorized the feel of my son's tiny hand in mine, and I let go.

As fast as I could, I hurtled toward Henry and Calliope, knocking him out of the way. Grabbing her fist, I smashed her knuckles against the wall to make her let go of the dagger. She wasn't human though, and just like me, she couldn't feel pain. No matter how much force I used, it was pointless.

But I had to buy Henry enough time to grab Milo and leave. Together we struggled, goddess against goddess, and I let out an enraged cry. Something inside me took over, something primal. As Calliope fought, so did I, with everything I had.

"Cronus!" shrieked Calliope, but he vanished into an eerie fog. His true form. With a dozen screaming gods surrounding the castle, no matter how powerful he was, he had no choice but to fight. He wouldn't be any help to her now.

Calliope must have realized the same thing, because with a surge of power, she shoved me, and we toppled to the ground. She twisted my neck, and I scratched her face, attempting to gouge out her eyes, but neither of us could hurt the other.

"You bitch," she snarled. "You conniving, useless bitch."

"Can't kill me." I worked my fingers around the handle of the dagger and struggled to pull it from her grip. "I die, you die, remember?"

"Father won't touch a hair on my head."

"Are you willing to bet your entire existence on that?"

She screeched and wrenched the dagger from me. I had no chance against her immense strength, and I watched in horror as my grip slipped and the tip of the infused blade plunged into my arm.

White-hot pain ripped through me, burning everything in its path, infinitely worse than the brush of fog against my leg during my botched coronation ceremony nearly a year before. This was inside me, fusing together with my very being, choking it until only a few pitiful gasps remained.

I was dying. Two more seconds, and I'd be—

A black blur slammed into her. As the weight of Calliope's body disappeared, the choke hold vanished. Agony burned inside me, leaving me breathless, and fire replaced the ice of the blade as I bled freely. What was happening?

I opened my eyes, half expecting to see wherever gods went when they died, but instead all I saw was Calliope's maniacal grin as she lay on the floor beside me.

No, that wasn't all. Henry hovered above her, pressed oddly against her body at an angle I didn't understand. His eyes widened, his mouth dropped open, and his hands clutched something against his ribs.

"I win," whispered Calliope. And as she pulled the bloody dagger from Henry's chest, I finally understood.

CHAPTER 3

THE DARKEST HOUR

For four years, I'd stayed by my mother's bedside and watched her fade away. Her once strong and healthy body had withered into a poor imitation of the woman I remembered, and not an hour had passed without me imagining what it would be like the day death claimed her.

I'd lived in constant fear of waking up and finding her gone, a shell where my mother had once been. I would watch the clock flip over to midnight and wonder if that was the date I would mourn each year for the rest of my life.

I knew what it was like to lose. I knew what it was like to fight the inevitable.

But none of that had prepared me for watching Henry die.

Blood spurted from the wound in his chest. He fell to his knees, one hand clutching his rib cage, the other reaching for me. I'd never seen such real terror in his eyes. Gods weren't supposed to die. Not unless they wanted to.

I reached for him with my good arm as the life drained from him. Was the blade strong enough to kill me, too? Once it was over, would we be together on the other side, wherever that might lead?

Was there even another side for the Lord of the Dead?

The moment our fingers met, my body lurched. It was a familiar feeling—much more jolting than I'd ever experienced before, but the instant it happened, I knew. We were going home.

One second, I was only feet away from Milo as he cried. The next I lay in a heap with Henry, and silence surrounded us. We weren't in Calliope's palace anymore. We weren't even on the island. But we weren't in the Underworld either, or at least any part of it I'd ever seen.

Instead we were in the middle of a massive room devoid of anything but a sky-blue ceiling and sunset floor. The golden walls seemed to stretch out forever, and with the sun in the middle of the ceiling as if it were a real sky, everything glittered with light. It should've taken my breath away.

But Milo was gone. Wherever we were, I knew instinctively he wouldn't be joining us, and unspeakable pain spread like acid inside me. I would have gladly been stabbed a thousand times over rather than feel this for even a moment.

There was nothing I could do, though. My mother was on the island with him, along with James and the rest of the council, and that would have to be enough. The only person I had a prayer of helping now had me pinned to the sunset floor.

"Henry." Even though the last thing I wanted to do was hurt him, I had no choice but to roll him gently off me. Blood soaked through his shirt, and I pressed my hands against his chest in an attempt to stop the flow, but it was useless. After everything we'd gone through together, after everything he'd done to protect me, I couldn't do a damn thing to save him. It wasn't fair. It wasn't *fair*.

"Kate?" His voice was thick and hoarse, as if he were ill, but he wasn't. He was dying. "Are you—are you all right?"

"I'm fine," I lied, and my voice broke. "Don't sit up. You're losing too much blood." How much did gods have in them? The same as mortals? How much could they live without?

"I didn't know," he whispered. "I thought— Ava said—"

"It's not your fault." I shakily brushed my mouth against his. He tasted like rain. "None of this is your fault. I should've never trusted her. I should've never left you. I'm sorry."

He kissed me back weakly. "Was that—was that baby…"

A lump formed in my throat. "Yeah. He's your son." I managed a watery smile. At least Henry knew. "I named him Milo. We can call him something different if you'd like."

"No." He coughed, and a few droplets of blood stained his lips. "It's perfect. So are you."

I leaned against his chest, putting as much weight on the wound as possible. I refused to say goodbye like this. Not to Henry, not to our life together, none of it. I wasn't ready, and Milo deserved to have a father. I hadn't had one growing up, and like hell would I let him experience that same emptiness and uncertainty. He deserved more than that. He deserved to have a family.

My arm bled freely, and within moments the room began to spin. Henry's moonlit eyes remained open, and he smiled. "Never thought I'd have a son." His voice trembled. "Never thought I'd have you."

I gritted my teeth against the dizziness, my body growing weaker by the second. "You're going to have me for a hell of a lot longer than this." My vision blurred, and I struggled to look around us. Where was everyone? Why couldn't they feel the life drain from Henry the way I could?

Because it wasn't his life I felt draining away. It was mine. "Kate? Henry?"

My mother's voice washed over me, and I let out an exhausted sob. "Mom?"

She knelt beside me, radiating warmth and the scent of apples and freesia. "Let go, sweetheart," she murmured. "I've got you."

I couldn't force my hands from Henry, though. He was cold now, his eyes wide and unblinking, and his chest was still. Gods didn't need to breathe, but Henry always had. His heart had always beaten, but now I saw no hint of a pulse.

He was dead.

I didn't remember the others appearing. One moment my mother held me against her chest, her hand wrapped around my bleeding arm as I screamed and cried and disappeared into myself. The next, Walter hovered over us, and Theo knelt beside Henry's body, his lips moving at a furious pace.

"Get her out of here," said Walter, his booming voice distant as I cowered in a dark corner in the recesses of my mind. Gentle hands lifted me, and I thought I heard James's voice murmuring words of comfort I didn't understand, but outwardly I thrashed and shrieked. I couldn't leave Henry. If I left him, I would never see him again, and then he really would be gone.

He couldn't be, though. He just couldn't be.

Another pair of hands joined us, but I was so completely submerged into myself that I might as well have closed my eyes and disappeared in the dark. In here, nothing could touch me. In here, Henry was everywhere. In here, it was winter again, and we curled up together underneath the down comforter in the Underworld as the hours passed by. His chest was warm under my palm, and his heart beat against my fingers, steady and eternal. In here, no one died.

A whimper caught my attention, and I opened my eyes again. The golden room was gone, replaced by the sunset nursery in Calliope's palace, and my heart sank. There, lying in the cradle, was Milo. My mother hadn't saved him, after all.

I stood beside him, pretending I could touch him and rock him to sleep. Pretending that it wasn't just a matter of time before the Titan fire in my veins consumed me and Milo would be orphaned. I had never known my father, but I treasured the time I'd spent with my mother. Milo would never have that either. The only time we would have together were those few seconds before Calliope had killed his father, and he would never remember them.

No, we had now. Even if he didn't know I was with him, I could be there. I would be. Settling in beside his cradle, I watched him unblinkingly, soaking in every second.

And I waited for the inevitable to come.

Kate.

James's voice floated toward me and wound its way through what was left of my heart. I blinked. How long had it been? Minutes? Hours? Days? No, Calliope might have been a monster, but she wouldn't have left Milo alone for that long. He slept soundly in the cradle, his little chest rising and falling. I took comfort in each breath.

Come back, Kate.

His words were a whisper against my ear, but I stayed put. There was nothing left for me in reality. My mother had lived for eons before I'd been born; she could do without me once more. She would have to.

The air grew thick with annoyance. *Kate, I swear, if you don't come back, I will tell Henry you kissed me. And that you said I have a nice ass.*

"Henry?" My eyes flew open—my real eyes this time. As it had each time before, the wrench of leaving Milo took my breath away, and fuzzy shapes floated in front of me until I managed to focus.

A sky-blue ceiling and undoubtedly a sunset floor. But unlike the room bathed in golden light, this was different. Smaller, muted, and darker somehow.

Frantically I looked around the room for any sign of Henry, but he wasn't there. James's sick idea of a joke then, to pull me away from the only thing that gave me any small measure of comfort now.

"How are you feeling?" My mother hovered beside my bed, applying a compress of something that smelled like honey and tangerines to my arm. Noticing my stare, she smoothed my hair back and offered me a small smile that didn't meet her eyes. "A compress to stop the pain. You'll have to wear a sling, but it won't spread anywhere else for now."

I shook my head. "Take it off."

"What?" Her brow knitted. "Sweetheart, this is saving your life—"

"I don't want it." I sat up, and my body screamed in protest as I ripped the compress from my arm. It didn't matter. Henry was dead, and I would never hold my son again. I didn't want anyone to save my life.

My mother set her hand against my good shoulder, and firmly but gently, she guided me back onto the bed. I didn't have the strength to fight her. "Too bad. I'm your mother, and whether you like it or not, I'm not going to let you die on my watch."

I sniffed, staring at the cloudless ceiling. "I can't do this, Mama." I hadn't called her that since the second grade, when the most popular girl in my New York City private school had overheard and proceeded to tease me for the next four years.

"Can't do what?" She laid the compress on my arm again, and though it hurt like hell, the pain didn't spread.

"I had a baby," I whispered. Did she even know she was a grandmother? Did she know about Calliope's plot? Or did she think I'd run off with Ava for nine months and forgotten about her?

She hesitated, not meeting my eyes. "I know. I'm so sorry, Kate."

That was it. Simple acknowledgment. No offer to find him. No promise to take him from Calliope the first chance she got. I swallowed thickly, half an inch away from hysteria. "His name's Milo. Henry—Henry liked that name."

"I'm sure he still does." James's voice filtered through the haze around me.

"Still does?" My voice cracked, and though my mother held me down, I raised my head. James leaned against the open doorway, his blond hair tousled and his cheeks flushed, as if he'd run a marathon. Or maybe it was because I hadn't seen him in the sunlight for so long.

"He's in another room. Theo's tending to him," he said. Theo, the member of the council with the ability to heal wounds caused by Titans. Or if not heal, at least make them less painful.

Was it possible? The way Henry's eyes had stared unseeingly, the lack of heartbeat, of any effort at all to keep his body going—it couldn't be. "Is Henry alive?"

The moment between my question and James's answer lasted for an eternity. All at once I needed to hear it, yet I didn't want to know. I could have clung to the delicious hope James gave me for the rest of my endless life. Henry could always be in the next room over, alive and waiting for me.

"Yes," he said, and I let out a soft sob. My mother touched my cheek, but I looked past her, focusing on my best friend.

"Can I see him? I need to see him." Forget lying still. I struggled to sit up again, but for a second time, my mother held me down, more insistent than before.

"You can see him as soon as you're well enough," she said, but she glanced at James, and they exchanged a look I didn't understand.

"What?" My neck strained with the effort of keeping my head upright, but I couldn't look away. "What's going on?"

James faltered, and that delicate balloon of hope inside me burst. "He's unconscious, and there's a chance he might never wake up."

I gripped the sheets with my good hand. He wasn't dead, but he wasn't alive either. Caught between, like my mother had been during the time I'd spent at Eden Manor when the council had tested me. Except Henry was immortal, and he would have no release.

I didn't know what was worse—death or this.

"Theo stopped the spread, but Henry was stabbed in the chest," said James. He approached the bed and took my hand, grasping it gently. My fingers twitched. "We don't know how bad the damage is. Or if Henry will ever recover enough to wake up."

"Is—is there a cure? A way to fix him?"

"There's nothing we can do," said James, and on my other side, my mother dabbed the corners of her eyes with a tissue. "We just have to wait."

My throat constricted. There had to be a way. There always was. If Henry could bring me back from the dead, then I could find a way to do the same for him. "What about Cronus? Couldn't he do something?"

Dead silence. Seconds ticked by, and without warning, my mother and James started talking at once.

"I can't possibly allow—"

"Even if he could, do you really think—"

They both stopped and stared at each other, and finally my mother went first.

"You are not going back there, sweetheart," she said. "It's a miracle Henry got you out in the first place, and he risked everything for you. He wouldn't want you to walk back into that. You know he wouldn't."

If it was just me, then my mother would have been right. However, it wasn't just about me anymore. It was about Milo, too. I might've been powerless to rescue our son, but if Henry could save me, then he could save him, as well. And if there was a way I could help Henry—if there was a way I could give Milo the father he deserved, then I had to try.

"Can Cronus help Henry?" I said again in as steady a voice as I could muster.

James leaned in closer, clasping my hand in his. "Yes," he admitted. "He could. But even if you did go back to Cronus, he wouldn't undo the damage he's already done to Henry. You know he wouldn't."

"Right," I whispered. James was wrong, though. If Cronus had enough incentive, he might. And I wasn't going to give up just because they insisted there was no point in trying. Even if it meant marching straight up to Cronus and giving him everything, I would really do it if it meant Henry might live.

While bedridden, I planned.

Every word I'd say, every argument I'd use, everything I'd offer Cronus to make him save Henry. Layer after layer of blueprints that would give Henry his life back and our son a father. Whatever it took.

I spent my hours with Milo, watching him sleep, watching as Ava changed him, watching as Calliope attempted to coax him to eat from a bottle. To my immense satisfaction, he refused.

"You must eat," said Calliope sternly as she offered yet another warm bottle to my son. He turned his head away, his face scrunched up and bright red from crying, and she narrowed her eyes. "Callum, you must."

Callum after herself, undoubtedly. He was Milo, not Callum, and no matter how long he stayed with that bitch, he would never be hers.

However, as the hours turned into one day, then two, my worry surpassed my hatred for Calliope. Milo wasn't eating. He fussed in his sleep, and when he was awake, his eyes constantly leaked with tears. He was miserable.

I didn't know what to do. Was there anything at all, other than storming the palace and demanding Calliope give him back to me? It wouldn't work anyway. I could have the entire council backing me up, but without Henry, it would be nothing more than an exercise in defeat. Cronus would keep me, Calliope would hide my son away, and he would only grow weaker.

"Come on, Milo," I whispered as I leaned over his crib. For the umpteenth time, I tried to touch him, but once again my fingers passed through his cheek. "I'm sorry I'm not here. If I had any choice…" My voice caught in my throat. "I know Calliope's horrible, but you need to eat. You need to be healthy and strong for when I finally get to be with you again."

At last he opened his blue eyes, and in that moment, I swore he saw me.

"There you are." I gave him a watery smile. "You're beautiful, you know. You put Adonis to shame."

His whimpers quieted, and he lifted his arms, as if he were reaching for me. I tried to touch him again, but it still didn't work. I'd never stop trying, though.

"Think you could do that for me?" I murmured. "Just eat a little bit. You can be as unhappy as you want. I don't blame you. It won't last forever though, I promise." It couldn't. I wouldn't let it.

"He has your eyes."

My heart damn near stopped. Slowly I turned, and despite the dim light, I could see every feature of his face. "Henry?"

He smiled grimly and opened his arms. I didn't think. I went to him, burying my face in his chest and inhaling, but he smelled like nothing. He wasn't here either. I could touch him, though. I could feel his silk shirt and the heat radiating from his body.

How?

"I've missed you," he murmured, brushing his lips against my cheek. When I tried to turn my head to kiss him properly, he pulled away, just out of reach. Rejection and doubt washed over me. Was he angry I'd gotten caught? That I couldn't save him? Did he know about my plans to give myself up to Cronus in exchange for his life?

When I followed his gaze, however, I relaxed. Milo.

I tucked myself underneath his arm, and together we approached the cradle. When the baby saw us, he reached for us. For me. And a piece of my heart melted.

Henry reached for him in return, and before I could warn him that it wouldn't work, his fingers made contact with Milo's. Not lingering in the unoccupied space beside him or hovering a millimeter above his skin and pretending.

He was really touching our son.

"Hello, little man," said Henry solemnly. "I heard you have not been eating."

Producing a bottle seemingly out of nowhere, Henry let go of me and picked Milo up. I stood back, stunned, as Henry offered him the milk. Several seconds passed, and at last Milo began to eat.

"How—" A wave of dizziness washed over me. This couldn't be happening, not unless he was dead or—or something I didn't understand. "How is this possible?"

Sometimes we misjudge what is possible and what is not.

Henry's voice rang in my head, clear as anything, and I waited for him to say those words again. To insist that just because I didn't know how it worked didn't stop it from happening.

Instead he smiled, and Milo ate greedily. "Because it is. What more of an explanation do you need?"

I wanted to know everything. I wanted to know how to save him, how to put our family back together, how to stop Cronus and Calliope from taking over the world. But at that moment, I only needed to hear one thing. "Will you stay with him?"

In his arms, Milo gurgled, and I tried to touch him once more. Nothing. "Of course," said Henry, and he pressed his lips to my forehead. "Always."

I opened my eyes, more content and relaxed than I'd been since the winter solstice. Despite the bright blue sky above me, this place—whatever it was, wherever it was—was quiet. My mother hadn't left me alone since I'd returned from Calliope's castle, but glancing around, I noticed her empty chair.

Finally, the chance I'd been waiting for.

Swinging my legs out of bed, I tested the sunset floor. It was warmer than I expected, and while my arm burned, my mother had been right; nothing else hurt. Whatever was in that compress had stopped the agony of the dagger wound from spreading.

While I'd been unconscious, someone—hopefully my mother and not James—had dressed me in a white silk nightgown, so smooth it might as well have been water against my skin. I took a few tentative steps, and once I was sure I wasn't going to collapse, I headed for the door. I had no idea where I was, but I wanted to see Henry. I had to make sure he wasn't dead. That my vision hadn't been his last goodbye to me. To our son.

No. He'd promised to stay with Milo, and he would. Gods didn't turn into corporeal ghosts when they died, or at least I thought they didn't. Had a god as powerful as Henry ever died before?

I opened the bedroom door to reveal a corridor on the other side, with the same blue ceiling and sunset floor. The colors underneath my feet changed as I walked, and I had to tear my eyes away to check the various doors that stood some twenty feet apart through the hallway.

Empty bedroom after empty bedroom. Some were plain, like mine, but others were decorated—one with light blue accents and white silk that matched my nightgown, and another with deep greens and bright flowers growing everywhere. It looked exactly like the sort of bedroom my mother might have if she'd—

Wait.

I pushed the door open wider. It wasn't just a bedroom; it was a suite, with several other doors decorating the walls, far more than space allowed with the other rooms surrounding it. I inched forward toward the nightstand, where a picture stood.

No, not a picture—a reflection, like the one Henry had had of Persephone in Eden Manor, one that captured a moment, not a still photograph. With a trembling hand, I picked up the wooden frame and stared at it. My mother and I stared back.

We were laughing in the middle of Central Park. I didn't need to see the cupcakes or the mess that remained of our picnic to know what it was.

It was the reflection Henry had given me our first and only Christmas together.

"Kate?"

The frame slipped from my hand, and the glass shattered as it hit the ground. I swore and bent to pick it up. "Mom, I'm sorry, I didn't mean—"

"It's all right," she said, kneeling beside me, and she waved my hand away. "What are you doing out of bed?"

I stood as the glass repaired itself under her guidance. How long would it take me to learn how to control my powers that way? I'd tried to figure out what I was capable of while Calliope had held me captive, but without someone to teach me, the best I'd managed was controlling my visions. "I want to see Henry."

"Fair enough." My mother straightened and set the newly repaired frame back on her nightstand. And it was her night-stand; I was sure about that now. This was her suite. This was her home.

This was Olympus.

"Do you mind taking a side trip with me before we go see him?" said my mother, wrapping her arm around my shoulders.

"What? Why?" I blurted. "I want to see Henry, Mom. He was in my vision, and he held Milo and got him to eat and everything."

Her brow furrowed, but instead of telling me I was crazy or that it was my imagination, she said gently, "We can talk about it later, sweetheart. Walter's called an emergency council meeting, and I was just on my way to fetch you."

To fetch me? What could I possibly help the council with? I'd only been immortal for a year and a half. That was nothing compared to the rest of the council, some of whom were older than the dawn of humanity. Like my mother. Like Henry. Like each of the original six siblings—five now that Calliope had abandoned them. Four now that Henry was lost in a world between the living and the dead. "What happened?"

My mother hesitated, and taking my good arm, she guided me to the door. "I don't want to worry you, but…"

"But what?" My insides seized. Had the worst happened? Were Henry or Milo dead? "Mom—*but what?*"

Her eyes flickered shut. "It's Cronus," she said, her voice cracking. "He's declared war."

CHAPTER 4
THE COUNCIL DIVIDED

Only half the council showed.

Irene, my tutor during my time in Eden, wept while Sofia, my mother's home care nurse and another of the original six, tried to comfort her. On the opposite side of the circle, Walter and Phillip, Henry's brothers, sat with their heads bent together, and they spoke quietly. James and Dylan, Ava's boyfriend from Eden High, remained silent on their respective thrones.

No one else showed.

"Where is everyone?" I whispered to my mother, though in the endless room, my voice carried.

"Some have chosen not to join us. We will not begrudge them that." She sat down and gestured for me to take a seat beside her, in the throne made of white diamond straight from the Underworld. Persephone's.

I hesitated. I'd sat there a few times in Henry's palace,

but I'd assumed it was there because it was his realm. Was it simply a place for me to sit, or did this mean I was a member of the council now? Despite the honor, the thought of having that kind of responsibility—that kind of *control* over the lives of others made me sick to my stomach. But if they trusted me enough to make me one of them, then I would do everything I could to help.

"We're waiting for you, dear," said my mother, and I forced myself to snap out of it. Perching on the edge of the chair, I cradled my arm to my chest and waited. I knew why Nicholas wasn't there, of course, since Calliope was holding him hostage. Ava was helping her—to save Nicholas, I realized, but that didn't make it easier to stomach her betrayal. And Henry...

They all had excuses for not being there, and after Ella had lost her arm the day Cronus escaped from the Underworld, I didn't blame her for not wanting to be part of it either. But what about Theo? What about Xander? The council without Calliope had argued and been at odds, but no one had flat-out abandoned their position.

Walter stood and cleared his throat. He looked older somehow, despite his agelessness. His shoulders slumped underneath the burden of everything that had happened, and beside him, Phillip, usually so gruff and impermeable, didn't look much better. "Brother and sisters, sons and daughters..."

Daughters? Only Irene was his daughter. Sofia and my mother were his sisters. Unless he meant me, too.

No. It was a slip of the tongue, nothing more. Because if he did mean me, too, then why hadn't anyone ever—

"It saddens me greatly to report that Athens has fallen."

All my questions about my father flew out of my head. Athens had fallen? Irene sobbed, and Sofia hugged her, rubbing her back and murmuring words of comfort I couldn't make out. Bewildered, I looked from them to Walter. How could Athens fall? This wasn't ancient Greece—what did that even *mean?*

"How?" said my mother. "Why? We have no army there. No soldiers to threaten Cronus's hold over the Aegean Sea. Why would he attack unprovoked?"

It wasn't unprovoked, though. Cronus had promised no one would die as long as I stayed by his side, and now I'd abandoned him. My hands began to tremble, and I shoved them between my knees. Across the circle, Walter's eyes met mine. He knew.

"We cannot pretend to understand how Cronus thinks," he said, and a rush of guilt-laced gratitude overwhelmed me. He wasn't going to tell.

"As for how he attacked," said Phillip, rising to stand beside his brother, "he used my domain. It was a calculated attack with Athens pinpointed specifically—no other area was touched. However, the damage he did…"

Irene cried even harder, and Phillip raised his voice so we could all hear him.

"The tidal wave washed nearly everything away."

My body went cold, and the golden room spun around me until I couldn't stand it any longer. "Did—did anyone die?" I whispered.

Walter said nothing for a moment, and I thought I saw a spark of compassion pass over his face. "Yes. Nearly a million people lost their lives."

Something twisted inside me, sharp and unforgiving, and if I could have thrown up, I would have. Nearly a million people were dead because of me, because I'd lied to Cronus. I'd known there would be consequences, yet I'd done it anyway.

No, I hadn't known it would be anything like this. This

wasn't war between two equal opponents; this was a massacre of people who didn't even know that gods and Titans were real.

"A purely symbolic attack then," said Dylan, his brow furrowed. A three-dimensional map of Greece appeared in the center of the circle, complete with mountains, islands and seas, all to scale and colored exactly like they would be if this were an aerial shot. For all I knew, it was.

The map zoomed toward Athens until the damage was visible. During my first summer away from Henry, James and I had visited Greece, and we'd spent weeks in the city. My memories of paved streets, kind people and the modern nestled alongside the ancient might as well have been a dream.

Nothing was left. Debris and mud replaced what had once been a vibrant city, now washed out to sea. Tears slid down my face, and I wasn't the only one crying. Beside me, my mother slipped her hand into mine, and even James's eyes grew red.

Athens was really gone.

"Look," said Irene suddenly, her voice thick. "Closer."

The map zoomed in, and I averted my eyes. I couldn't see the bodies, if there were any left to begin with. I couldn't see the faces of those who were dead because of me.

"The Parthenon," said Irene. "He left it standing."

I cracked open an eye. The temple of Athena—of Irene—remained standing, untouched except for the ravages of time and history.

"A message?" said James, leaning forward.

"I cannot say," said Walter gravely. "Perhaps he has a small amount of respect for all we have done for the world."

"Or maybe it means he'll keep us alive if we don't stand in his way," said Irene, dabbing her eyes with a handkerchief.

"We must not fall victim to the belief that removing ourselves from this war will prevent it from happening," said Walter with surprising gentleness. "He intends on killing us—*all* of us—for keeping him locked in Tartarus. Humanity is nothing to him, but he will not hesitate to wipe them out as well, knowing our existence is now linked to theirs. We have no choice but to fight until it is over."

"One way or the other," whispered Irene.

Walter nodded. "One way or the other."

"Isn't there something we can do?" The words were out before I could stop them, and each council member focused on me. "Cronus must want something."

"You know what he wants," said Walter, and my cheeks burned. Yes. He wanted me.

"We all know what he wants," cut in Dylan. "Death. Destruction. Mayhem. War. To rule the world once more. Usually I'd approve, but not when we're the targets."

"So what do we plan to do about it?" said James. "Let him get away with this?"

"I have already called a meeting among my subjects," said Phillip. "They know not to bow to his will no matter the cost."

"Cronus has more power than all of us combined," said Irene, a determined edge in her voice now. "We cannot fight back as we are and expect to achieve any measure of success."

"What about the other gods?" said James. "They could help."

"They have nearly all signed a petition insisting they will not," said Walter. "Besides, they could all join us and put everything they have into this war, but it would still not be sufficient. They are not powerful enough to make up for the loss of Henry and Calliope."

I gritted my teeth. Henry wasn't dead yet. "I could talk to Cronus," I said. "He—he was nice to me. He might listen."

"No," said my mother. "Even if you did have that sort of hold over him, he will stop at nothing until he has what he wants. He has waited and planned for eons. You will not change his mind no matter how fond of you he might be."

Across the circle, James focused on me. I ignored the question in his stare and concentrated on the floating image between us instead. "It could work," I said.

"That is a risk we cannot take," said Walter. "Calliope has already proven she will kill you if given the opportunity, and Cronus may not be willing to protect you any longer. No, we must focus our efforts on coming up with a way to even our odds despite our missing members."

Frustration, hot and unyielding, rose inside me. Of course they would invite me to join them only to dismiss every idea I had. What else did I expect? "What about Rhea?" I said. It felt like years since I'd decided to leave the Underworld to ask for her help. She was the only one who could match Cronus in power, and if anyone could win this war, it was her. "What did she say?"

Silence. Walter and Phillip exchanged an uneasy look, and finally James piped up. "No one's tried to find her."

"What? Why not?"

"We did not know you were not—" started Walter, but my mother cut in.

"*Most* of us did not know Kate was not searching for her," she corrected, fire in her eyes. Walter's lips thinned underneath her stare.

"Yes. Most of us did not know you were not already searching for her."

Right. That moment between Henry and Walter in the office. Henry had hinted Walter may have known what was going on. "And that entire time, you didn't stop to think it might be a good idea to send someone else instead?" I said.

Walter cleared his throat. "Our efforts were focused on trying to stop the impending war, not escalate it."

"Oh, yeah? How did that turn out?" I said, and my mother squeezed my hand, a silent command to stop talking.

This was my fault though, every last bit of it. I'd won immortality and stolen Henry from Calliope, or at least that was how she saw it. My stupid mistake had forced Henry to release Cronus from Tartarus in the first place. Now, because I'd left Cronus, nearly a million people were dead, and more would undoubtedly follow.

No, I wasn't going to shut up.

"While the rest of you flounder and try to figure out what to do, I'm going to find her," I said. "And I'm going to get her to help us."

I expected an argument, but instead the council was silent. "It's our greatest chance at obtaining a powerful ally," said Sofia after a long moment. "We can't hope to sway Calliope back to our side, and without a balance of power, more cities will crumble, and more people will die. I don't know about the rest of you, but I'm willing to try anything that might bring us peace."

Walter sighed wearily. "Very well. If you are able to convince Rhea to assist us in containing Cronus, then you will do us a great service, Kate."

And possibly prevent millions—maybe even billions—of people from dying. Yeah. No question. "I'll do it."

"I'll go with her," said James. Our eyes met again, and this time I didn't look away. "Like it or not, I'm the only one who can find her, so don't argue."

"I wasn't going to," I said. "I trust you." If there was one person I knew wouldn't betray me, it was James. He had nothing in this fight except his own survival, and his ability to find anyone meant we wouldn't waste time searching for Rhea. He would know exactly where she was.

"We must all trust each other now," said Walter. "Those who are here and those who are not." He focused on Ava's empty seashell throne for a moment before turning his gaze to me. "We all have made mistakes. We all have a burden to bear. But unless we are united, we will fall, and we must find forgiveness and understanding within ourselves. Pure evil does not exist. Even Cronus has his reasons for doing what he does, and the better we understand each other, the better chance we have at finding a solution before our foundation crumbles."

I averted my eyes. Once upon a time, when I'd first faced the council, I'd forgiven Calliope for killing me. I'd been able to see past her crimes and examine the reasons underneath, and in a way, I'd been able to understand her. But if Walter was really asking me to do the same with Ava...

It wasn't my life she'd threatened. It was Milo's, and some things were unforgivable. But despite my anger, I *wanted* to forgive her—I wanted to sympathize with her. I wanted her to be on our side again. And I could understand why she'd done it, even if I didn't want to admit it to myself. Calliope was blackmailing her, using Nicholas's life to ensure Ava's cooperation. The day she and I had left the Underworld, the signs had been obvious, and if I'd taken a moment to think about it, I would have known something was up. Ava's strength was in how she loved others. I'd known Calliope had taken Nicholas and she'd spoken to Ava alone, and I should've realized that Ava would do whatever it took to protect him. I should have done something to help her before she'd had to betray me.

That was over with now, though. She'd made her mistakes, and I'd made mine. I would do whatever I could to fix them, and I could only hope she would do the same, as well.

"We will all do our best," said my mother, and she squeezed my hand again, her gaze focused on me. I gave her a slight nod. I would try.

"Then it is settled," said Walter, and somewhere deep inside the palace, thunder rumbled. "Kate and James will attempt to ally the council with Rhea."

"And we will prepare for war," said Dylan with a gleam in his eye.

"No," said Walter. "We have prepared enough. Now we fight."

I spent the next three days by Henry's side as I regained my strength. He was in an undecorated room a few doors down from mine, and while my mother tended to both of us, I lay curled up beside him. I'd nearly lost him—still might if I couldn't convince Cronus to undo the damage he'd done—and I wasn't leaving him again until I absolutely had to.

The wind howled endlessly, and somewhere in the distance, the seas crashed against the rest of the world. Despite the sunny blue skies above me and the sunset below, thunder raged at all hours of the day and night, and even if I'd wanted to, I wouldn't have been able to sleep.

I split my time evenly between my present and my visions with Milo. Henry didn't break his promise; each time I arrived, he was there, sometimes holding Milo, sometimes keeping watch at his cradle as he slept. We stood side by side for hours and simply watched him, and Milo gazed at us in return. Somehow, someway, he knew I was there, I was sure of it now. I envied Henry his ability to hold him, but at least he would have a chance to know our son. If the worst happened, Milo would have these moments with him.

"You're going to come back to me, aren't you?" I said on the evening my mother had finally decided I'd healed enough to travel. James and I would set out to find Rhea in the morning, and in all likelihood, this would be the last night I'd have with Henry and Milo for a while.

"What do you mean?" said Henry. "I am here now."

"I mean here for real," I said. "Are you going to wake up? I know Cronus hurt you, but—you're here, and maybe if you tried really hard…"

Henry kissed my forehead, his palm pressed against the nape of my neck. "I will always be here for you, my dear. Nothing will change that."

I took a deep breath, refusing to cry in front of Milo. Even if he was sleeping and would never find out, I would know. "Please wake up," I whispered. "We need you. Not—not like this. We need *you*. We can't defeat Cronus without you."

"You cannot defeat Cronus with me. Not without Calliope," he pointed out.

"We're trying. He killed an entire city full of people. Athens is gone, and he's going to kill again and again until he gets what he wants."

"And what do you think that is?" said Henry, and I faltered. I couldn't tell him about the deal I'd made with Cronus. It was too complicated, and if he slipped away, I wouldn't be able to live with the guilt of knowing that was one of the last things I'd said to him.

"I don't know," I lied. "The council thinks he wants to kill them for keeping him imprisoned in Tartarus."

"Perhaps." He ran his fingers through my hair, his touch so gentle that it felt like a warm summer breeze. "All I want is you."

I shivered. Milo's lips parted in his sleep, and he made an

adorable suckling motion. "All I want is to be a family. A real, live family, together and safe from all of this."

"We will be," he promised. "I will make sure of it."

I leaned against him and wrapped my arm around his waist, his silk shirt tickling the inside of my wrist. How long would it be before we got to spend time together like this again? "James and I are leaving to find Rhea tomorrow morning."

Henry's fingers stilled in my hair, and for a moment he said nothing. "What is so important that you have to put yourself in such a dangerous position?"

"The same reason as before," I said. "If we can convince her to fight on our side, we might have a chance at winning."

"But Cronus is ravaging the world. If you leave Olympus, you will not be safe."

"I don't care anymore," I said with as much conviction as I could muster. "Besides, he's mostly trapped on the is- land with Calliope. He's powerful enough to cause natural disasters that kill millions, but Africa isn't close enough to Greece to be a problem."

"Are you sure about that?"

I hesitated. "No."

He turned from Milo to hug me tightly, almost posses- sively, and he buried his nose in my hair. "Please do not go. Rhea will not fight for anyone, much less against her own husband. It is not worth the risk."

"I have to try. You know I do."

"Even though it might kill you?"

"I'm not planning on letting that happen, but—yes. Even though it might kill me."

His expression clouded over. "Very well," he murmured. "All I ask is that you remember what happened the last time you left the safety of the council."

I scowled. "I get it. Something bad might happen if I leave Olympus. Cronus might catch me, Calliope might kill me or the sky might fall and land on top of me. But I can't stand by and watch millions of people die because of me, all right?"

"Humanity is nothing compared to you," he said, touching my cheek, and I stepped back.

"Even if that were true—and you know it isn't—Milo deserves a happy life, and that means making sure there's still a world for him to live in. I have to do this, Henry. I'm sorry. I love you and Milo more than anything, and if I had any choice in the matter—"

"You do," said Henry. "You have as much choice as you are willing to give yourself."

I huffed. "Fine. I've made my choice. I'm going to fight."

"You should not be fighting in the first place," he said. "You are too delicate, too—"

"Too what? Too young? Too inexperienced? I don't need to be ancient to be worth something, and I'm doing this whether you like it or not." I glared at him, but he averted his eyes. Several seconds ticked by, and at last I said in a softer voice, "I get why you don't want to fight, Henry. I do. But that was before all of this happened. That was before Milo was born. If you won't fight for me, then will you at least fight for him?"

Henry was quiet for a long moment, and not even the rise and fall of Milo's chest comforted me. This was impossible. Half-dead or not, Henry was as stubborn as ever. After caring for the baby all this time, he knew Milo even better than I did, and that was the part I didn't understand. How could anyone look at that face and not want to rip the world apart to get him back? How could Henry not need to protect his own son and give him the future he deserved?

"We will discuss it once you have made contact with

Rhea," he finally said. "I will not promise anything, but if there is a way I can help, I will. As it stands, I am rather stuck."

That was as much of a concession as I was going to get. I stood on my tiptoes to try to kiss him, but like he had every other time during our visits with Milo, he turned his head so I only captured the corner of his mouth. "Thank you," I said, refusing to let his distance faze me. Maybe he was Sleeping Beauty, and a kiss would wake him up and take him away from his son. If only it were that easy.

"You are welcome." He reached into the crib and picked up the baby. "We will be here waiting when you return."

"You'd better be." I held my hand above Milo's forehead, as close as I could get without going through him. "I love you both so damn much. You know that, right?"

Milo waved his arms, as if reaching for me, and Henry kissed his hand. "We do," he said. "And we cannot wait to be with you again."

I poked him in the ribs. "You can count on it."

"Kate?"

I opened my eyes. James leaned toward me, his nose inches from mine.

"There you are," he said with a hint of relief. "You were smiling."

I straightened and adjusted the sling wrapped around my burning arm. It was easier to ignore the pain as it became the norm, but when I focused on it, it made me wince. "I didn't realize that was a crime."

"It's not." James offered me his hand, and I took it. "I just thought you weren't coming back. I've been calling your name for ages."

My cheeks grew warm. I didn't know how I acted during these visions—no one had bothered to explain it to me, and

I was too embarrassed to ask. Could James hear everything? "Then why didn't you break in like you did last time?" I muttered.

"What, you mean when I was trying to drag you back from total oblivion?" he said. "I *am* sorry about that, you know. It's rude. But if I hadn't, you'd still be in there, convinced Henry was dead. So all in all, I figure it was worth it."

I scowled at him, but he was right. "How did you do that anyway?"

He tapped his nose. "My secret. Maybe if you're good, I'll explain it later. Are we leaving? I packed a bag for both of us. Actually, your mother packed yours. I figured Henry might smite me if I went through your underwear."

"I thought Walter was the one who did the smiting," I said with a faint smile.

James's eyebrows shot up. "Did you or did you not see the black cloud of doom when Henry broke onto Cronus's island?"

My smile vanished. "Of course."

"And you still think he doesn't have it in him?"

I frowned. James didn't have to rub my nose in the fact that I didn't know what my own husband was capable of. Or what I was capable of, for that matter.

"Come on," said James, gentler this time, and he took my good arm. "Let's go say goodbye."

My mother wasn't the only one waiting for us. Walter stood at her side, and his smooth expression didn't betray whatever it was he was thinking. My stomach twisted. I'd avoided him since the council meeting, unable to forget how he'd addressed me—as his daughter.

It seemed impossible. It had to be. If I was the daughter of Zeus, I'd know it. But the more I thought about it, the less I could deny it. James and Ava had mentioned that only his children joined the council; and if I was a member, then the answer was obvious.

But regardless of the evidence, part of me wanted to stay in denial. I'd lived my whole life thinking my father had left my mother early on, that he may have not even known I'd existed. It was easier than facing the possibility that he'd known and just didn't care. And if Walter was my father, then there was no question that he'd not only known I'd existed, but he'd been acutely aware of everything my mother and I had gone through, as well. And he'd never cared enough to help.

As I walked toward him and my mother, resentment made my blood boil. He said nothing as my mother embraced me, and I buried my nose in her hair, inhaling deeply. It didn't matter who Walter was to me. I had my mother, and she was the only parent I'd ever need.

"Where are the others?" I said. Not that I expected them to care that I was leaving, but I figured they'd at least want to give James a decent send-off.

"Attempting to corral Cronus fully back onto the island," said my mother grimly. "We will be joining them once you leave."

Fear swept through me. I had never thought of her as a soldier—she'd fought hard against the cancer that had eventually taken her mortal life, of course. But this wasn't cancer. This was war, and the thought of my mother fighting alongside the likes of Dylan and Irene and Walter made my head spin. She was the gentlest person I knew.

No one could afford to sit this one out, though. If I knew how to fight like they did, I'd be on the front lines, too, using every bit of power I had inside me to get my son back. As it stood, the only way I had to help was this. And that was why no one, not even Henry, would ever talk me out of it.

"Kate," said Walter, and my mother let me go. "You understand that Rhea is equally as strong as Cronus, do you not?"

I eyed him. We looked nothing like each other, but when the gods could and did change forms, that didn't mean much. "Yeah, I know. Isn't that the whole point?"

"Yes," said Walter, giving my mother a look I didn't understand. "That also means if you press her to do something she is not willing to do, or if you upset her in any way, she has the potential to be equally as devastating to our cause."

"So you want me to suck up to her?" I said. "We're in the middle of a war."

"Yes, I am aware," said Walter dryly. "I am merely asking that you show her the respect she deserves. She is our mother. Your grandmother twice over—"

"Excuse me?" I blurted. My mother squeezed my elbow, but I shook her off. It was one thing for me to at least have the choice to pretend to be blissfully unaware of his role in my life, but for him to force this on me now…something inside me snapped. "If you're finally going to admit that you're my father—"

"Now is not the time, Kate," said my mother.

"It's never the right time," I said sharply. "It's a simple yes or no, Walter. Are you my father?"

He raised his chin and looked down at me. "Yes. I never thought there was a question."

As if it was no big deal. As if the years I'd spent taking care of my mother on my own didn't matter. I'd cried myself to sleep countless nights, terrified I'd wake up and be alone in the world, and all this time, not only had my father known about me, but he had known exactly where we were and what we were going through.

"Then I guess it's a good thing I never thought I needed

a father," I said. "Now, if you don't mind, I've got a Titan to find."

"Kate," said my mother, reaching for me, but I yanked my arm away. Her lips parted in surprise, and guilt gripped my heart, more painful than anything Cronus could possibly do to me. But I stood my ground.

"We need to go." I slid my hand into the crook of James's elbow and took a step back, ignoring the way my throat tightened. I wasn't going to cry. Not over Walter, and especially not in front of him.

For the first time in our friendship, James kept his mouth shut. Instead he nodded in Walter and my mother's direction. My parents' direction, I realized. For the first time in my life, I had parents.

That should've made me giddy with excitement, or at least it should have given me a glimmer of happiness during one of the worst times of my life. Instead it made me nauseous.

"Goodbye, sweetheart," my mother whispered. Before I could say goodbye in return, golden light flashed from all directions, and bright spots of color burst in front of me as the sunset floors vanished.

James and I appeared on a grassy hill, and I blinked. Sheep's Meadow in Central Park, the exact spot I'd met with my mother every night I'd spent in Eden. We were surrounded by people, but none of them so much as glanced up at our appearance. Could they see us? Or had James done something to make them think we'd been there the whole time?

"Why are we in New York?" I said. "Is Rhea here now?"

"Rhea? What would she be doing here?" said James, and he guided me down the hill. "She's still in Africa."

"Then why aren't *we* in Africa?" I said, and James smirked. Clearly he was enjoying my ignorance.

"We're here because this was where Olympus happened to be."

I hesitated. "I thought Mount Olympus was in Greece."

"Mount Olympus is, but Olympus, the council's home, isn't in a fixed spot. Well, no, it is," he amended, gesturing to the sunset that stained the New York sky. "It's caught eternally between day and dusk."

Right. Hence the interior decorating. "So why can't we just...appear there?"

"Because I miss traveling, and it happens to be what I'm good at." James took my elbow, his hand warm even through my sweater. "We're handling things the old-fashioned way and catching the first flight to Zimbabwe. It'll give us some time to map out our game plan, and I figured stretching your legs would do you some good. Besides, only the six siblings can disappear and reappear in another place. And you now, too, I suppose, once you learn how," he added. "I bet Walter would teach you once we get back."

The mention of Walter turned my stomach. "Why can I do it, too?"

James raised an eyebrow. "You're complaining?"

"Of course not." I bit my lip. "It can't be because both of my—my parents—" I could barely force the word out "—are part of the original six. Then Nicholas and Dylan could, too. So why?"

"Because otherwise you're not going to be very good at traveling through the Underworld, are you?" James untangled his arm from mine and wrapped it around my shoulders instead. "I'm sorry, Kate. Walter should've told you ages ago."

A bitter taste filled my mouth. Sorry wasn't going to fix anything. "Doesn't matter. I don't need him."

"He is a bit of a womanizer," agreed James. "Definitely

not a good role model for the baby. Thankfully Milo has Henry to look up to."

For a moment I was silent. James didn't know whether or not Henry would ever wake up again. We didn't even know if he'd still be alive by the time we got back. "Your optimism continues to defy reality," I mumbled.

"I was right about your mother," he said, and I shook my head.

"No, you weren't. She died. Her mortal form, anyway, and you had no idea I was going to pass the tests. You didn't know if I'd ever see her again."

James waved off my objections. "Either way, this isn't optimism. This is fact. Henry's going to make it."

He was baiting me, the jerk, but no matter how badly I didn't want to give him the satisfaction of knowing he had me hooked, I couldn't resist. "Fine, I give. How can you possibly be so sure?"

Grinning, James leaned toward me, his lips brushing the shell of my ear. "Because," he whispered, "Rhea can heal him."

CHAPTER 5
UNDERNEATH

"Did you know?"

I stood beside Milo's crib, gazing down at his sleeping form as Henry stood across from me. He looked different— more distant somehow, as if he was somewhere else, as well. He barely looked at me, and he stared unblinkingly down at the baby.

"Did I know what?" he said after a long moment. Was he even listening?

"Did you know that Rhea could heal you?" I said, keeping a stranglehold on my temper. Everything that had happened wasn't Henry's fault, of course, but still. Had he known this whole time? Was Walter aware? Was my mother?

"I...suspected," said Henry, and his eyes glazed over again. Wherever he was, I sure as hell hoped it was more important than his own life. "I did not want to give you false hope."

"Bullshit," I said. "You didn't want to give me any hope at all."

Several seconds passed, and finally his gaze met mine. "Are you going to try?"

"Try what? You're her son, aren't you?" I said.

"In a manner of speaking."

"Then why would she say no?"

"She does not like to bother herself with our affairs," said Henry.

"I'm sure she won't mind pulling herself away from whatever it is she does in order to heal you," I said. Why was he being so difficult?

Kate?

I froze at the sound of James's voice, but Henry didn't so much as frown.

Kate, come back, said James, the words no more than a whisper. *It's important.*

It was always important. I sighed inwardly and leaned over the cradle to give Henry a kiss on the cheek. "I have to go. I'll be back soon."

"Of course," he said distractedly, once again staring down into the crib. His gaze wasn't focused on Milo's face, though; it was as if he was looking through him. What was going on?

The nursery faded, replaced by the interior of an airplane. Despite the ample room first class provided, my arm ached from the way I leaned against the window, and I winced. These were the only tickets we could get, and James had insisted Henry would pay him back. During my first summer away, I had been reluctant to spend Henry's money and forced James to fly coach. This time, I didn't argue. I'd learned my lesson about spending twelve hours crammed between a screaming baby and a snoring passenger who treated my shoulder like a pillow.

"There you are," said James. "Hungry?" He sat beside me, and on the tray table in front of him sat two actual plates of cheeseburgers and fries. Fancy. James hadn't bothered with one of them, undoubtedly meant for me, but on the other he'd stacked the fries into a teetering structure.

"Depends," I said, stretching my legs. "Did you pull me away from Henry just to ask for my fries?"

"'Course not," said James cheerfully, and he pulled a plastic bottle of ketchup from his backpack. "If I wanted them, I'd steal them. Ketchup?"

"You really brought a bottle of ketchup on the plane? How did you get it through security?"

He grinned. "My secret."

I moved my plate onto my tray table. Unlike coach, it came out of my armrest, and on the back of the seat in front of me was a wide screen playing a movie I didn't recognize. "You're crazy."

"I prefer the term *resourceful*." He squirted a moat of ketchup around his French fry fortress. "Anyway, I woke you up because you were mumbling something. What were you dreaming?"

I picked up one of my fries and popped it into my mouth. Not half-bad for airplane food. Then again, the few meals I'd had on airplanes before hadn't been served with white china and silverware. "I wasn't dreaming. I was with Milo and Henry."

James frowned. "How often is Henry there with you?"

"All the time. I asked him to stay, and he did."

"Can you touch him?" said James, and I nodded. "What about Milo?"

"He can. I can't."

"Right." His frown deepened. "What have you been telling him?"

"What, I can't have a private conversation with my husband without you butting in?"

James set his bottle aside and faced me. "Did you tell him where we're going and what we're doing?"

"Of course," I said. "Well, no, I mean, I told him what we're doing and that we're going to Africa. I didn't mention Zimbabwe specifically."

"Good." He brushed his fingers against mine, and I pulled away, folding my hands together and setting them in my lap. Friends or not, he'd intentionally hurt Henry all those years ago by having an affair with Persephone. While Henry might've been willing to forgive, he undoubtedly hadn't forgotten, and I wasn't about to give him any more of a reason to worry. "How has he been treating you? Has he said anything strange? Done anything that didn't seem quite right?"

"What is this, twenty questions?" I leaned back in my seat, leaving my plate all but untouched. "It's none of your business."

"Yes, it is. We've never had a situation like this before. During the first war—obviously I wasn't alive back then, but Walter—"

"I don't want to hear it." Not when it had anything to do with Walter.

"You need to." James's voice was surprisingly kind. "It doesn't matter who Walter is to you, all right? Forget about him. He's not important right now."

"He's never been important." As far as I was concerned, he never would be.

"I wouldn't go that far," said James with a wry smile. "He *is* King of the Gods and head of the council, after all. We're all his children. You know that."

"So what, are you saying I'm stupid for not figuring it out sooner?" I said, and though James shook his head, I still felt like an idiot. He was right. He and Ava *had* told me that every younger member of the council was one of Walter's children.

"You're not stupid," said James. "Not at all. Walter, he's the stupid one for not stepping in to act like your father when Diana told us her mortal body had cancer. Your mother wanted him to," he added. "So don't be pissed off at her for this, all right? She fought hard to get him to show up. Phillip even volunteered to step up as your uncle, but in the end, Walter decided going through that alone would give you a better chance of passing the tests."

"He's a bastard," I whispered, half expecting a bolt of lightning to tear through the sky and knock us out of the air.

"Most of the time," agreed James. "He doesn't understand emotions well, I guess. Wasn't a great father to any of us, except for maybe Ava, and she was adopted. Can't blame him too much, though. He didn't exactly have the greatest role model either."

That didn't make up for abandoning me when he knew I'd needed him, but it did help to know that I was part of the rule rather than the exception. "Good to know I didn't miss out on anything," I mumbled.

James snorted. "Hardly. He makes Henry look like a clingy, doe-eyed schoolgirl."

At least I knew Henry was a good father, and in the end, that was what mattered—that Milo had a dad. My childhood was already over. His was just beginning, and I wasn't about to let him go through the same thing I'd endured. He would have a father, one who loved him, one he saw every day. I would make sure of it.

"We need to talk about your visions now," said James quietly. "Will you let me go with you and see?"

"Go with me? It's not like I travel, you know. I'm still here when I have them."

"You can take someone with you if you want, though. Persephone did it with me sometimes."

"I'm sure she did," I said, rolling my eyes.

He groaned. "Not like *that*. I mean—you can slip into it now, right? You've gained control?"

After nine months of nothing else to do? "Yeah, I've got it down."

He set his hand over mine again, and this time I didn't pull away. "I don't know how Persephone did it, exactly, but she described it to me as swimming through nectar. Instead of breaking the connection so she was alone, she took me with her."

Right. Wasn't helping. "If you need me to get there, then how did you manage to talk to me when I was there before?"

"That's different. I did that mentally." *Like this.*

His voice echoed in my head, louder than it'd ever been before, and I jerked away from him. "What was that?"

"Shh," hissed someone in the seats behind us.

James laughed quietly, but there was nothing funny about this. "That was me, of course."

"But how—" I stopped short and lowered my voice to a whisper. "How did you do that?"

"It's easy. We can all speak mentally one on one. Not all at once, of course, because that would get crowded and very, very loud, but if we focus our thoughts on one person, we can do it." He offered me his hand again. "You try."

I hesitated. "How?"

"Just think of something, and push that thought my way."

I closed my eyes and concentrated on the feel of his skin against mine. His hand was warm, his fingers impossibly smooth, and there was something comforting about it. Familiar.

This is crazy.

"We're all a little crazy, when you think about it," said James, and my eyes flew open.

"It worked?"

"Congratulations, you've mastered the art of thinking. Now let's take this connection one step further. Go into your vision and take me with you."

Apparently it was too much to hope for that he'd forget about invading my privacy like that. "It isn't going to work. Why do you want to go with me anyway?"

"Several reasons," he said in a cagey way that meant he was hiding something from me. Then again, I was fairly sure he always was.

"Like what?"

"So I can get a good idea of what the layout of Calliope's fortress is like," he said. "So I know where Calliope and Cronus spend their time. So I can see where—"

He stopped, and I frowned. "So you can see where what?" I said, and his expression turned distant.

"Did you ever meet Iris?" he said, and I shook my head. "She was another one of Walter's messengers."

"Was?"

He cleared his throat and stared at his fort of fries, but his heart didn't seem to be in it anymore. "Calliope killed her the day Henry rescued you."

My mouth opened, but for a long moment, nothing came out. It didn't matter that I hadn't known her; James's pain crept through me as surely as if it were tangible. "I'm sorry," I said at last. "I can't imagine what you must be going through."

"She was one of my best friends," he said softly. "It's different when you're immortal—you always take people for granted. I mean, they'll be there in a century or two, right? No need to tell them how you feel, because there'll always be another opportunity."

I squeezed his hand. "I'm sure she knew, even if you never got the chance."

"Walter should've never sent her in the first place." James took a shuddering breath, and at last he looked at me. I pretended not to notice the redness in his eyes. "I want to see where she died. But I also need to get an idea of what's going on so the council can form a strategy. If we're going to rescue Milo, we need to know where he is."

"You'd really do that?" I said.

He gave me an odd look and smiled. "Of course. He's your son."

That was all I needed to hear. Tightening my grip on his fingers, I closed my eyes and concentrated on his hand, all the while sliding into my vision. He held me back though, as if we were moving through quicksand. This was impossible. "I can't do it."

You're almost there. Keep going.

I pushed on. Milo's warmth lingered in front of me, waiting, and I couldn't disappoint him.

Finally, as if emerging from an endless ocean of mud, we surfaced together. I planted my feet firmly on the floor of the nursery, but James stumbled, and it took him a moment to right himself.

"Whoa. Forgot about the aftershock." He glanced around the sunset nursery. Henry stood in the corner, feeding Milo with a bottle, and James's eyes widened. "Pretend I'm not here."

"What—" I began, but Henry turned toward me, a blank smile on his face. Anxiety pooled in my stomach. Was he fading? Was that why he was barely there anymore?

"Welcome back, Kate," said Henry, his quiet voice somehow reverberating through the nursery, as if he were speaking in a deep valley. "Milo began to fuss."

"Right," I said, glancing at James. Wasn't Henry going to say hi? "Sorry about leaving like that earlier. Something came up."

Henry nodded once, his eyes unfocused. He barely seemed to notice he was holding Milo. "Nothing terrible, I hope."

I shook my head. "Just lunch."

James moved toward Henry, one slow step at a time, until he was barely half a foot away. Henry didn't so much as blink. How could he see me and not know James was there?

Without saying a word, James slipped out of the nursery. Did he expect me to follow him? Or was he memorizing the hallway Milo was in? With luck he'd look out the window, too, else there was no way he'd know which level we were on. Unless Calliope hadn't fixed the massive hole in the floor yet.

For the next several minutes, neither Henry nor I said anything. Instead I moved to his side and watched Milo eat. It wouldn't be much longer before I would be the one holding the bottle for him. We were almost to Johannesburg, and from there it was a much shorter flight to Zimbabwe. As soon as Henry was healed and Rhea was on our side, we would end this war.

Movement near the doorway caught my eye. I looked up, expecting James to come sneaking back into the room. Instead a girl walked in, carrying a pile of blankets that obscured her face, but I would've recognized her anywhere.

Ava.

She set the blankets down on a dresser shoved in the corner, a new addition since Milo's arrival, and she jumped. "Wh-what are you doing here?"

My mouth dropped open. She could see me? "What do you think I'm doing here?"

Instead of answering me, she hurried toward us, her arms

outstretched. "If Calliope finds out you've been in here again, she'll be livid. Give him to me."

Without warning, she stepped right through me and took Milo from Henry's arms. My insides turned to ice. She could see Henry, but she couldn't see me.

And she was holding our son.

"Give him back," I said, reaching for him, but of course my hands went straight through them both.

Henry held on to the bottle, and devoid of his meal, Milo began to wail. His cries were louder and healthier than they'd been the first few days, but as reassuring as that should've been, they fueled every instinct I had to help him.

"Henry." I grabbed his hand. "Don't let her take him away. He's still hungry."

Finally Henry blinked and shook his head slowly, as if pulling himself out of a daydream. "I am doing what has been asked of me," he said to Ava, ignoring me. "I am taking care of my son."

"He is *not* your son," hissed Ava, cradling him to her chest and turning her back on Henry. Hot fury washed through me, replacing my astonishment.

"You bitch," I snarled, advancing on Ava. I didn't care that she had no idea I was there. I'd tried to see things her way, but if she was going to take Milo away from his father, if she was going to insist Calliope was his real mother—

"Kate?" James's voice cut through my rage. "Don't move. Don't say anything."

"Not this time," I said, but my footsteps faltered. Ava hunched over Milo, as if she were shielding him with her body. From what? His own father? "She stole Milo straight out of Henry's arms."

"She's only trying to protect him," said James.

"Protect him?" I exploded. "That's his father, and she's stealing Milo—"

"She isn't stealing him."

"Look at her! Henry, why aren't you—"

I whirled around to face him, but his expression was as blank as ever. Like he was nothing more than a lifeless wax model. "Henry?" I said uncertainly. "Henry, what's—"

James stepped between us, and he glared at him with such hatred that I stopped in my tracks. "I'm sorry, Kate," he said. "That's not Henry."

CHAPTER 6
RHEA

Not Henry.

The words rattled around in my head like they were stuck in a labyrinth and couldn't find the way out.

"Of course that's Henry," I said. Who else would it be? He'd touched me. He'd stayed with our son. He'd done everything Henry would have done.

He hadn't kissed me, though. Some of the things he'd said hadn't sounded right—they hadn't sounded like Henry. Something had felt *wrong* this entire time. I'd dismissed it as a consequence of my vision, of him barely hanging on to this world in the first place, but what if it wasn't?

Cold horror filled me. The only person capable of mimicking him so completely—

Cronus.

Of course. Of *course*. I was an idiot, and all this time he'd played me. He'd taken care of Milo. He'd fed him when he wouldn't take a bottle from anyone else. He'd rocked him to sleep. He'd stood with me for hours, watching Milo's chest rise and fall steadily.

"Come on," said James gently, taking my trembling hands. "Let's get out of here."

"I can't." I stared at the mockery that was Cronus in Henry's form, and hot rage unlike anything I'd ever felt coursed through me. "I can't leave Milo."

"There's nothing you can do for him here," said James. "Ava will make sure nothing happens to him."

Despite my bone-shaking fury, I knew Cronus wouldn't hurt him either. Whatever reason he had for doing this, he'd been good to Milo so far, and James was right. There was nothing I could do, not when I couldn't so much as touch the baby.

"We'll go to the council about it as soon as we find Rhea," promised James. "But right now I need to talk to you, and we can't do it in front of him."

I glared at Cronus over James's shoulder. "He's not listening. He's practically a zombie."

"He's always listening." He touched my shoulder. "Come on, before he snaps back and makes things worse."

In other words, before he could threaten me into silence or inaction. After saying a silent goodbye to Milo, I closed my eyes and slid out of the nursery, fighting through the quicksand to return us to our reality.

After the salty Mediterranean breeze, the stale air of the plane smelled foreign. Beside me, James looked as pale as I felt, and hot tears ran down my face. James silently offered me a napkin from his tray. When I didn't accept, he dabbed my cheeks for me.

"I should have known," I whispered.

"It isn't your fault," said James. "Cronus could have fooled any of us, and you needed hope that Henry was out there somewhere. It isn't unreasonable. It's human."

"I knew something was off. He kept saying strange things, he wouldn't kiss me, and the way he could hold Milo when I couldn't touch him..." I shook my head. "I should have *known*."

"You do now, that's the important part," said James. "I need to know what you told him."

A lump formed in my throat. "Everything."

I'd told him about Rhea. I'd told him the council's plans to fight. Everything they'd trusted me with, I'd blabbed directly to the enemy. Once again, because of my stupidity, any advantage we'd had over Cronus was gone.

James hugged me, and I stiffened. I didn't deserve his sympathy. "It will be okay," he said, an empty reassurance. Regardless of whether or not there was something he could do, he couldn't guarantee everything would turn out all right. He couldn't promise me that Henry would live or I would ever hold Milo or that the council would recapture Cronus and make sure Calliope never hurt anyone again. He couldn't make up for the countless lives already lost because of me.

"I'm never going to see them again," I whispered.

"Yes, you will. I'll make sure you do."

I curled up in my seat and rested my head against his shoulder, lost within myself. I could only take so much before I broke, and Calliope knew it. Cronus knew it. Staying strong for my mother while she'd been dying had been easy—it was staying strong for myself that had been impossible. Now I had no one to stay strong for, not even Milo. Not even Henry.

James was staying strong for me, though. I owed it to him—and to Henry and Milo and my mother and everyone— to try not to crumble. I swallowed, and my dry throat protested. "Did he know you were there?"

He shook his head. "He can see you, but only because he expects you and has already forged that connection with you. He'll know someone came because you were talking to me, but unless he figures out who I was, he won't be able to see me if we go back again."

"How did you know it wasn't Henry?"

"I didn't," said James, running his fingers through my hair. "Not until I saw him. The only question is why?"

My chin trembled. "I did something really stupid."

"How stupid?" said James, his hand stilling.

I pressed my lips together, fighting the urge to slip back into the sunset nursery. "I promised Cronus I would stay with him and—and be his queen if he didn't kill anyone. And if he gave me Milo."

James exhaled. "Oh, Kate."

"I'm sorry." I tried to draw away from him, but his arm around my shoulders tightened. "I'm so sorry, James. I had no idea. I thought— I didn't know what I was thinking—"

"You were thinking you had a chance to do what you always do," said James with kindness I didn't deserve. "You were going to give yourself up in order to save the people you love. It's a bit of a problem with you, you know."

I sniffed. "I just wanted to see Milo again."

"I know," he murmured, kissing the top of my head. "You have nothing to apologize for."

"But all of those people—Athens—"

"—would have happened no matter what you did. Cronus always intended on causing as much destruction as possible. That has nothing to do with you, Kate, I promise." He paused. "In fact, your deal could work for us."

"How?" I wiped my cheeks with my sleeve. "He knows we're going to Rhea to ask for her help. He knows she can heal Henry, and the first chance Cronus gets, he's going to kill him."

"Probably," said James. "We'll make sure he never has that chance though, and in the meantime, we have a direct line to Cronus."

"He won't listen to reason."

"No, but he might listen to you. Especially if you can convince him you're still on his side."

A wave of nausea swept over me. "I was never on his side."

"Doesn't matter when he doesn't know that," said James. "He's always willing to believe the worst in us. Use that against him. Say you want to rejoin him, but Walter's holding you hostage. You want to be with Milo, so it won't even really be a lie."

Unless he could see the lie in a truth, like Henry could. "He'll come after you," I said. "He'll attack Olympus."

James chuckled. "Last time Cronus tried, he wound up in the hottest, deepest pit on earth. I doubt he'll give it another go."

But no matter how hard he was trying to convince me that it wasn't a big deal, I heard the worry in his voice. This was his entire family, too. This was his home, and he was gambling it all on what? On the slim chance Cronus might be willing to listen to me? If James was right and Cronus had heard everything that had gone on in the nursery, then he would know I knew. And he would know I was angry.

"What if it doesn't work?" I whispered, finding his hand and lacing my fingers through his. A friendly touch. Nothing more, but I needed that much, and so did he.

James rested his head against mine. "Then we'll just have to figure something else out."

Six hours and one connecting flight later, we touched down in Zimbabwe. James hailed a cab on the curbside of the airport, and soon enough we were on a remote road traveling to a place I couldn't pronounce no matter how many times James tried to teach me.

"You'll get it eventually," he said with a chuckle, but after a moment he turned serious. "None of us have contacted Rhea in a very long time. I have no idea how she'll react, and I can't make you any promises."

"I don't need promises," I said, but my insides churned. What if I couldn't convince Rhea to help us? What if she wouldn't heal Henry?

I straightened in the back of the hot cab. No matter what it took, no matter what I had to promise her, I would find a way to make this happen. I would find a way to save Henry. If Rhea was really so unconcerned about the rest of the world that she wasn't willing to step up and help us fight...

She would. She had to.

The Zimbabwe landscape, for the most part, looked surprisingly familiar. Drier and wilder, with scragglier underbrush, but closer to home than I'd expected. I pressed my forehead against the cracked window of the cab. A few people walked along the side of the road holding signs made out of battered cardboard, but the cabdriver sped past before I could see what they said.

We stopped at the edge of a village that looked more like a slum than a town. James held my hand tightly as we walked down the narrow way between cobbled-together buildings, some of which leaned dangerously to one side. Trash lined the makeshift streets, and a few children dressed in worn clothes began to follow us.

"Don't we have anything we can give them?" I said. James paused long enough to take off his backpack, and he pulled out several apples that I was positive hadn't been in there before. He handed one to each child, but the crowd continued to grow, and he frowned.

"Kate, I want to help as badly as you do, but we're on a timetable."

"We just wasted over a day flying when you could have dropped us off much closer," I said. "We have a few minutes for this."

James continued to hand them out. "You know how to create. Reach in and help me."

"Actually, I don't," I said, but I reached into the bag and tried anyway. What was I supposed to do, just imagine it was there? I closed my eyes and pictured a juicy yellow apple. And then—

Nothing. Perfect.

James chuckled. "You're the worst goddess I've ever met."

"Calliope's the worst goddess you've ever met. I'm just the most incompetent." I scowled. "It'd help if anyone bothered to teach me how to do things, you know."

"Hey, I showed you how to think." He grinned, and I shot him a look. "In all seriousness, everyone's sort of busy right now, but I'll see what I can do. Most of it takes decades to learn."

We didn't have decades, not if I had any chance of helping in the war. James handed out a few more apples, but the crowd continued to build. Were they really so hungry that an apple was enough to stop what they were doing and come running?

A child shouted in a language I didn't understand, but instinctively I knew what he was saying to the boy he wrestled. *Mine.*

"Whoa, hey, hold up," called James, trying to wade through the wide-eyed boys and girls to reach them. "No fighting, there's plenty more where—"

"Calm down, my children," murmured a voice that seemed to come from everywhere and nowhere at once. Immediately the boys stilled, and James let out a deep breath. He didn't need to say a word for me to know what was going on. Rhea was here.

The crowd parted, and a girl who couldn't have been older than thirteen walked barefoot down the path. Her eyes stood out against her dark skin, and she wore a colorful scarf around her head. She moved with inhuman grace, and though she blended into the crowd purely by her appearance, she radiated warmth and comfort. Not power and pain like Cronus. As she passed, the children reached out to touch her, as if that alone could cure illness or bring them luck.

"Grandmother," said James reverently, and as she approached us, he knelt down. "I've missed you."

Rhea touched his cheek. "Hermes," she murmured. "I have been waiting for you. It has been far too long."

"I meant to come sooner, but..." James trailed off. There was no excuse for not coming to see this girl. This Titan. "I'm sorry."

"No need to apologize. You're here now. Stand," she said, and James did so, slipping his hand into hers. "Let us speak privately."

They walked past me as if I weren't even there. James seemed to be in a trance, and I hesitated. Should I follow?

"You, too, daughter of Demeter." Rhea's words whispered through the air, and my feet moved without me telling them to. In that moment I would have followed her off the end of the world if she wanted me to.

"We don't go by those names anymore," said James, and I trotted to catch up to them as they rounded a corner. None of the children followed, but every person we passed stared at us openly. Because of Rhea? Or because James and I were strangers?

She led us to what amounted to a large blue shanty with a white cross painted on the sign above. We entered, and James had to duck to avoid hitting the top of the doorway. Inside, instead of the church I expected, was a hospital.

Over two dozen men, women and children rested in cots and makeshift beds shoved so close together that the doctors and nurses—or at least I assumed they were doctors and nurses—had no room to slide between them. Instead, each patient was faced with their head near the aisle and feet to the wall. Several were coughing, and a few looked so frail and close to death that I tried to memorize their faces. Would I see them in the Underworld? Would I even have the chance to return if Henry didn't make it? What would happen to the dead then?

No. I couldn't think like that. Rhea would help us.

"This way," she said, and we walked through the narrow aisle to a door toward the back. I expected an office, but instead we stepped into a cramped garden blooming with all sorts of flowers and herbs I didn't recognize. My mother would've loved this place. "Now, why have you come?"

"You know why," said James, albeit respectfully, and he sat down on a crate that served as a bench. "Cronus has destroyed Athens. Hera has abandoned us to fight with him. Hades is on the brink of fading. We are desperate, and we need your help."

Rhea began to tend a bush with tiny white flowers. "You know my stance on war," she said. "I cannot support it in any way."

"Please." James screwed up his face. Going against her was clearly painful for him. "If you don't help us return Cronus to Tartarus, he will destroy humanity and kill us if we're lucky. If we're not, we'll spend the rest of eternity as his slaves. Without Hera, we aren't strong enough to fight him on our own."

Placing the blossoms she picked into a basket, Rhea said nothing. After nearly a minute, James's shoulders slumped, and I knew it was hopeless. Not even the threat of extinction was enough to convince Rhea.

I scowled. It was one thing to not want to fight on either side of a war—I wasn't crazy about wielding a sword and running screaming out onto a battlefield either. But this was different. "We're not asking you to fight," I said. "We're asking you to help us prevent more deaths."

"I know my husband," said Rhea. "If I were to get involved, I would be forced to fight, and I will not hurt a living creature no matter their intentions. That includes Cronus."

"Even though he'll kill billions of people and nearly the entire council in order to get what he wants?" I took a deep breath, forcing myself to stay calm. Getting upset wouldn't help matters. "You know as well as I do that inaction isn't supporting peace. It's turning a blind eye to what's really going on. And without your help, we *will* lose."

James reached for my hand, but I pulled away. If he wasn't willing to fight, then I would.

Rhea slowly turned toward us. Her serenity vanished, replaced with frigid disapproval, and I steeled myself against it. She could dislike me as much as she wanted. I wasn't going to back down.

"I would be no help to you regardless of what I did. My husband will not listen to reason," said Rhea. "I will not raise a hand against anyone. My children are much better served by what I do here."

"But your children are *dying*," I said. "You could stop that.

You could save their lives—you're the only one who can. If you don't, they'll die, and it'll be because of you."

The moment the words left the tip of my tongue, I knew it was the wrong thing to say, but I couldn't take it back now. I glanced at James, a silent apology and plea for him to help me. He stayed silent.

Rhea straightened, her powerful gaze focused directly on me. "No, daughter of Demeter. They will die because of *you*."

My face burned, and it took everything I had not to run out of there as fast as I could. How did she know? Could she sense the guilt floating inside me, buoyed by every life already lost because of my stupidity? "My name is Kate. And I'm sorry. I'm *sorry*. I didn't know—"

"Ignorance is not an excuse for the consequences that result because of it."

"You don't think I realize that?" Hot tears stung my eyes. I'd never hated anyone as much as I hated Rhea in that moment. Not Walter. Not Calliope. Not even Cronus.

No, that was wrong. I hated myself more than I could ever hate any of them.

"He has my son." My voice grew thick, and my hands trembled. "For some unfathomable reason, he wants me to be his queen—"

"It is not unfathomable," said Rhea with unnerving calm. "You showed him kindness and understanding when no one else has in millennia. Even the most blackened and twisted of souls cannot help but respond to compassion."

I hesitated. "How do you—"

"I know everything I wish to know."

I bit my lip. "Then you must realize why this is so important to me. You know what I promised Cronus. You know what he's been doing to me, the sick—"

"I am aware," said Rhea. "And you have my sympathy. Standing at his side does not make you his equal in his eyes, and it is a hard life, one you do not have the power to fight."

"I don't, but you do," I said. "Henry's your son, right? He's dying. He needs you, but instead you're here with strangers—"

"No one who walks this earth is a stranger to me." Her eyes flashed, a strange combination of the sun and the ocean. "I am not neglecting my son. He knew the consequences of his actions when he committed to them, and it was a risk he was willing to take to save you."

I exhaled sharply. She wasn't listening. She didn't understand—or maybe she did, and she just didn't care. "What about my son? He's Henry's, too, you know. And he's your grandson. His name's Milo, and he's not even a week old. Why does he deserve to be raised by Cronus?"

Rhea said nothing, and I couldn't stop the flow of words that poured from me now.

"He'll never know me. He'll never know his father. He'll grow up calling the bitch who kidnapped him his mother, the egomaniac who's killed millions of people his father and he'll never know that I'm out here loving him more in a moment than they could in an eternity. What could he have possibly done to deserve that?"

"Nothing," said Rhea softly. "Your son has done nothing to deserve that, as the people of this village have done nothing to deserve brutality and starvation."

"Then help him like you're helping these people," I begged. "Please, I'll do whatever you want—"

"I want you to leave me in peace."

"Okay." I took a shaky breath. She wasn't going to help the council with the war. If she wouldn't do it for the billions of helpless people in the world, then nothing I could possibly say or do would change her mind. "I'll go away, I promise. Just—please. Help Henry. At least give my son a chance to know his father."

Once again, Rhea was quiet. Her eyes grew distant the same way Cronus's had in the nursery, and her hand stilled halfway to the basket. I glanced at James. Was that our cue to go? He shrugged, and together we waited.

"Very well," she said at last, breaking the silence. "It is done."

"What's done?" I said, giving James another bewildered look, but his brow knitted in confusion. "Rhea, please— what's done?"

"Give your mother my love," she said, touching my shoulder. The pain in my arm from the dagger vanished. "You are strong, Kate. Stronger than you know. As long as you resist my husband, you do not need me to have what you most desire."

"It isn't about what I want," I said, seconds from bursting. How could she heal me but not help save the people who really needed her? "He's going to kill everyone, this village included."

She didn't respond. Instead she picked a few more blossoms and turned to reenter the clinic. I started to go after her, and James grabbed my wrist with an iron grip.

"Don't," he said. Before I could protest, another voice whispered through the garden, hoarse and cracking. But real. So, so real.

"Kate?"

My heart hammered, and I spun around, yanking my hand from James's. Nestled between a gnarled tree and a patch of ferns stood Henry.

CHAPTER 7
ATHENS

I flew across the garden and into Henry's arms, kissing him like it was the last chance I'd ever get.

It was really him. His skin was warm, his moonlight eyes focused on me, and the way he lifted me into the air and kissed me—no one, not even a Titan, could make my insides turn to mush the way he did. He splayed his hand over my back, his palm so hot that I could feel it through my shirt.

"I missed you." My voice broke, and he pressed his forehead to mine so all I could see was him.

"You're all right." He ran his fingers through my hair the same way James had on the flight over, but that was nothing more than a distant memory. Henry was here now, and part of me clicked back into place.

He stumbled, and I immediately dropped back to the ground, searching his face for any sign of pain. Instead of grimacing, he smiled and took my hand. "I'm all right. Just need rest."

I wasn't so sure I believed him, but James stood and gestured to the door Rhea had disappeared through. "We should thank her and get on our way," he said, eyeing Henry. "I reckon you aren't in any condition to get us back to Olympus, so we'll have to do it the old-fashioned way. Sunset's in a few hours."

"Wait," I said, helping Henry forward. "There's someplace I want to see first."

Henry and I sat against the wall in the Zimbabwe airport, my fingers laced through his. I hadn't let go since I'd flown into his arms in Rhea's garden, and he hadn't tried to make me.

I'd sneaked kisses in the cab all the way back to the airport, ignoring the faces James made in the front seat. Now that we were in public, Henry seemed hesitant, but he never refused me. How could I have ever believed Cronus's ruse? No one, especially not the King of the Titans, could ever replace Henry.

"Do you want to see Milo?" I said as we waited for James to return from the ticket counter.

"Yes," said Henry without hesitation, though the exhaustion on his face gave me pause. Rhea had removed every last trace of Cronus from his body, but he still moved as if he were in pain. What would going through that quicksand barrier do to him? Would it make him worse?

"Once you rest," I said, gripping his hand. "You can sleep on the plane."

His expression flickered with disappointment, but he didn't argue. If he'd been well enough to see him, he would've fought like hell to get me to agree, and uneasy satisfaction settled within me. At least I'd made one right choice today.

"What happened?" He spoke quietly, but even in the middle of the loud airport, I heard every word. "Why are we going to Athens?"

I hesitated. There was no easy way to say it and nothing I could do to make it less painful, so I pulled no punches. I told him everything that had happened since Calliope had attacked him. The assault on Athens, my visions, everything Cronus had said and done—everything except for the part where I'd promised myself to him. I couldn't bring myself to say it, and with the way the muscles in Henry's jaw twitched as I described how Cronus had held our son, I didn't want to make things any worse than they already were.

"I will kill him," whispered Henry. "If I have to tear the world apart to do it, I will."

"And then you'll be no better than him," I said. "We'll figure out how to get Milo back without anyone else dying, I promise."

Henry nodded and seemed to relax against the wall. At least I thought he was relaxing until I felt the telltale waves of dark power emanating from him.

I touched his knee. "Henry, as badly as I want to rip the bastard's head off, you're in no condition to get into a pissing match with a Titan. Rest first, and we'll figure something out later."

After a long, tense moment, that resonating power vanished. I looked around nervously, searching for any signs that the people milling around us had noticed anything, but no one seemed any the wiser.

Twenty feet away, I spotted James talking to a woman wearing a massive backpack. He pointed down the length of the terminal, and she gave him a grateful smile and ran off in that same direction. I frowned.

"Not exactly the best time to stop and give directions, is it?" I said as he rejoined us. James shrugged.

"Not exactly the best time to gather enough power to wipe out half of Africa either," he said, looking pointedly at Henry. They glared at each other. "Besides, giving directions is what I do. Among other things."

"Like rob banks," said Henry.

"That was *once*." James shook his head and produced three tickets. "The airport in Athens isn't there anymore, but I got us as close as possible. Are you sure you want to do this, Kate?"

I nodded numbly. As important as reporting to the council was, I had to see the damage. Cronus had left the Parthenon untouched for a reason, and maybe there was a clue there, or something that could help us. Besides, I had no doubt Henry would dive into the war the moment we returned to Olympus, and he needed a break before he went head to head with Cronus. Keeping him away for as long as possible was the only solution I could think of.

Henry pressed his lips to my temple. "Going to Athens won't help," he said quietly. "It won't change anything."

"It could. We might find something. Those people died because of me—"

"Of course they didn't." Henry's frown deepened. "It has nothing to do with you. Cronus would have attacked humanity eventually, and nothing you could have done would have prevented it."

James gave me a look, but I averted my eyes. I couldn't tell Henry how wrong he was.

"Come on," said James, offering Henry a hand. He refused, and James's arm dropped to his side. "Our flight boards soon. We should arrive with enough time to reach Athens before the next sunset."

"Why does that matter?" I said, steadying Henry by the elbow as he stood shakily.

"Because the closer we are to Cronus, the more danger we're in," said James. "I don't know about you, but I'm not willing to risk it for very long."

Part of me didn't care, the part that had died along with the people of Athens. But the part of me that held Henry's hand and dreamed of holding Milo cared, and I nodded. The less time we spent in Greece, the better. I had to go, though. I wouldn't budge on that.

"Maybe you should go back to Olympus," I said to Henry. If Cronus discovered Rhea had healed him, Henry would be dead the moment he stepped within reach. How wide was it now? How far could Cronus extend? To Athens? To London? To New York City? How long before he broke out of the island prison the others had managed to construct? He'd broken out of the Underworld on the winter solstice. Would he do the same this December?

Of course he would. That was why the council was fighting him now.

"No," said Henry with gentle firmness, and his fingers tightened around mine. "I will not leave you again."

And selfishly I couldn't ask him to either, even though it might cost us everything.

Our flight was nearly empty. It was like the reports I'd watched on television hours before a hurricane was supposed to hit a town; the freeways leaving were crowded with more people than they'd ever been designed to handle, but the roads leading into town were deserted.

That was us. We were alone in first class, a necessity now that Henry was with us and needed space to rest. I sat in the seat beside him, watching him sleep and trying to coax him to eat something once the fancy meals came around, but he didn't do much more than pick at his chicken and remind me gods didn't need food.

"He'll be fine," whispered James from the seat in front of me. Though Henry had fallen back asleep, he continued to squeeze my hand. "Should've never left Olympus in his condition, the stubborn ass. Once we get back, he'll recover a lot faster."

"You think?" I pursed my lips. "That's part of the reason I wanted to go to Athens. I figured the minute we get back, he's going to want to fight with the others. He won't give himself the time he needs to recuperate. At least this way he'll get some rest."

James eyed him. "You really think he'll change his mind about fighting?"

"Of course. They have Milo." And no matter how stubborn Henry could be, he wouldn't abandon our son. "Are there any others?"

"Any other what?"

"Titans," I whispered. "There were others in the myths, right?"

James scowled, the line between his eyebrows deepening. "Yes, there were others, but they won't be any help. They were buried in Tartarus with Cronus." He must have seen the look on my face, because he added hastily, "We don't have to worry about them. Cronus would never allow them to leave, first of all—he wants to be king, and they'd challenge his rule. Second, they were all captured before Cronus was, and the measures the original six took to make sure they'd never see the light of day again…" He winced. "The only reason they didn't take those measures against Cronus is because Rhea begged them not to. It more or less kills them," he added. "Or at least as much as a Titan can be killed. And because she's their mother, they listened."

"Is that why they didn't imprison her?"

"She didn't fight in that war either."

"Right," I said. At least she was consistent.

"You should get some sleep," said James. "Busy day ahead of us."

"You, too," I mumbled, and for the rest of the flight, I tried to follow his advice. But sleep either meant visions and Cronus or nightmares of Titans rising up from the earth, and I couldn't stomach either right now.

The plane landed, and I reluctantly woke Henry. Without any checked luggage, it was an easy trek through the airport to catch a cab, and once again we settled in for a drive.

Athens hadn't been the only place affected by the aftermath of the tidal wave. Signs of devastation were everywhere: refugees huddled together in large tents on the outskirts of the airport, debris of what had once been Athens was scattered across the coast, and the towns we drove through were practically empty.

"The earthquakes, they have scared our people away," said the cabdriver. Once again I recognized that the words he spoke weren't English, but I understood them anyway. That ability must have developed between my summer in Greece and now. "After what has happened to Athens, many believe we have been cursed."

"Earthquakes?" said James and I at the same time, though he spoke in what must have been Greek, while I used English.

"You have not heard?" said the driver, and for a moment James's eyes grew distant. I couldn't hear what he was saying or who he was saying it to, but it was obvious he was communicating with someone.

"Phillip says there have been dozens of minor earthquakes around the Aegean Sea since the attack on Athens," said James in a hushed voice. "Two major ones."

"He is trying to escape our barriers by going through the earth," said Henry on my other side.

"It isn't working, is it?" I said, and both he and James shook their heads. "Good."

I spent the rest of the cab ride in silence. The hours slipped by as we drove through the Greek countryside, heading toward the destruction while everyone else was leaving. I couldn't bring myself to fall asleep. I sat rigidly beside Henry, whose eyes slipped shut for long periods of time, and not even our driver seemed very chatty once he'd updated us on everything that had happened. James told him which turns to take, and despite looking annoyed at being given directions by a tourist, he didn't argue.

At last, after I'd wondered if we would ever reach Athens, the taxi came to a stop on a road that wound up a steep hill. "I cannot go any farther," said our driver apologetically. "There is nothing left for us to go toward, and I have barely enough fuel to make it back."

"That's fine," said James, handing the man a wad of bills. "Keep the change."

The three of us piled out of the car, and I hugged Henry's arm as James led us down the road. It slanted upward as it circled the hill, and I didn't see any sign of the city, but he seemed to know where he was going.

"You need to prepare yourself," said James as we rounded the corner. "This won't be easy."

"I didn't come here for easy," I muttered. Henry didn't say a word, but he slid his arm from my grip to wrap around my shoulders instead. Warmth spread through me, and though it wasn't enough to make me relax, it did help. Just Henry being there did wonders.

We reached the other side of the bend. I don't know what I'd been expecting—more green landscape, more trees, more Greece, but the moment I saw what lay before us, I stopped cold.

The ocean glittered in the distance, churning threateningly

as dusk approached. Before it, where Athens had stood, was nothing. Land that had once been covered in buildings and homes and people going about their daily lives was now barren and brown. Rubble stood where skyscrapers once had, and though rescue crews were scattered across the ruins, I would have never guessed that less than a week before, this had been Athens.

"It's gone," whispered James, and I groped around until I found his hand. His fingers were cold. "It's just—gone."

On my other side, Henry met the scene in front of us with stony silence. Pulling myself away from the destruction long enough to gauge his reaction, a wave of nausea swept over me. He didn't look any different. His expression was impassive and his eyes distant, but there was no horror in his eyes. Only the same sadness that was always there.

This was his reality. He'd surrounded himself with death for eons; why would witnessing it on the surface be any different from seeing the dead in the Underworld? From ruling over them, judging their lives, choosing the fates of those who couldn't choose for themselves?

In spite of reason, the way he stared at the ruins with silent acceptance chilled me. I never wanted to look like that. I never wanted to feel like death was no great loss, because for the family and friends and loved ones the people of Athens had left behind, it was terrible.

I leaned against him, and the three of us stood there, linked together. How could anyone who claimed to be capable of love do this?

Cronus wasn't mortal, though. He didn't understand the bonds of humanity or the fear and impact of death. To him, he'd done nothing more than brush away an anthill on a sidewalk, not realizing the ripples would be felt by millions.

No, he knew. He knew exactly what he'd done. He simply didn't care.

"Can we—can we get to the Parthenon from here?" I said. "Maybe Cronus left something or—"

"There's nothing there but rubble and dust," said James.

"I know, but—"

Henry squeezed my hand. "I will take you."

Before I could protest, the world around the three of us dissolved, and we landed in the middle of the ancient ruins. Above us, the sky was a symphony of color, a stark contrast to the devastation below.

"Are you okay?" I said, watching Henry. He was pale, and a thin sheen of sweat covered his forehead, but he nodded.

"I will live. Let us search for this clue."

The tone of his voice made it obvious he was with James on this one—that there was no way Cronus would've left any sort of sign for us, but we had to try. I walked around the crumbling structure, searching for anything that looked out of place. James and I had visited the Parthenon during my first summer away from Henry, but I'd barely glanced at the details then, more enamored with the view. Now I wished I'd paid more attention.

What was I looking for? The pillars looked the same. Despite the destruction below, the council had been right: Cronus had left these ruins alone. Why?

Maybe it really was just a sign. An offer of peace if they stepped aside. But Walter had been adamant that Cronus would slaughter them all regardless of their efforts against him. Was he wrong? Or was Cronus trying to lure the others into inaction?

I kicked a bit of dirt. No way of knowing without asking, and the likelihood of Cronus telling me the whole truth was minuscule. Except—

I squinted. The floor hadn't been made of dirt the last time I'd been here. Kneeling down, I brushed it away, revealing the worn stone underneath. My heart sank. Just debris from the tidal wave then. But that didn't make any sense. How would that have gotten up here?

"Is there a way to clear all of this dirt out of here?" I said, and a few feet away, James waved his hand. A gentle wind swirled across the ground, revealing the floor below—along with a series of drawings etched into the stone. There was no way a human had done them. They were too intricate, too sophisticated, too impossible. The images seemed to warp the very stone, as if those things really existed within it.

"What the hell is that?" said James. He and Henry stepped back, and I rose. These hadn't been here last time either.

On the ground, it was impossible to see them all as they stretched across the Parthenon. Instead I focused on the one nearest my feet: a drawing of fifteen thrones, all consumed by fire. Even though the lines didn't move, it was easy to see the flicker of the flames.

My pulse raced, and I hurried over to another. A massive figure hovering over a crack in the earth as a dozen tiny figures fought it.

Cronus, escaping from the Underworld.

"It's his version of history," I said, stunned. "Not just history, but his plans for the future, too."

Slowly Henry, James and I walked around the ruins, examining each picture. Some were of a time long before I was born—some before the birth of humanity—and Henry and James quietly explained them to me. But others I recognized. The drawing of a gate in Tartarus made me shiver, and I turned away. Each bar had a bloody handprint on it.

"Kate?" said Henry. "Come see this."

I moved to his side and slid my hand in the crook of his elbow. "What's—"

I stopped short. Below my feet, an etching of Cronus stared up at me, and he wasn't alone. Standing beside him, holding on to him as I held on to Henry now, was a girl wearing a crown.

Not just a girl.

Me.

That girl was me.

CHAPTER 8
QUEEN

Silence. I held my breath, waiting for Henry to say something, but he didn't. He didn't blink, he didn't move, he didn't look away from the image. He just stared, and the same black waves of power that appeared in the airport began to gather.

Terrific. There went any chance I had of stopping Henry from riding his cloud of doom back to Cronus's island.

James sauntered over and let out a low whistle. "Nice. Cronus really captured your essence. And look at that tiara."

I elbowed him. "It isn't me."

"Who else would it be? I mean, look at her—the nose is a bit off, but other than that, it's perfect."

"It isn't me," I said stubbornly, giving him a look. We both knew it was a lie, but Henry couldn't find out about the deal I'd made. "Calliope's been shifting her appearance, and she looked exactly like an older blond version of me. You can't tell what color hair this girl has, but that is definitely her nose."

James held my stare for a long moment, and finally he refocused on the picture. "You're right," he said. "It must be Calliope."

I wanted to hug him for lying and smack him for doing it so badly. Instead I settled on a smile and wrapped my arm around Henry's waist. "See? It's Cronus and Calliope. Nothing else makes sense anyway."

Henry exhaled, as if he'd been holding his breath this entire time. Maybe he had. "Of course," he murmured. "My mistake."

Henry wasn't stupid, but I hadn't lied—Calliope did look a lot more like me and my mother these days. With luck, that would cover my lies long enough for Henry to recover. And by then, maybe his involvement would be enough for the council to take Calliope down and recapture Cronus, after all.

I couldn't stomach staring at that image any longer, and I drew Henry and James over to the edge of the Parthenon. Together we gazed down at the devastation once more, but this time Henry's grip felt like steel. He wasn't letting go for anything, and neither was I.

I didn't know how long we stood there. Minutes. Hours. Years. I was lost in forever, waiting for something to happen to remind me that there was still a world out there, a place to fight for even though Athens was gone, and a future beyond the one Cronus wanted for me. It wasn't hopeless, not yet, and I couldn't afford to forget that. The ocean grew surlier, whitecaps forming and waves raging against the shore, and something streaked across the sky.

I blinked. "What was that?"

"What was what?" said James, and another spark sped across the purple horizon.

"That," I said as another followed, and another. "Rescue flares?"

"No," said Henry. "It is dusk, and Olympus is overhead. The council is attacking the island."

My blood ran cold. I'd never seen the other members of the council attack in their own realm. Down in the Underworld, their abilities had been muted, but on the surface they must have been giving it their all.

At what cost? Who would be next? My mother was among them. Would it be her?

I swallowed hard, and my vision blurred. The last time I'd spoken to her, I'd been a selfish brat. I hadn't given her the chance to explain why she'd kept the identity of my father secret. What if those were the last words I ever said to her?

"I should help them," said James, and he tried to let go of my hand, but I held on.

"Be safe," I said. "And make sure my mother comes home."

He kissed my cheek. "Always. I'll see you in a few minutes."

A few minutes? James started toward the center of the Parthenon, and several feet away, he began to glow. Before I could utter a word of surprise, he, too, turned into a blaze of light, and he took off after them.

"Oh, my god," I said as I followed his path across the sky. "I had no idea we could do that."

"They are most powerful when Olympus is nearby," said Henry. "As James said, the battle will not last long. Come. We must return to where it is safe for you."

"You, too," I said firmly. He could pretend he was fine all he wanted, but he wasn't fooling me. I could see the exhaustion in his eyes. He wouldn't have a chance if Cronus discovered we were here, if he didn't know already. "Can we still visit Olympus sometime, once you're healed?"

Henry gave me a puzzled look. "We are not returning to the Underworld. We are going to Olympus. Cronus and Calliope believe me to be dead, and we must encourage that belief."

He was wrong; Cronus didn't think he was dead. He knew we were going to find Rhea, and he had to realize that Rhea wouldn't refuse to help her son.

Though what if he didn't? He knew nothing about a parent's bond to a child. He cared about control and power, not affection and love. If I told him Rhea had refused to help, would he believe me?

"All right," I said. I would talk to James about it later. Henry was too tired, and he needed rest, not a late night of planning how best to screw with Cronus's head. He'd be all too willing to do it, too, after that image of me beside Cronus. "I don't know how to get back to Olympus."

"Lucky for you, I do," said Henry with a faint smile. "Close your eyes."

I gazed out across the ruins of Athens one last time. I would make this right. I couldn't give the people back their lives, but I would do everything I could to make their stay in the Underworld a happy one.

Focusing on the streaks in the sky attacking the island prison, I said a silent prayer that they came home safely. To whom, I didn't know. To anyone who would listen. There had to be a way to stop Cronus's version of the future from happening, and I would do everything I could to figure it out.

At last I closed my eyes, and Henry wrapped his arms around me. A warm wind surrounded us, and my feet left the ground. This wasn't Henry's usual disappearing–reappearing act, but it didn't matter. We were together, and for one beautiful moment, we were flying.

★ ★ ★

I'd spent countless hours in hospitals, waiting for a doctor to tell me how my mother was doing after her latest round of tests and surgeries. Anxiety had become my closest companion during those years, and no matter how many times I played the game, it never got any easier.

I'd never been able to read or make small talk with the others waiting for news. Sometimes I'd filled in the empty spaces of coloring books with cheap packs of crayons I'd found in the gift shops. Sometimes I'd stared at a television, unable to focus on what was showing. It never seemed nearly as important as what was happening to my mother.

Sometimes I had imagined I could feel everything she felt. I'd imagined what she could see if she was awake. If not, I'd imagined what she'd dreamed. And always, always, time had stood still while I waited for the inevitable bad news.

I'd known I would lose her someday, but then came Henry. Then came the seven tests. Then came the rest of my life. The moment I'd passed, the moment I'd swallowed my pride enough to admit defeat, my mother had appeared in all her immortal glory, and I'd thought it was the universe's way of promising I would never lose her again.

That promise was a lie.

Henry eased down onto his black-diamond throne in the vast room inside Olympus, and without saying a word, I curled up in his lap. He kissed me, the sort of warm, soft kiss that normally washed away every worry I had, but not today.

We waited. He ran his fingers through my hair, toying with the ends, and I stared at the center of the throne room. The faint sounds of battle filtered in from the world below us, and the clouds on the sunset floor swirled, as if they, too, could sense the world's discontent.

It never ceased to amaze me how quickly a few minutes

with my mother could pass. When I knew I might never see her again, however, those few minutes turned into hours, and my entire world narrowed until all I could think of was her.

"Tell me about him," whispered Henry, his voice muted as if he were half a world away.

"Milo?" I said.

"Yes." He threaded his fingers through mine. "What's he like?"

He was trying to distract me, and my heart swelled with gratitude. "James taught me how to show you. Do you feel up for it now?"

The smile on his face was worth every drop of guilt I felt for caring about something other than my mother right now. "Yes. I would love that."

"And—and you're sure Cronus won't be able to see you?"

He brushed my knuckles with the pad of his thumb. "I'll make sure of it."

Pulling Henry into my vision of the nursery felt like dragging him through quicksand, exactly like it had with James, but I was almost too distracted to notice. I had no idea what I was going to say to Cronus. Would I let him keep up his ruse? Or had I already given myself away with James? And what about Henry? What if Cronus said something that gave my lie at the Parthenon away? But I needed Henry to meet Milo. I needed him to see our son for more than a fraction of a—

Something tugged me sharply back to Olympus. Lost in the middle of that quicksand, I had no choice but to return to the throne room, once again feeling as if I were surfacing after a long swim. I opened my mouth to complain, sure it was James again, but my mother pulled me into an embrace before I could utter a word.

"Kate." Her voice surrounded me, soothing away my frustration. Her skin was cold, but she was alive.

Fighting tears, I hugged her as tightly as I dared. Her body felt as delicate as it had during the last days of her mortal life. "I'm sorry—I'm so sorry, Mom. What I said before, I didn't mean—"

"I know," she whispered. "It's all right. I'm just relieved you're safe."

I could've held on to her forever, waiting for her to warm up again, but she pulled away. Behind her the others gathered, all the worse for wear, but no one was bleeding.

"I told you not to go to her," said my mother, and it took me a moment to realize she was talking to Henry. "You shouldn't have gone anywhere in your condition."

Henry grimaced, and he set his hand on my back, as if he couldn't go a moment without touching me. I wasn't about to complain. "You would have been just as angry if I had not," he said.

"Likely so," admitted my mother, and she kissed us both on the forehead. "Thank you for taking care of her."

"Hey, what about me?" said James, and she moved aside so he could join us. "I did most of the work."

"You insisted on dropping off in New York City instead of Africa, like I told you to do," said my mother sternly. "You could have had her back days ago."

James shrugged sheepishly. "Yeah, well. Henry was stable, and it isn't a trip if there's no traveling involved, you know."

"Do not pretend it was anything more than you wanting to spend more time with her," said Henry.

James grinned. "Can you blame me? She's the only one of you who bothers with me for more than a few minutes at a time."

"I wonder why that is," said my mother, nudging him with her hip, and he smirked.

Behind them, someone cleared their throat, and my mother's

smile faded. Walter stepped forward. "Brother," he said to Henry. "Welcome back. You are well?"

Something flickered in Henry's eyes, as if he were making a decision. No real question what that was—the last time they'd spoken, it'd been an argument over me. But I was safe now, and there were more important things to worry about. Like rescuing Milo.

Be angry with him after the war, I thought, pushing it toward Henry. *The council is fractured enough as it is.*

Henry's eyebrow quirked, and though he didn't look at me, his shoulders relaxed. At last he addressed his brother. "I will be well soon enough. How was the battle?"

"It was what it was," said Walter, exhaling. Even he couldn't hide his relief at Henry's apparent forgiveness. "Tomorrow we will attack again, and we will continue to do so until we have made the progress necessary to allow for a winning strategy. James told us of your discovery at the Parthenon. Perhaps that will give us clues as to Cronus's plan."

"Perhaps," said Henry. Walter eyed him as if he was sizing him up, and I automatically shifted in an attempt to protect Henry from that calculating stare.

"And you, brother," said Walter. "Will you be joining us as soon as you are well?"

"As I am outside my realm, I cannot imagine that my contribution will be any great thing. But yes," he said quietly. "I will join you."

"Me, too," I said, and before anyone could protest, I added, "I have a right to fight for my family. While Henry's recovering, he can teach me."

"No." Henry's voice was little more than a whisper in my ear. "I will not have you fight in this war."

Once again, we were back to this, to Henry insisting I couldn't take care of myself. To the entire council refusing to accept that I might be able to help them, if only a little. Maybe a little would be enough to change the tide, yet they refused to consider the possibility. Hadn't I just proven I wasn't completely incompetent? I'd been the one to suggest going to the Parthenon in the first place. I'd been the one to discover the etchings. I didn't know how to fight like them yet, but I could learn. And in the meantime, I could do a hell of a lot more than sit around and twirl my hair.

I opened my mouth to protest, but my mother beat me to it. "Kate can fight if she wants," she said. Her eyes locked on mine. "If Henry won't teach her, I will."

Henry scowled, but Walter was the first to speak up. "Very well. If that is what Kate wants, so be it." He touched my mother's shoulder and turned to join the others on the opposite side of the circle.

I stared after him. That was it? After everything that had happened, that was all he was willing to give me? No offer to teach me himself—not that I expected one, and I would've turned it down anyway, but still. No attempt to insist I stay safe. Just permission to go out and die if that was what I wanted.

Maybe if I hadn't already been so on edge, it wouldn't have stung as much as it did. My mother knew I would've gone anyway. She knew who I was, and she knew it was pointless to try to argue. Walter didn't know me though, and if he was really any sort of father, he should have cared.

"Kate," started Henry, but I stood, pulling my hand from his. He could only shield me for so long before he paid the price, and I wasn't going to let that happen. I had to learn how to control my abilities. I had to learn how to protect myself, if only so I could protect Henry and our son.

"You need to rest," I said sharper than I intended. Leaning down, I kissed his cheek, a silent apology. "I love you. I just need to be alone right now."

He caught my lips with his, and a long moment passed before he finally broke away. After giving him a small smile, I ducked my head and hurried off toward the suites, silently praying no one would follow me. Of course they would, though. If Henry didn't, James would, and if James didn't—

"Sweetheart."

If James didn't, my mother would.

I slowed to give her the chance to catch up, but I didn't stop. What would she do if she found out about the deal I'd made with Cronus? Would she help? Tell the rest of the council? I couldn't be sure, and that mistrust hurt like hell. I should've been able to confide in my own mother without worrying about the consequences.

"I just want to be alone," I mumbled, but she draped her arm across my shoulders and fell into step beside me. I didn't pull away. I couldn't. Even if the anxiety of waiting and worrying for her to come back was gone, there would be a next time. There was always a next time, and I didn't want to beat myself up about turning her away now like I had before I'd left with James.

"You shouldn't be alone right now," she said, and there was something underneath her words I didn't understand.

She was right, though. If I had my way, I'd never be alone again, but I no longer had any guarantees. If the worst happened—if the council didn't discover a way to stop Calliope and imprison Cronus once more—then I might have Milo, but I would be Cronus's plaything for eternity. And I would rather Milo die and spend the rest of forever oblivious in the Underworld than be subjected to the same fate.

My mother led me to her bedroom, and as she entered, the branches of her bed frame flowered with magenta blossoms. I sat down on the edge of her mattress and inhaled. They smelled like summertime.

"I'm sorry I didn't tell you about your father sooner," she said, rubbing my back, and I let myself relax under her touch. After years of wondering when her last moment would be, I no longer had it in me to be angry with her.

"It's all right," I said, although it wasn't. "Why didn't you tell me?"

"Because I selfishly wanted to keep you for myself." Settling in behind me, she combed her fingers through my hair and began to braid it. "I loved our life together. I missed the council, but having you more than made up for it. I hadn't been that happy since—"

She stopped short, and I stared at my hands. She didn't need to finish for me to know what she was going to say. "Since you had Persephone," I mumbled.

"Yes. Since I had Persephone." She shook out the braid she'd managed in those few seconds and began again. "I raised you as a mortal because I believed that kind of life, away from this grandiose existence, would give you the best possible chance of passing the tests. But along the way, I discovered how much happier I was when it was just the two of us lost in the sea of humanity. And if I ever allowed Walter into our lives, that would have shattered."

"But if Walter's immortal, and you're immortal, then why wasn't I?" I said. It seemed like such a small, unimportant question in the scheme of things, but I needed small and unimportant right now.

"Because I had you in my mortal form." She began on a smaller braid, weaving it together with the larger one. "That was part of my bargain with the council. Demigods—and you have always been a demigod, darling—are not immortal, but they can earn immortality, as can mortals."

"Why have Henry marry a mortal to begin with?" I said. "Why not—I don't know. Why not just have me and marry me off to him?"

She laughed softly. "And how well would that have gone over, do you think? I learned my lesson with Persephone. Henry wanted a willing queen, one who understood the price of death, and he insisted on mortal candidates. The council did consider having you born immortal, of course, since the others died very mortal deaths, but Calliope was the one to insist that you not be born a goddess." Her voice dropped as if she'd just realized what it meant, two decades too late. "I thought it was because she wanted the same things as Henry—that she did not want to push another girl toward a marriage and a role they did not want, only to once again end in disaster."

That wasn't why though, of course. She'd wanted competition she could kill off. "Did Walter know you were going to get sick?" I whispered.

"What? No, honey, no." Her hands slowed. "I was never supposed to get sick. You were supposed to be older. You were supposed to have the chance to live, to choose a life for yourself. Deception was never supposed to be part of it. I planned on telling you on your twentieth birthday, and at that point you would've taken the tests if you'd wanted to. When I found out I had cancer, I went to the council, and they decided to speed up the schedule. I held on so long because Theo helped me. None of that was planned, I swear."

I nodded. She wouldn't lie to me, not about something like that. And everything she went through, everything she'd suffered—no one in their right mind would put themselves through that for a stupid test.

I would've never passed if she hadn't developed cancer, though. I would've never been so afraid of death that I was willing to give up six months of my life to save Ava's. Had the council known that? Had they gone behind my mother's back to give me a fighting chance?

I pushed the thought from my mind. It was ridiculous. Not even the council was capable of that. I hoped.

"Walter knew I was alone," I said. "Why didn't he come help me?"

"Because he's the King of the Gods, honey, and as much as he might love his family, he has the weight of the world on his shoulders." She finished my braid, and after tying it off with a bit of ribbon from her nightstand, she picked a magenta flower and tucked it into the end. "Walter has never been much of a father to any of his children."

"So I've been told." I turned to face her. "What would've happened if I hadn't passed?"

"You know what would have happened, darling. Your memory would have been erased, and you would have gone on living your life."

"But you would have still been alive," I said. "Your mortal body would have died, but you would still be there. And you would've visited me, right?"

My mother's eyes became unfocused. "Perhaps in your dreams, if the council allowed it."

I inhaled sharply, and pain worse than anything Cronus could throw at me burrowed into my chest. She would have left me. My own mother would have willingly abandoned me if I hadn't passed.

Then what? I would've lived the rest of my mortal life thinking I was completely alone. I would've been, too, because dreaming about my mother—if the council *allowed* me to—wasn't the same as having her with me. She knew what I'd gone through, taking care of her and watching her slowly fade away all those years. She knew that I would have done anything to give her more time to stay with me. And she would have abandoned me like that anyway.

I stood, my legs unsteady. "I need to go."

"Where?" said my mother, standing with me, but I stepped back. Confusion and hurt flashed in her eyes, and I looked away. She was my rock. My constant. She'd sworn she'd had me because she wanted to, and I believed her. I wasn't Persephone's replacement—but only because I'd passed those tests. If I hadn't, I would've been nothing but a disappointment, too, and she would have left me exactly like she'd left Persephone. Like Persephone had left her.

I needed my mother's love and support more than ever, but for the first time in my life, I doubted her. And it killed me.

"I'm going to get Milo back," I said. "Someone around here deserves to have parents who love them more than anything, including their own immortality."

I headed toward the door, tears stinging my eyes. Silently I prayed she would tell me to stop, that she would hug me and insist she would have defied the council whether or not they'd allowed her to see me. That she would have been there for me no matter what.

"Kate."

My heart caught in my throat.

"I'm sorry. I love you."

I blinked rapidly. Not enough to have stayed with me for the length of my measly mortal life, though. Not if it'd meant disobeying the council. "I love you, too," I mumbled, and without saying another word, I walked out of the bedroom and closed the door behind me.

A soft hum filled the sunset nursery when I arrived. I'd rehearsed over and over what I wanted to tell Cronus, my last-ditch effort against the impending war. Rhea might have refused to help us, but that didn't mean battle was inevitable, and I had to try. As my vision adjusted to the darkness, however, I let out a strangled gasp, all of my carefully formed phrases forgotten. Calliope paced back and forth through the nursery, holding Milo to her chest.

I lunged for her, but as always, I went straight through her and landed half a foot away from Cronus. For the first time since I'd escaped, he wore his face instead of Henry's. So he'd absorbed everything I'd said to James, after all. He stayed silent, only quirking his lips. At least someone found my rage amusing.

"Of course Mother will heal him," said Calliope, her brow creased with worry. "I know she has her reservations about fighting, but she wouldn't let one of us die like that, right?"

She looked to Cronus for confirmation, but he said nothing. Good. That meant he didn't know.

"Father, I *need* Henry. Can't you undo it?"

"Perhaps you ought to have taken that into consideration before you attempted to kill him," said Cronus neutrally, and Calliope tightened her grip around Milo, her scowl deepening.

"I was aiming for his shoulder, not his heart. And he wasn't supposed to *leave*. You swore you'd heal him."

She hadn't meant to nearly kill him? I narrowed my eyes. Of course she'd been bluffing this whole time. She'd been in love with Henry for millennia—she wasn't the type to give up on that. Like Cronus wanted me by his side, Calliope wanted Henry by hers.

"Then it seems as if things did not go according to plan," said Cronus plainly. "You cannot hold me responsible for that."

Milo started to cry, and Calliope let out a frustrated sigh. "Callum, be *quiet*. Mother's trying to think."

"His name isn't Callum, and I'm his mother, you bitch," I

snarled, but of course she didn't hear me. She deposited the baby into Cronus's waiting arms.

"Here. He likes you better anyway. I need Henry, Father, and you need to get him back for me. He can't die."

Milo quieted. At least Calliope didn't have him anymore. "If he is in Olympus, it is out of my control," said Cronus.

"Then you'd better hope he isn't," she said.

Cronus tilted his head. "You dare speak to me in such a manner? I am your father, your ruler, your king, and yet you treat me with as little respect as you do your enemies."

To my immense satisfaction, Calliope froze, her mouth forming a small circle. "I didn't—" She paused, flustered. Served her right. "You know I respect you, Father, more than anything in the world. I just— Nothing's going *right* anymore. Henry was supposed to be mine by now, but Ava couldn't be bothered to fulfill her promise when he was here rescuing that hag."

I stilled. What else had Ava promised Calliope?

"Such insolent behavior will not get you what you want, my daughter," said Cronus. "Surely you must know that by now."

She nodded, and for half a second, she appeared almost meek. "You're still on my side, right, Daddy? You won't stop loving me, too?"

I could've thrown up at her saccharine manipulation, but Cronus didn't bat an eye. "No, daughter, I will not. We are in this together, and it would serve you well to remember that."

"Of course." Calliope bowed her head, the first sign of deference she'd shown since I'd arrived. "I'm sorry for upsetting you, Father."

He waved dismissively, and she headed out of the nursery, closing the door behind her. For a long moment, the only sound that filled the room was Milo's whimpers.

At last Cronus focused on me. His face morphed into a copy of Henry's once more, though he now wore a mask of false concern. "My dear, what is wrong?"

Everything I'd planned to say was gone, but at least I didn't have to pretend to cry. My eyes were red and puffy, and my cheeks flushed from arguing with my mother. Watching Calliope with my son had renewed my frustrated tears, and a lump formed in my throat. There was nothing fake about my grief.

"You know I know who you really are," I whispered. "Change back to your normal face. Please."

Cronus eyed me, and at last his appearance shifted until it was his own again. "I thought you would prefer it this way."

He knew damn well he was fooling me the entire time, but maybe it wasn't just to trick me—maybe he thought it would bring me some comfort, as well. Maybe that was his version of consoling me. I shook my head. "Henry's dead. Rhea couldn't help him. And she won't—she won't help us either."

"I am sorry," said Cronus. He set a sleeping Milo down in the crib and wrapped his arms around me. I held my breath, refusing to hug him back. He could say he was sorry all he wanted, but we both knew he wasn't. He couldn't be. He didn't have it in him. "I was certain Rhea would help him."

"We—we were too late," I said in a broken voice, allowing the tears to flow. "By the time we got there..." It was so close to the truth that it wasn't hard to imagine what it would have felt like to lose Henry completely. If Rhea hadn't healed him, he would have been dead by now. I was sure of it.

We stood there in silence for several minutes. Cronus made the usual gestures someone did when comforting a loved one; soothing words, a gentle touch, promises that it would be all right as I wept into his shoulder. But I wasn't crying about Henry's supposed death, and Cronus didn't really love me. How had I ever believed he could possibly be Henry?

"What did Ava promise to do for Calliope?" I said once my sobs had subsided. "Did she do something to make him die?"

Cronus shrugged and loosened his grip. "I am certain she did not, though I could not begin to guess what her intentions are."

He was lying, but there was nothing I could do to call him on it. "Are you really loyal to Calliope?" I said in a small voice. "I thought you wanted me."

"I do," he said. "I am loyal to no one but you. I tell her what I must to keep her happy, but I live to see you smile."

Bullshit. I hiccupped and pulled away from him, though he didn't let me go completely. "Stop killing people. Please. No one else should have to die because of a stupid family argument."

Cronus paused. "I would like nothing more than to grant your request, my darling, but surely you must know that is not possible. What do you expect me to do? To retreat back to Tartarus without so much as a second thought?"

"Of course not," I mumbled, wiping my eyes with my sleeve. Cronus produced a handkerchief out of nowhere, and only because refusing him would do me no good, I took it. "Why does there need to be a war in the first place? Why can't everyone coexist?"

"Because, my dear Kate, they will not stop until I have been imprisoned once more, and I cannot allow that to happen."

"What if they promised not to try to send you back into the Underworld?"

"If it were that easy, we would have reached a solution eons ago. Unfortunately it is not. Zeus will never agree."

"He's a stubborn jackass," I muttered, and Cronus chuckled.

"Right you are, my darling. Surely you understand that as long as he rules the skies, I cannot stop."

"But what if he and the rest of the council promised not to attack?" I said. "If I could get Walter—Zeus to agree to leave you alone as long as you didn't hurt anyone else?"

Cronus shrugged. "If you are capable of doing the impossible, then perhaps I might consider a truce, though I certainly cannot speak for my daughter."

Without Cronus, Calliope was all but powerless against the other members of the council. "Someone once told me that anything is possible if you give it a chance," I said softly. "If Zeus agrees, you'll back off and let the council take Calliope?"

"Yes," said Cronus, snaking his arms around my waist and gently drawing me toward him again. "I have no use for her any longer. You are all I need."

My entire body went numb. Of course he still expected me to be his queen. He thought Henry was dead.

I stared into the cradle. I'd never held Milo. I'd barely even touched him, and now he would be doomed to a lifetime with Cronus as a father. Then what would everything I was fighting for mean?

Nothing.

"Okay," I whispered. "I'll come back to you as soon as you call a truce and the others have Calliope in custody. But I want you to let my son leave."

"If he leaves, I cannot allow you to go with him."

I nodded tightly. "I know."

He studied me. "You do not want to be his mother?"

I wanted to be his mother more than anything in the world, but if I let Cronus near him, I would be anything but. "I want my mother to raise him in Olympus," I said firmly.

That way Milo would be with Henry, and I could breathe easier knowing they would have each other.

"I see," said Cronus. "You do not want me to be his father."

I balled my hands into fists. "You'll have me. You don't need anything else."

He brushed his knuckles against my cheek in what I was sure he meant to be a loving caress. It sent shivers down my spine, but not the kind he was aiming for. "I need you to be happy. It would give me such great pleasure to show you the honesty and compassion you have shown me."

"If you want to show me any of that honesty and compassion, then you'll give me my son," I said. "And you'll promise to stop killing all of those people."

"Have Zeus agree to a truce, and you have my word," said Cronus with a bow of his head, and he produced a scroll out of thin air and set it in my hand. "A token of my intentions."

I began to untie the black silk ribbon, but he placed his hand over mine.

"It is a list of names of those who have turned traitor and pledged their allegiance to Calliope. With your husband dead, it is only a matter of time before I overthrow the council," said Cronus. "If they wish to survive, my forgiveness is their only hope. And for that, all I ask is you."

I clutched the scroll, and even though it tore me to shreds, I whispered, "Thank you."

"No, my dear," said Cronus, and the fog in his eyes swirled malevolently. "Thank *you*."

CHAPTER 9
MESSENGER

What was left of the council gathered in the throne room of Olympus. It was well past midnight in Greece now, and after the battle at sunset, several of the members looked like they hadn't slept in months. They were there though, and that was the important part. Even Henry had gathered, though he was silent and still looked the worse for wear.

"Well, Kate," said Walter from his throne of glass, "we have all gathered. What is so important that it could not possibly wait?"

I stood. James sat across from me, and I focused on him as my nerves fluttered. Start simple. No need to tell them what I'd bargained until it became necessary. I couldn't give them any reason to turn Cronus down.

"Cronus wants to call a truce," I said, and a ripple of stunned whispers spread throughout the council. Only James didn't move, his eyes locked on mine. He knew the price.

"Absolutely not," said Walter, his voice booming with thunder. "We will not negotiate with a Titan."

"Kate, what's going on?" said my mother quietly, but I didn't waver. If I looked at her, if I saw the concern in her eyes, if I let the confusion in her voice crack my determination, I had no idea what I would do. And I couldn't take that chance.

"He's sent a list of gods who have sided with Calliope," I said, holding out the scroll to Walter, but he made no move to take it. "As a token of his intentions."

"I'm sure he did," said Walter. "And as soon as he has our complacency and his freedom, he will turn on us and once again attempt to destroy the council. I will not allow it to happen."

"He's going to destroy the council anyway," I said. "We don't have the power to fight him and win. You might be able to drag this war out another ten years, but you'll lose eventually. Humanity will be destroyed, and Cronus will kill us all. That's inevitable. So what's the harm in trying to negotiate? He's willing to make a deal. Doesn't that mean something?"

"Not when you are asking us to negotiate with a Titan," said Walter. "Cronus does not settle. His endgame will always be our destruction, and he will not stop until he has his way. I understand you are new to this, Kate, but that is no excuse for such stubborn ignorance."

"Walter," said my mother sharply, "that's enough. Kate has a point. Perhaps it would be wise of us to at least consider—"

"Father's right," said Dylan, rising to his feet. The purple circles under his eyes did nothing to hide the way they sparkled with bone-chilling zeal. "There is no sense in attempting to bargain with Cronus. He will see it only as a weakness, and we cannot allow him to believe we have any holes in our armor that he could exploit for his own gain."

The way he eyed me as he said it made my skin crawl.

"And by that, you mean me," I said. "You think I'm a liability."

"You've been no use to us so far," said Dylan. "If anything, you've only made things worse. Cronus didn't touch Athens until you left—"

"She distracted him for us and bought us more time," snapped James.

"—you seem to delight in distracting the council and insisting we do things we know won't work—"

"She's the one who came up with the idea of searching the Parthenon."

"—and to top it off, you nearly got Henry and your own son killed—"

"He's the one who decided to go after her without backup—"

"You will both silence yourselves immediately," said Henry, but it was too late. Dylan might as well have punched me in the stomach.

"I know," I said in a strangled voice. "I *know,* all right? I'm trying to make things right. I don't want seven billion people to die because of my stupidity. I don't want to lose any one of you. And I'm *trying*—"

"Then maybe you should try a little less," said Dylan, and two thrones down from him, Irene rose.

"That's *enough,*" she said in a dangerously soft voice that mirrored her father's. Our father's. "There is no shame in exploring other avenues. One who jumps into combat purely for the thrill of the fight is a fool, particularly when he risks innocent lives while doing so."

"Are you calling me a fool, daughter?" said Walter. Irene's hand twitched at her side, but she didn't back off. I could have kissed her.

"No, Father. I'm merely pointing out that you have options. We do not even know what Cronus wants or why he wants it. Surely he must have given Kate some kind of hint."

Every pair of eyes in the room turned toward me once more. Great. I wiped my palms on my pants. "He wants a life," I said, mustering up as much conviction as I could. They had to believe me. "He's been stuck in the Underworld for so long that he just wants a chance to live again. He thinks you won't let him."

"No, we will not," said Walter. Irene gave him a look and gestured for me to continue.

"He's agreed to stop attacking us if you stop attacking him. He won't hurt anyone else. And—and he'll turn over Calliope, or at least he won't stop you from taking her back."

"In exchange for what?" said Dylan, and though Irene shushed him, he continued. "We let him go? Do you know what it took to contain him in the first place?"

I hesitated. "He won't go back on his word. He knows the consequences if he does."

"And what, pray tell, are the *consequences* for the most powerful being in the universe flexing his muscles?" said Dylan. "What could he possibly want more than total control over everything?"

Silence. My heart—my stupid, useless heart that cared too much about everything and everyone—hammered painfully, and my breathing grew ragged. I wasn't mortal anymore, but at that moment, I felt more human than I ever had in my life. "He wants me."

The seconds ticked by. Walter frowned deeply, and Irene looked confused. From behind me, I could sense Henry's stare, but I didn't turn around. I couldn't.

At long last, Dylan snorted. "You? You're nothing to him."

I focused on James again, silently pleading with him to explain. He nodded and stood grimly.

"During our trek through the Underworld, Kate had an... encounter with Cronus," said James carefully. Dylan whistled suggestively, but he stopped when he caught sight of Henry behind me. Whatever look he was giving Dylan, I was glad I couldn't see it. "She spoke to him and stopped him from attacking us. Ava and I didn't believe it at first, but he let us go through the Underworld unhindered after that."

"The encounter in Henry's palace," said my mother, her splintered voice damn near breaking my heart. "Calliope left Ava untouched because of what she'd done to Nicholas. But we never did understand why Cronus did not harm Kate."

Once again, everyone focused on me, waiting for me to speak. It was the silence behind me that was unbearable though, and I reached for Henry. All I touched was air.

After an eternal moment, however, his warm fingers found mine, and I let out a sigh of relief. He understood. I could do this. "When Milo was born and Calliope took him from me, Cronus was there," I said. "I begged him to help, and he said—he said if I promised to be his queen, he would let me have Milo again. And he would protect him."

Walter's frown deepened, and a few seats down from him, Dylan rolled his eyes. "Aren't you the little siren?"

I ignored him. "I agreed. I didn't mean it," I added quickly. "But I said yes because—"

"Because Milo's your kid," said James. "You don't need to explain."

I gave him a grateful look. Henry's grip on my hand tightened, and I continued. "When I go see Milo, Cronus is always there. He took Henry's form at first, and I thought— I didn't realize who he was. I thought he was Henry. It was stupid, I know, but James told me who he really was. And I told him Rhea refused to help us."

"Fantastic," said Dylan. "While you were having your

little affair, did you happen to tell him any other closely guarded secrets?"

"That's enough, Dylan," said my mother.

Dylan opened his mouth to retort, but before another fight broke out, I blurted, "He thinks Henry's dead. He doesn't know our real numbers, and he believes we have no choice but to agree to a truce. And we don't," I added. "Not unless we want to risk the entire world."

"If we surrender and allow Cronus to be released, you do realize that he will want you?" said Walter, and I nodded. "Yet this is something you are willing to do?"

"Yes," I whispered. "I don't like it, but if it's the only way to stop this war, I'll do it." And Milo would be safe. That alone would be worth it.

James winced. "You really need to get over your martyr complex. One of these days it's going to get you killed."

Behind me, a pair of feet shuffled, and Henry let go of my hand as he stood. "Brother," he said to Walter, wrapping his arm around my shoulders and pulling me to him. "If you allow Kate to do this, you will no longer have my cooperation. She is my queen. I have already completed her coronation, and I will not allow anyone, not even a Titan, to usurp my claim."

His *claim?* Before I could say a word, Walter cut me off. "Very well. Then we will not accept Cronus's truce."

"And the list of traitors?" said Dylan, eyeing the scroll with an unsavory gleam in his eyes. What did he plan on doing, hunting down each and every one of them? Somehow that didn't feel too far from the truth.

"I will deal with them personally," said Walter, and with a wave of his hand, the scroll vanished. "We have already lost the alliance of most of the other gods. That is not news."

"So what? You're going to let all of those people die while

you fight a war you know you can't win?" I said, and Henry's grip around my shoulders tightened. But I wasn't his *claim,* and I wouldn't let something like this go just because Walter decided the discussion was over. He wasn't always right. My childhood was proof of that.

"No," said Walter. "I intend on winning the war. Now if you will excuse us, Kate, we've got tomorrow's attack to discuss. Given your closeness to Cronus, it would be best if you did not hear our plans."

No one spoke up in my defense. Not Henry, not James, not even my mother. After several seconds, I swallowed the knot in my throat and twisted out of Henry's grip. If they didn't want me around, then fine, but I wasn't going to twiddle my thumbs for the next decade while they got everyone killed.

I was halfway to the guest room when Henry caught up to me. He put his hand on my arm, and I shrugged it off, too furious to say anything. He'd promised that our relationship would be between equals. That I wouldn't *belong* to him. That wasn't how we worked, and how dare he insinuate I was his for any reason other than the fact that I wanted to be?

I stormed into my room and tried to slam the door, but he caught it. "Kate, please, will you listen to me?"

"Why should I?" I prowled from one end of the room to the other, glaring at him and silently daring him to come closer. He only moved forward enough to close the door behind him. "You won't listen to me—why, because I'm young? Because I'm a girl? What is it, Henry? Why am I suddenly nothing more than your *claim?*"

He exhaled. "You know I do not think of you in that way—"

"Sure could have fooled me lately."

"That is not fair. I am trying to keep my family intact,

and the only way to do so is to speak a language my brother understands."

"Oh, so he's the misogynist?"

"Yes," said Henry. "He has never understood partnership. Not in his marriage, not within the council, not even among his siblings. It is not fair, but he is the head of the council, and we must play this game his way."

I collapsed on the bed. "Great. I spend my entire life wanting a family, and when I finally get one, it's full of people who think I'm no better than dirt."

Henry took a few cautious steps toward me, but stopped when I gave him a look. "I wish you would have told me about your deal with Cronus."

"Up until two days ago, you were in a coma," I pointed out.

"Yes, but you have had ample opportunity to do so since. And it seems to me as if the details of your arrangement were made much more recently."

He watched me with his unwavering gaze, and I looked away.

"I am not angry with you, Kate," he said gently. "I cannot imagine what you endured while they held you captive, and truthfully I would have done the same if our positions were reversed. But as you are my partner, I am yours. Regardless of the circumstances, it should have been a decision we made together."

Tears sprung in my eyes. Not because I was mad at him, but because he was right. "I'm sorry. I was afraid you'd take off after him, and you're still so weak—"

"I accept your apology," said Henry. "And I ask that you accept mine, as well. I will not let you go, Kate, because I love you. Not because I believe you belong to me. Anyone who has been around you for five minutes knows better than to think that."

"Apparently my own father doesn't," I mumbled, and Henry sighed.

"Yes, well. It's easy to chalk this whole mess up to Walter. He is the one who never gave Calliope the respect and love she deserved, after all."

"You'd think he would've learned from that."

"You would think." He sat down on the bed, and I didn't move away. "I want to get our son back as badly as you do, but this is not the way."

My eyes welled up again. When would I stop being on the verge of tears? When I finally held Milo? When Calliope was defeated? When Cronus was back in his own personal corner of hell? "I don't know how to be me without him," I said. "Everything I do, it's like —it's like this need is pulling me in one direction, and I can't function without going toward it. And when I'm not, I'm empty. He needs me. He needs us, and we're not doing anything to get him back. We've practically abandoned him."

Henry lay down on his side so he was facing me. "Do you really believe that?" he said, sandwiching my hand in his. "I am certain Milo does not. You said so yourself that you believe he knows when you are there."

I rubbed my eyes with my free hand. "I want him back, Henry. I want us to be a family."

"We are a family." He kissed my forehead, my cheek, and finally brushed his lips against mine. "We cannot pretend it has been easy, but we love each other unconditionally, and that is what matters. We will get him back. I swear it."

My chin trembled. "How?"

"I do not know yet, but I will find a way. We will find a way together."

I kissed him back, not caring if he could taste my tears. "How am I supposed to help you when everyone thinks I'm worthless and won't teach me how to use my abilities?"

"I do not think you are worthless," he said, his breath warm on my cheek. "Far from it, I assure you. I will teach you anything you desire."

"Really?" I said, and he nodded.

"Really."

I hugged him, burying my face in the crook of his neck, and let out a soft sob. That was all I allowed myself, though; one sob, and now it was time to get to work. Now it was time to prove I deserved my place on the council.

I only had to do one thing first. "Do you want to see him?"

"Do you really have to ask?"

I managed a watery smile. "Make sure Cronus can't see you."

"I will."

Once again I sank into my vision, pulling Henry along with me, and this time no one interrupted us. Together we fought through the quicksand until the bedroom dissolved around us and we surfaced on the other side.

Milo lay in his crib, his eyes shut. It had to be well past midnight on the island. Cronus stood in the corner closest to the door, his arms crossed as if he was waiting for me, but I ignored him. I didn't know how to tell him that Walter had turned him down. If he didn't know already.

Henry and I leaned over Milo's crib like I thought we had a dozen times before, but this time it was really him. The three of us were together, or at least as together as we could be for now.

"He's beautiful," whispered Henry. I didn't say anything. I couldn't, not with Cronus hovering nearby. I smiled, careful to keep my eyes on Milo, and Henry touched my back. He understood.

"My darling," said Cronus, appearing on my other side and taking my hand. "Have you news of the truce?"

I couldn't tell him the truth, not yet. I had no idea what he would do to prove his dominance—kill another million people? Destroy all of Greece? Even if everything else stemmed from the way Walter had treated Calliope, this was on me. And I had to stall.

"They haven't reached a decision yet," I said, my stare not wavering from Milo. "They need time."

Out of the corner of my eye, Henry gave me a searching look. I ignored it.

"Very well. I hope they do not take too long." He began to knead my shoulder, and I winced. "Why are you so tense, my dear?"

Because Henry was alive and standing two inches from my elbow. Because the council—or at least certain members—blamed me for everything. Because if I made one wrong move, all of this would be over. "Do you really have to ask?" I said, echoing Henry.

"No, I suppose I do not," said Cronus, and he moved behind me to massage both of my shoulders. Henry scowled and stepped away.

"Please don't do that," I said softly, but Cronus continued anyway. Henry moved to the other side of the crib so he could look me straight in the eye, and I pressed my lips together. Did he understand that I didn't want this?

"Soon you will be my queen," said Cronus, his lips tickling my ear. The look on Henry's face was murderous. "You have not changed your mind, have you, my dear?"

My eyes locked on Henry. He had to understand it was all an act. "No," I said. "I haven't changed my mind."

"Good girl," murmured Cronus, and Henry straightened, his hands balled into fists as if he were seconds away from decking Cronus.

"I'm going to find Calliope," said Henry. "You stay here."

My eyes widened, but despite my silent protest, Henry leaned across the cradle to kiss my cheek. At least he understood.

As he left the room, Cronus ran his hands down my back before returning to my shoulders. "When you and I are together, you will never know tears," he murmured. "You will never know pain. You will only know joy and happiness. Everyone will bow to you. Everyone will know that you, Kate Winters, are my queen. And they will all love and fear you for it."

I didn't want to be feared. I didn't want anyone to bow to me, but Cronus would never understand what it meant to be happy without absolute power. He would never understand why I would always love Henry and never love him. But at least Henry wasn't here to hear this.

"What are you doing?"

Cronus's hands stilled. I tried to turn, but he blocked my way. Not that it mattered. I would've known that voice anywhere.

Ava set a load of blankets down on the dresser and moved toward us, her eyes focused on Cronus. She couldn't see me. "Who are you talking to?"

"The baby," said Cronus smoothly. "Someone must ensure his education."

"No, you weren't," said Ava, advancing on him. Her hands trembled. She was as afraid of Cronus as everyone else. "You said Kate's name."

"So I spoke of his mother." Cronus straightened and dropped his hands. Apparently he'd realized that massaging an invisible person's shoulders didn't do much to support his argument. "What of it?"

Ava eyed him. "Kate's here, isn't she?"

"Perhaps," he allowed. "Perhaps not."

My stomach twisted into knots. She was so close that I could reach out and touch her if I wanted to.

"I want to talk to her," said Ava. "I know you two communicate. I know you can hear her and she can hear you, and—and I want you to tell her something."

How could she possibly know that? Cronus hadn't mentioned it to her, else she wouldn't have sounded so determined to be right. Who else knew? The council, but none of them had been in contact with Ava. Unless there was another traitor.

No, impossible. I trusted the council with my life. Except for Dylan, but he wouldn't have done anything to risk losing a battle, especially feed information to the enemy. Unless it was all a ruse and he really was reporting to Cronus, after all.

I bit my lip. I couldn't think like that, not unless I had proof. With how much he seemed to hate me, it was easy to suspect Dylan of being a snake, but that kind of thinking and suspicion would tear us apart. The last thing the council needed was someone else backing down. Dylan and I might not have liked each other much, or at all, but that didn't mean we couldn't work together toward a common goal. As long as he wasn't doing what he'd accused me of and telling his girlfriend secrets behind the council's back.

"If you would like to speak to her, then speak," said Cronus, and the false note of warmth he used with me evaporated. "She is perfectly capable of hearing you."

Ava took another tentative step forward, focusing somewhere over my right shoulder. "Kate—Kate, I'm so sorry.

I swear I didn't know what Calliope was doing. I would've never risked your baby's life if I had."

I shifted protectively in front of Milo's crib. Fat lot of good that would do, but it made me feel better, at least. "It's too late for apologies," I said, and to my surprise, Cronus opened his mouth and spoke those same words, exactly as I'd said them.

Ava's expression grew stricken. "Please. I'll do anything."

"Come back to Olympus," I said, and once again Cronus repeated me. "Leave Calliope."

"I can't," she said. "You don't understand—she has Nicholas, and if I don't cooperate, she's going to kill him like she killed Iris and Henry."

The moment she said those words, a cold silence settled over the room, and she blinked several times.

"I'm so sorry," she said, and I could hear the sob bubbling up inside her. "I'm so, so sorry, Kate. I can't tell you…"

"Then don't," I said. "If you're really sorry, then do something to prove it. I don't care what. But stop acting like a helpless victim and stand up for what you believe in before you have nothing left at all."

Tears flowed down her cheeks, and she didn't try to stop them. "I just want things to be okay again. Please, Kate—you have to understand. You would've done the same thing for Henry, wouldn't you?"

"Yes," I said softly. "But I would have hated myself every moment for it, and the instant I realized you were pregnant, I would've fought Calliope to the death to protect you. I would've never let her destroy you like she's trying to destroy me."

Silence settled over the room once Cronus finished repeating me. Ava sank to the ground, hugging her knees to her chest, and I pressed my lips together. As hurt as I was, mine wasn't the only life Calliope was trying to destroy.

"You have my understanding," I said quietly. "Do the right thing, and one day you will have my forgiveness. But you won't have anything if you don't start acting like the Ava I know and stand up to Calliope."

Ava was sobbing now, her entire body shaking. "I can't. I *can't*. She'll kill him. Please, Kate. You're my best friend. You're the only one who understood before. Please try to understand now—Callum, he's safe with her, she won't hurt him—"

Something ugly uncoiled inside me, something vicious and dark where every terrible thought I'd ever had lay dormant, waiting to come out again. "She hurts *Milo* every second she keeps him from me and Henry, and you're the one who let her take him in the first place. You didn't raise a finger to stop her, and because of you, he's here, and he will never be safe with her. Ever. If you can't see that—if you're so blind to your own actions that you can't take responsibility for them—then as far as I'm concerned, we were never friends at all. And we never will be again."

Her eyes flew open. Instead of the anguish I expected, they filled with magenta fire, as surely as Henry's glinted with moonlight and Cronus's swirled with fog. She unfolded her legs and stood, and a pale aura glowed around her.

"You're a liar." Her words echoed throughout the nursery, and Milo let out a startled cry. She ignored him and went toe to toe with Cronus, unaware I was less than a foot away. "Kate would never say those things to me, and your pitiful attempts to sever my loyalty won't work. Even if Kate did say those awful things, she doesn't really mean them. Calliope's using her powers to make her hate me, isn't she?"

Calliope didn't have to cut the strings of our friendship.

Ava was already fraying them beyond repair. But no matter how much I understood why she was doing this, no matter how much I wanted to forgive her, I'd never had such conflicting feelings for someone in my life. I constantly wavered between irresistible fury and the deep desire to understand, as if those two parts of me were at war with each other. And while I'd been on the island, close enough for Calliope to get to me whenever she wanted, forgiving Ava had never crossed my mind.

Maybe Calliope was behind this, after all. I took a deep breath. Acknowledging it didn't make the tension in the pit of my stomach lessen, but I would force myself past Calliope's influences if Ava did the right thing.

"Is that so?" said Cronus with eerie calm, pulling me back into the present. "What makes you so certain? You are already on our side. I have no reason to lie."

"You have every reason to lie," said Ava. "I've told Calliope, and now I'll tell you. I am not your bitch. I'm here for my husband, and I'm here for Kate's baby. I won't let you or Calliope poison him."

A shadow moved in the doorway, and Henry appeared. He was safe. Wordlessly he crossed the room and took my hand.

"You can tell me as many awful things as you want. I won't believe you." Ava's voice trembled, but power radiated from her. "She's my best friend, and I love her. Not that you would understand the first thing about love."

She reached into Milo's cradle and picked him up, and his cries grew louder. His arms flailed toward me, and I held my hand over his forehead. "It's all right," I whispered. "I'm here."

As the words left my mouth, however, Ava stormed toward the door, and it was only Henry's tight grip on my hand that kept me from going after her.

"Where are you taking him?" said Cronus without any hint of anger. If anything, he sounded amused.

Ava glared at him. "To give him a bath and a bottle. Someone needs to make sure he knows he's loved, and you and Calliope sure as hell aren't qualified."

I stepped toward her, yanking on Henry's hand in an attempt to get him to follow, but he stood firm. "Come, Kate," he said, and the world around us began to fade. "There's nothing more we can do."

And though I said nothing while he brought me back to Olympus, I knew he was wrong. There was something more, and now I had no choice but to do it.

CHAPTER 10
DESTRUCTION

I wasn't sure how long I lay there, staring at Henry in the middle of our bed. Long enough for my heart to ache the same way it did whenever I was gone from Milo for too long. Long enough to be certain that the council meeting was over by now, but my mother still hadn't come to find me. Maybe she knew I didn't want to be found.

"Why do you think she did it?" I said, breaking the silence between me and Henry.

"Ava?" he said, and I nodded. "Because she loves Nicholas, and because she was naive enough to trust that Calliope would keep her word."

"But why did Calliope go after Ava to begin with?"

Henry leaned over and kissed me. "Calliope sees Ava as her greatest rival. Walter loves her more than anyone else on the council, and Calliope has always been jealous of the sway she's had over him. Ava is powerful in her own right, as well. Calliope has control over a person's loyalty, but Ava controls love. Not even Calliope can touch that."

Realization dawned on me. "She wanted you. Calliope was going to capture you and force you to be her partner. That was her endgame—to lure you in and keep you like some kind of pet or something. Maybe that's why she wanted Ava on her side."

Henry said nothing. I waited for him to speak, but his gaze grew distant, and eventually it became obvious he wasn't going to respond.

I hesitated. Another topic then. "Do you think Ava's right and Calliope's using her abilities to make me hate Ava?"

"I don't know. The only person who can answer that is you."

But I didn't have an answer. I didn't even know the right questions to ask. My anger wasn't irrational, but I'd never been so furious and frustrated with anyone in my entire life. Not even Calliope after she'd tried to kill me. If I could forgive her, then why couldn't I forgive Ava?

Because Calliope had only taken my life. Ava had ripped the most important thing in the world away from me.

"It still doesn't make sense," I said. "If she's using Ava's powers somehow, then why haven't we heard about it? Why hasn't Cronus told me?"

"I don't know." His hand slid down my side to rest on my waist. "There's nothing we can do about it right now except prepare ourselves for the possibility that Calliope still has an ace hidden up her sleeve."

Miserable as I was, I snorted into his shoulder. "Hearing you use poker metaphors is bizarre."

"I'm much better at it than you might think," he said.

"I believe it."

He kissed me again and ran a finger above the waistband of my jeans, leaving searing heat wherever he touched me.

It didn't take a genius to figure out what he wanted, and I kissed him back, but set my hand over his. He sighed.

"I'm sorry," I said. "It's just—last time we did this, Calliope used it against us. And I can't go through that again."

Instead of protesting, Henry drew me in closer, shifting his body so it rested against mine. "Is this your way of offering me more incentive? Win the war, and you'll sleep with me again?"

I rolled my eyes. "Please. If that's what I was trying to do, I'd be way more obvious about it. Winning the war's a little vague, after all. I'd go for something more solid."

"For example?" he murmured.

"I'd say something like...I'll sleep with you after you teach me how to disappear and reappear."

He peered down at me, and for the first time in ages, I thought I saw a real smile on his face. "Is that a promise? Because with that kind of motivation, I'm certain we could have it down by next sunset."

"You're ridiculous," I said. "But if you're offering..."

He immediately sat up and smoothed his shirt. "There must be somewhere in this place we can practice without getting scolded."

I started to suggest returning to the Underworld, but we were as trapped here as I'd been on the island. If we left Olympus for any reason, it would only be a matter of time before Calliope and Cronus discovered Henry was alive. We'd gotten lucky in Africa and Greece, and we couldn't afford to risk it a second time.

"Do you think we'll ever see him again?" I said, and Henry's smile faded.

"Milo?" he said, and I nodded. "Yes. We'll see him anytime you want."

"You know what I mean."

He drew me toward him again, his arms tightening around me. I'd been an idiot to ever think he didn't love me just because he didn't say it. He told me a hundred times a day without having to utter a word. "I promised you we would find a way to get him back, and we will. Whatever it takes."

"Except you dying," I said firmly, wrapping my fingers around the hem of his black shirt. "I mean it."

Henry kissed my forehead. "So you are allowed to offer yourself to Cronus for all eternity to get Milo out of there, but I am not allowed to offer my life to do the same?"

"I'd still be alive," I said. "And I'd find a way out of there eventually."

"I admire your bravery, but James is right. You must find a solution to this martyr complex of yours."

I gave him a halfhearted glare. "You weren't complaining when my martyr complex gave you a second chance."

"But the time has come to fight not just for the lives of those you love, but for your own, as well," he said. "If only so you do not hurt those same people by leaving them the way you're so afraid they will leave you."

That wasn't fair and he knew it. If someone had to die, I would much rather it was me than suffer that kind of loss. Henry, my mother, Milo—I couldn't come out of that and still be me.

"I'll do my best," I said.

"Promise me."

But I couldn't, and neither could he. We would both do what we had to in order to protect each other, and no promise in the world could stop either of us.

By the time Olympus once again hovered over Greece and the council departed for another minutes-long battle against Cronus, I managed to disappear from one side of the throne room and reappear on the other. With the amount of concentration it took, I had no chance to worry about my mother and the rest of the council. And I was too frazzled to be annoyed that this must have been Henry's plan all along.

"Why didn't you teach me this sooner?" I said, pulling my hair into a ponytail. "This would have come in handy nine months ago, you know." It didn't take any physical exertion at all, but the amount of willpower it required made me dizzy every time I crossed the room. How did Henry travel through the entire Underworld like this?

"We did not have the opportunity," he said. "Now try to go into the bedroom. I will meet you there."

I gave him a look. "I told you, I don't want to do that until—"

"Is that all you think about?" he said with a faint smile before disappearing, and I huffed. Completely unfair.

Closing my eyes, I focused on the air around me. In the throne room, it was still and warm, but not unbearable. Slowly, agonizingly so, I pieced together an image of the bedroom in my mind. The plain bed, the dresser, the closet, the white door, the sunset floor and the sky-blue ceiling exactly like the throne room. Gathering myself together, feeling every inch of my body from the tip of my nose to the bottom of my heels, I exhaled.

And then I opened my eyes.

"Very good," said Henry, standing dangerously close to me. "You were faster that time. Less than thirty seconds."

It was difficult to take a compliment from someone who could do it in the blink of an eye. "What if we appear in the same space?"

"That will not happen," said Henry. "The laws of the universe won't allow it."

Oh. Well, that was good to know. I leaned up against the

bedpost and stuck my hands in my pockets. "Once I have this down, could you teach me how to fight?"

"It takes centuries to learn how to fight the way that would make any difference in the battles," he said. Damn. So James hadn't been lying. "This—learning how to travel—is your best bet."

"How can this help?" I said, and he shrugged.

"Any number of ways, really. Never underestimate the value of being able to go wherever you'd like with a single thought. That coupled with your visions…well, you could be a very formidable opponent indeed."

"You're just saying that to try to make me feel better."

"Perhaps," he allowed with a smile. "But it doesn't make it any less true. Now, before you get the wrong idea of me, I will meet you back in the throne room."

Once again, he disappeared, and I sighed. If I were still mortal, I was sure I'd have a raging headache by now. Closing my eyes, I repeated the process, this time trying to focus faster and shave a second or two off my time. I had to get better, and I only had so much time to learn how.

I reappeared in the throne room twenty-two seconds later and grinned. "Next time we play tag, I get to be it," I said, and my eyes fluttered open.

Walter stood two inches in front of me, so close my nose was nearly pressed against his chest. "While it is admirable that you have found the time to play games during such a troubling period, I must ask that you take your seat now."

I stumbled back a step and hit someone else. James. He set his hand on my shoulder to steady me. "We're back," he said.

"Hadn't guessed," I mumbled before shuffling over to my throne. Henry stood beside his, and he extended his hand. I took it. The rest of the council each stood by theirs as well, and I did a quick mental count. They all looked worn down—my mother's skin was sickeningly pale, a painful reminder of her last few days back in Eden—but everyone had returned.

No one spoke. Their expressions ranged from deep sadness to inexplicable rage, and it took everything I had not to sink into a vision and make sure Milo was all right. "What happened?" I said shakily, too scared to wait for Walter to speak first.

"Cronus's reach is extending. He sent out another tidal wave," said Walter. "Alexandria is all but gone, and Cairo is half-drowned."

"But—" I tried to picture a map of Egypt. It'd been forever since I'd seen one. "Cairo isn't on the coast."

"With the power of a Titan behind it, there was nothing to stop the wave from reaching so far inland," said Phillip, and he took a great shuddering breath. "I am sorry. I have done everything I can to counter him, but—"

"There's only so much you can do," said Sofia gently, her eyes rimmed with red. "No one blames you, Phillip."

From the way he bowed his head, it was obvious Phillip blamed himself. I shoved my shaking hands between my knees. Two cities this time, and everything in between.

"How many casualties?" I said.

"Millions," said Walter. "Several times the amount of destruction in Athens."

All the air left my lungs. Why hadn't they taken Cronus's deal? Maybe it'd only been worth a little more time to prepare, but that was still something. Cronus was escaping with or without their permission, and it wouldn't be long before he devastated Europe and Africa. And then where would he hit? Asia? Australia? North and South America? How long would it take him to destroy everything?

At least Calliope attacked me for a reason. But Cronus—

was he doing this just to hurt the council? To prove he was stronger and there was nothing they could do to stop him? They already knew that, even if Walter was too pigheaded to admit that he wasn't the biggest, baddest bastard in the universe.

I opened my mouth to demand that Walter do something— anything, I didn't care, so long as it stopped the attack. Henry took my hand though, stroking my knuckles with the pad of his thumb, and I fell silent. To Walter, I wasn't anything more than an incompetent pest. Because of that, no matter what I said, no matter how much logic and reasoning I used, he wouldn't listen to me. None of them except my mother, James and Henry would, and the council couldn't afford to be any more divided than it already was.

"Kate, you may go," said Walter, and I left the throne room without protest. I might have been young and inexperienced, but that didn't make me an idiot. And if they wouldn't fix it, then I would.

Shadows danced on the walls of Milo's nursery as it materialized around me, and Cronus hovered over his cradle. He looked paler than usual, but his eyes swirled with fog, and a faint aura of power surrounded him.

"I've been waiting for you." He set a hand on my lower back, and I recoiled.

"You're a monster," I snarled, reaching into the cradle for my son. "Do you realize how many people you've just—"

As always, my hand met empty air, but this time it was different. I squinted into the mess of blankets, and I froze. Milo wasn't there.

"What did you do to him?" I said, and my voice broke. "Where the hell is my son?"

Cronus gestured behind me, and I spun around. Ava sat

in a rocking chair that hadn't been there the day before, and she cradled Milo.

"She has barely put him down since you last left," said Cronus.

I hurried over to her, and Ava glanced up. For one horrible moment, I thought she could see me, but instead she looked right through me. "It won't work," she said to Cronus. "I don't care how many times you try it. Kate isn't here, and even if she was, you wouldn't be able to see her."

Still in denial then. For now, it didn't matter; I watched Milo happily suck away on the tip of her pinkie, and my heart melted. Opening his eyes, he stared right at me, and I could have sworn he smiled around her finger.

"Hi, baby," I whispered, kneeling beside Ava. The blade of her rocker sliced through my insubstantial thigh. "Look at you."

His eyes were bright, his cheeks pink, and he waved his little hands at me with more enthusiasm than before. He looked like a healthy ten-day-old baby. Whatever Ava was giving him, it was working.

"Why does he look so much healthier?" I said to Cronus, and he repeated the question.

Ava, who must not have realized that he was once again speaking for me, shrugged. "Everyone knows that newborns need to be held, and not by a walking void of emotion either. A little love does them wonders."

And right now, she was the only one who could give that to him. I bit the inside of my cheek and focused on Milo. He was so beautiful that it hurt to look at him, but I couldn't tear myself away.

"Why did you attack those people?" I said to Cronus.

"For the same reason I attacked Athens," he said. "To teach the council a lesson."

"And what lesson was that supposed to be?" I snapped. "The more you hurt them, the less likely it is they'll agree to your truce."

"We both know that will not happen," said Cronus, and in the rocker, Ava's brow furrowed with confusion.

"Stop it," she said, her grip on Milo tightening. "She isn't here."

"Tell her that you lied yesterday," I said. Ava was doing something no one else could or would for Milo right now, and if Cronus said the wrong thing, I couldn't risk Ava leaving the baby alone again. The last thing he needed was to lose someone else who loved him.

Cronus sighed and said in an annoyed voice, "My words yesterday were purely my own, not a reflection of what Kate expressed. My sincerest apologies."

Ava smirked triumphantly. "I knew it. You're scum."

"So I have been told," said Cronus with surprising ease. "My dear Kate, the fact remains that we all know a truce will not happen, not while Walter is in charge of the council."

"It isn't in my power to convince them to overthrow Walter, and even if I could, I wouldn't," I said.

"Then you know the consequences," said Cronus. "The time for inaction is over. I have given the council long enough to surrender, and now that they have chosen not to, I will do what I must to put them in their place."

My stomach dropped. "Please," I said. "Give them a little more time. Give *me* a little more time."

"It will not make a difference. The winter solstice is in less than three months. The council's bonds will no longer hold me then."

"I know."

"Then why did you come?" said Cronus. "Do not tell me it was merely to see your son."

I would've spent eternity locked in a room with Calliope if it meant getting to spend five minutes with Milo. But I didn't say that, because Cronus was right. He was always right. "You know why I'm here."

His footsteps echoed behind me, growing closer until he knelt beside me and snaked his arm around my waist. Ava pulled away from him. I didn't blame her.

"Kate?" she said, her voice trembling as she searched the space I was in. I ignored her. Now wasn't the time.

"I want to hear it from you," said Cronus huskily, and despite his lips lingering next to my ear, he no longer had any breath. Not warm, not cold—nothing.

I tightened my hands into fists and focused on Milo's blue eyes. Henry would understand. He had to. "I'm here to make a trade."

"For real this time?" said Cronus.

"Yes," I whispered. "For real."

CHAPTER 11

HORIZON

Cronus gave me seven days with Henry and my mother before he would attack again.

It wasn't out of the kindness of his heart. I had no way of reaching the island on my own yet, and I couldn't ask anyone to go with me. Besides, the more people I involved, the bigger chance it had of getting back to Henry.

So I had to learn how to get there myself. I could barely travel across the room without Henry's help; learning how to cross half an ocean in a week seemed impossible, but I had to.

As my mind returned to Olympus, I grew aware of two things: first, I was crying. And second, Henry lay beside me, his eyes locked on mine.

"Are you all right?" He brushed his thumb against my cheek, catching a stray tear. The urge to tell him everything overwhelmed me, making it hard to breathe, but I couldn't. This was for Milo. If one of us had to do it, I was the best choice. Cronus had already issued Calliope an ultimatum not to hurt me or Milo; Henry wouldn't have the same security, and he was too important, too powerful, too needed to sacrifice himself. I would find a way back as soon as I could. Maybe if I could learn how to travel properly, I would be able to take Milo and escape. It wasn't much, but it was something, and I couldn't have Henry risk himself in the meantime.

"I love you so much," I said, closing the distance between us and wrapping myself around him. "No matter what happens, no matter how this war turns out—I love you, forever and always."

Henry was quiet for a long moment, and I counted the seconds, taking comfort in each breath he took. At last he lowered his lips to mine, kissing me with aching tenderness.

"You are my life." Though his words were barely a whisper, they seemed to echo from somewhere deep within him, enveloping my body and infusing me with something unshakable. "There is nothing I would not do to make you happy. Before I met you, my world was a string of days that were gray and empty. I had nothing to look forward to, and I cannot tell you what it was like, facing down eternity alone. Every day I wished for you. Every day I held on in hopes that eventually we would meet. And when I finally found you..."

He leaned in and kissed me again, as tenderly as before. His hand slid underneath my shirt, splaying across my stomach, but the touch wasn't sexual. It was as if he were trying to memorize me, just as I was trying to memorize him.

"I have existed for more eons than I remember. I have seen the sun rise and fall so many times that the days lost all meaning. For so long, they passed me by in a blur. But that night we met by the river—the night you gave up yourself in order to save a virtual stranger—my heart began to beat again."

He took my hand and pressed it against his chest, and there it was—*thump thump, thump thump,* strong and beautiful. I would've given anything to keep his heart beating. The black abyss that had become my world in those hours I'd thought he was dead had faded, but it was a scar I would always bear. I couldn't go back to that. Even if I had Milo, I would never have another Henry.

"I see the sunrise now," he said. "Because of you, the days have color. Eternity has meaning once more. You found every broken piece of me and put me back together, even though I hurt you too many times for me to deserve it. You are the glue that holds me together. If I lose you, it will be the end of me."

A knot formed in my throat. "You'll never lose me," I said, my voice breaking.

"Promise." His gaze searched mine as he ran his fingertip up my spine.

"I promise." I closed the minuscule gap between us once more, capturing his lips and trying to show him how much I meant it. "I love you. I love our family. I love our life together, and I can't wait for the day when we're back home, just the three of us, and this whole war is over. I swear to you that will happen. That *will* be our future."

He cradled the back of my head, his palm searing against my skin. "I have waited an eternity for this love. I'm not going to let anyone, Titan or not, take it from us."

"Promise?" I said, and this time it was Henry's turn to kiss me.

"I promise."

"Then do me a favor."

"Anything."

I shifted onto my back, rolling him with me. His body pressed against mine in all the right places, and I lifted my head high enough to rest my forehead against his. "Live this love now," I whispered. "And never stop."

★ ★ ★

In those seven days, I spent every moment I could with Henry. Walter ruled that despite him being mostly healed, Henry would remain in Olympus until the last possible moment, to give the council the element of surprise. Though Henry had a tendency to pace around mumbling things about his brother that I was all too willing to agree with, it gave us more time together.

When we weren't playing our new brand of tag throughout the sun-drenched palace, we fought our way through the quicksand of my visions to see Milo. Cronus was always there, a silent reminder of the little time I had left with my family, but now Ava had become a permanent fixture, too.

The happier and healthier Milo became, the thinner and paler Ava grew, as if she was pouring everything she had into him. Maybe she was. Maybe she was the only thing keeping him alive. When I voiced that to Henry after returning to Olympus one day, however, he shook his head. "We are both immortal, and so is Milo."

"What?" I stopped in the middle of the abandoned throne room, the only place we could go that didn't feel stuffy. The sun shone a little brighter here, and the sunset at our feet seemed deeper, more real somehow. "But I thought everyone had to take the tests."

"Members of the council do," said Henry. "Demigods attempting to earn immortality usually have to prove themselves in some way. And royals take the test, as well. If Walter chooses to take another queen, regardless of her mortality, she will have to pass the same tests you did to earn her position. If Milo ever replaced me as King of the Underworld—"

"Why would he?"

"Just hypothetically," said Henry, and his fingers danced

down the curve of my back. "If he replaced me, he would have to take the test, too."

It wasn't just hypothetically, though. Was he planning the same thing I was—to sacrifice himself to get Milo back somehow?

No, he wouldn't do that to me, not after everything we'd been through, which made doing it to him all the more difficult. I'd find a way back to him though, no matter what it took. I rested my head against his shoulder. The silver scar from Cronus's first attack poked out from underneath his collar, and I traced it with a featherlight touch.

"Come," he murmured. "I want to show you something."

Before I could say a word, the now-familiar feeling of disappearing washed over me, and the throne room faded. However, a similar room replaced it, with sky that stretched out endlessly before us.

There was something different about this, though. Before it had been easy to tell the difference between the ceiling and the floor, but in here they blended together as if it were the real thing. Unless—

I blinked. It *was* the real thing.

"I am not supposed to bring you here, or even be here myself," admitted Henry. "This is the balcony outside Walter's private quarters. It's the pinnacle of his domain, and he is very protective of it. But there is nothing more beautiful in the world, and I wanted you to see it."

He led me to a glass railing, and I gazed out across the infinite sky. Caught between day and dusk, the colors swirled as if they were liquid, and flames seemed to dance in the clouds. "This is incredible," I said, stunned.

We stood there for a long moment, and at last he wrapped his arm around me, pulling me closer. "You can tell me anything, you know."

"I know," I said softly.

"Then tell me what has been bothering you."

I focused on the horizon. I couldn't lie to him. I didn't want to, and even if I tried, he would know. "We're in the middle of a war, and we're both being used as pawns in ways we don't understand."

"That is not atypical for my brother," said Henry with a hint of mirth.

"That's not what I mean. We're all on one big chessboard, aren't we? Cronus is on one side and Walter's on the other, using everyone like chess pieces. Except I'm not so much as a pawn on Walter's side."

Henry opened his mouth, but I interrupted him before he had the chance to speak.

"Don't tell me I'm wrong. We both know I'm not. I'm useless to Walter. I've tried to give him information, act as an envoy, learn how to fight so I can help everyone, but he isn't having it. Cronus though—he's moving me around like I'm a damn king piece. One step at a time in any direction he wants, but I can never venture too far on my own, because if I do, if he loses me..."

"He will not lose the war if he loses you, if that is what you are thinking." Henry turned so he was facing me, and he held my stare. There was something earnest and anxious in his eyes, as if he were desperate to make me understand. "You are not a king piece to him. If you are anything at all, you are a pawn. Something small and inoffensive, easily overlooked, nothing more than fodder. If he gets you where he wants you though—so deep into enemy territory that we don't even know you're there—then you will become more to him. But only because of the role you play, not who you are. Despite the illusion of whatever he is offering you, you will be nothing more than another piece of the game to him. Do you understand?"

I took a deep breath and released it slowly. There was no good solution to any of this. "Cronus wants me. Whatever ungodly reason he has for it, whatever he thinks of me, having me means something to him. I can't ignore that."

"I'm not asking you to," said Henry. "I'm asking you to think of me, to think of Milo, and realize that you're no good to either of us if he has you. You cannot trust a Titan."

"Now you're starting to sound like Walter," I mumbled.

"He has a point about Cronus. The only person who can stop him from reneging on a deal is Rhea, and she's already made her position on this war clear. In the meantime, it isn't worth the risk. Milo is safe. Ava's taking care of him, and she will not let anything happen to him."

"She already let something happen to him, though," I said. "And how do I know that the first chance she gets, she won't throw him into the ocean?"

"If she does, then we ought to consider ourselves lucky," said Henry, pulling me into another hug. "Phillip would find him, and we would have him back again."

"But what if Calliope decides to kill Milo, after all? She has the dagger. She has Cronus. She could do it. Cronus could do it if I refuse to go to him—"

"If Cronus or Calliope threatens to kill our son, I will rip them apart with my bare hands," said Henry. "You are not alone in this fight, Kate. Do not forget that. I have already failed you more times than I can count, and I will not do it again."

"You haven't—" The words caught in my throat. "You haven't failed me."

"You died on my watch," he said. "And my feelings for Persephone—"

"Ancient history. You haven't failed me, got it? And I'm not going to let you storm in there on your own."

He ran his fingers through my hair. "Nor will I allow you to do so either. We are in this together no matter what happens. I will not make the mistake of leaving you behind again. All I ask is that you do the same for me, as well."

Cold horror hit me. He knew. Somehow, someway, he knew what I was planning, and instead of admitting it and forcibly stopping me, he was trying to reason with me. He was giving me a choice.

But he'd also made the consequences of me making the wrong decision painfully clear. If I ran off on my own to try to protect Milo and stop this war, he would, too. And we both knew his attempts would be a hell of a lot bloodier than mine.

I tilted my head upward to capture his lips, kissing him with every ounce of passion and frustration and guilt inside me. He had to understand. "I love you, and I will always be yours."

"And I yours. We will have our future," whispered Henry. Despite everything that was happening around us, despite the wrenching choices we both faced, I believed him completely.

On my last day before surrendering to Cronus, my mother tracked me down. I'd been practicing for ages, and Henry had long since grown tired of chasing me around Olympus. In spite of the hours I'd clocked disappearing and reappearing in random places throughout the palace, I hadn't seen all of Olympus yet. Now I never would, but it was a stupid regret to have, all things considered.

"We need to talk," said my mother as I reappeared in the throne room.

"About what?" I said, forcing my voice to remain steady. No use giving her any reason to think I was up to something, and if anyone could figure it out, it was my mother. Unless Henry had already told her.

"You've been anxious lately," she said, and I swore inwardly.

"We've all been on edge."

She couldn't argue with that. Instead my mother pursed her lips. "Do you want to talk about it?"

Yes. I wanted to crawl into her lap like I had when I was a kid and admit every stupid thing I'd done and every idiotic thing I'd agreed to. I wanted her to tell me that everything would be all right, and I didn't have to worry anymore, because she would fix it.

This wasn't something she could solve with a wave of her hand or a few gentle words though, and for the first time in my life, I began to understand that she wasn't the all-powerful mother I'd always thought she was. She was human, or at least as close to human as a member of the council could be. She made mistakes, too, and she didn't always have the answers.

"I can't," I mumbled, and she motioned for me to join her. I curled up in her lap without a second thought. Why couldn't things be simple again?

They hadn't been simple for years though, not since I was fourteen and my mother had been diagnosed. And while I'd had the illusion of simplicity in the years before that, they'd never really been easy, had they? She'd had to raise me knowing what was coming. The council had always loomed over me, waiting until I was old enough to put me through a test no girl before me had survived. My mother had known the risks. She'd known what the inevitable looked like, yet she'd always been there and always loved me with everything she had. Now it was my turn to do the same for Milo.

"You're a good girl, Kate," she murmured, holding me close. "Do what you have to do to protect your family."

I hugged her back tightly. So Henry had told her, after all. Did the entire council know now? Did it matter, as long as they weren't trying to stop me? "I love you," I said, clinging to her.

"I love you, too, sweetheart." She rubbed my back in slow circles. "Everything will be all right in the end. Evil never lasts forever, and neither will this."

Even though I knew she was right, even though she said the exact words I'd needed to hear, she couldn't predict what would happen in the meantime. No one could. And that was what I was really afraid of.

Later, in our bedroom, Henry and I didn't speak. We lost ourselves in each other, a silent farewell that neither of us could bear to say. If I hadn't been certain before, I was now; he was letting me go, and it would only be a matter of time before I discovered the price we would both have to pay for it.

As my time dwindled to less than half an hour before I was due to surrender to Cronus, I still couldn't bring myself to say goodbye. I waited until Henry's chest rose and fell in the steady rhythm of sleep, but he didn't fool me. He was awake, and I gave us both one last moment of pretending and slipped away in silence.

James was waiting for me in the hallway, leaning up against the wall with a scowl on his face. "Going somewhere?"

"I—" I paused. "You can't stop me."

"No doubt about that," he said, taking my hand and leading me toward the throne room. As badly as I wanted to pull away, I couldn't. Not when this might be the last time I'd ever see him. "Are you sure about this?"

"If you were me, what would you do?"

"I would have left ages ago."

At least he understood, but I didn't have time for this.

If I wasn't in Calliope's palace in twenty minutes, Cronus would kill millions more. "If you're not trying to stop me, then what are you here for?"

"Everyone gets a goodbye except me?" he said, and I hugged him around the middle.

"I'm sorry. I meant to tell you."

"That's a lie, but thanks for the thought," said James without a hint of anger. "So what's the plan?"

I didn't speak. It wasn't any of his business, and if I told him, I ran the risk of him trying to interfere and screw everything up. I trusted James, but I'd trusted Ava, too. I'd trusted Calliope. Each time something terrible happened, that trust bit me in the ass. If this plan had any chance of succeeding, I had to keep my mouth shut.

James didn't press the issue until we reached the empty throne room. Stopping in the center, he searched my face for something he obviously couldn't find. "You can trust me," he said. "I want to help."

"The moment I tell you, you're going to do everything in your power to stop me," I said without anger or accusation. It was the truth, and we both knew it.

"I swear I'll only help," he said, tracing an *X* over his chest. "Cross my heart, word of honor, stick a needle…" He grimaced. "Actually, no, not that last part. Doesn't even rhyme properly."

I punched him lightly in the arm. "And how do you plan on helping? By running to Walter and telling him everything so he can stop me?"

James scoffed. "Is that what you think of me? You're sneaking away to live in sin with a mass murderer, and *I'm* the bad guy here?"

Any small amount of amusement I'd managed in those

few minutes with him evaporated. "You know I don't have a choice."

"You do have a choice," he countered. "You've just made it already, that's all."

"What else would you have me do?"

He shrugged. "Couldn't say. I'd do the exact same thing."

My anger deflated. "Then give me a hug goodbye and let me go. I might be an infant compared to the rest of you, but that doesn't make me an idiot."

"Most of the time," said James, and I punched him in the arm again. Wordlessly he gathered me up and buried his face in my hair. "I was supposed to be your first affair."

A lump formed in my throat, and I hugged him back fiercely. "I don't think it counts as an affair if the thought of Cronus makes me sick to my stomach."

"So there's still hope for me, after all."

I half laughed, half sobbed. "You're an ass."

"Runs in the family." He let me go. "Be safe, Kate. I mean it. If you die, Henry will—"

"—tear the entire world apart with his bare hands," I said. "Yeah, I know. Believe it or not, I really want me to stay alive, too."

"Despite all evidence to the contrary." He smiled faintly, and I touched his elbow.

"Do me a favor. Find someone for you, okay? Not a fling or a mortal to marry for fifty years before she dies, but someone to really settle down with. You're, what, several thousand years old? Don't you think it's time?"

His smile faltered for a split second. "I would've settled down with you, but then you had to go and marry my uncle. You're a little heartbreaker, you know."

I rolled my eyes. "You're terrible. I mean it. You deserve someone—someone who isn't already taken. Go out and find her. Or him. Just find *someone*." I drew myself up to my full height. "I'm going to be mad at you until you do."

"It took Henry a thousand years to find you," said James. "You think you could really be mad at me for that long?"

"Henry doesn't get out much. You do." I kissed his cheek. "I'm serious. There has to be a minor goddess out there somewhere who's absolutely head over heels for you."

"Who I haven't already deflowered— *Ow*." James rubbed his shoulder, where I'd punched him a third time. "You're awfully violent today."

"And you're awfully crass."

He captured me in another hug. "Too bad you didn't have a daughter."

"If I had, I'd have told her to stay the hell away from you."

"Even as a newborn?"

"You can never start too early."

Kissing the top of my head, he slid his hand into mine. "Fair enough. Now what do you say to getting out of here?"

We were back to that again. I sighed. "I don't need your help, James. I'm fine on my own. I've got it all figured out."

"Do you now?" he said, eyebrow raised. "Then tell me— how do you plan on getting off Olympus? By taking the stairs?"

I hesitated. "Can I?"

"This isn't a Led Zeppelin song, sweetheart. There are no stairways to heaven." He gestured to the sunset floor. "Walter has this place locked down right now, which means there's only one way out of here, and that's to have an Olympian escort you. Ready?"

I eyed him, searching for any sign that he was about to run off to Walter. But time was slipping away, and I didn't have much of a choice. "If I let you, do you swear you're just helping?"

"Everything short of the needle," he said. How was it possible he could make me smile even in the middle of the hardest thing I'd ever had to do?

Because he was James, and because I could have loved him like that if I didn't already love Henry. I did have Henry though, and I would never cheat on him. James knew it, I knew it—the only person who didn't was Henry himself.

Standing on my tiptoes, I kissed the corner of his mouth, lingering for longer than was strictly necessary. "First affair, I promise," I whispered. "Now let's do this."

James grinned. "Thought you'd never say so."

We arrived smack-dab in the middle of the busiest inter-section I'd ever seen. Hundreds of people moved together in varying directions, streams intersecting and merging like real traffic, and I squinted upward in hopes of gaining my bearings. Pink and purple clouds decorated the sky, which was barely visible through the thick forest of skyscrapers that surrounded us.

Standing still in the chaos wasn't an option though, and I wound up sandwiched between two Japanese businessmen in black suits, both carrying briefcases and chatting in a language I didn't know. However, like in Africa and Greece, even though I didn't know the words, I understood them anyway.

"…morning meeting with the executive from San Francisco?"

"Indeed, but wouldn't you say—"

"James!" I shouted, struggling against the flow of the crowd, but it was useless. With less than ten minutes left before Cronus's deadline, I couldn't find James anywhere.

The businessmen on either side of me gave me a dirty look, as if they'd only now realized I was there, and they shifted until I was behind them. Fine by me.

"James!" I shrieked again as I reached the sidewalk. Elbowing my way through the crowd, I reached the glass face of a building and leaned against it, directly underneath a neon sign advertising electronics. This was insane. How could there possibly be this many people in one place at one time?

"First time in Tokyo?" said an amused voice beside me. James leaned casually against the wall, and he held a bowl of noodles with his right hand while he maneuvered a pair of chopsticks with his left.

"Very funny. I'm leaving now." I closed my eyes and started to slip away, but James's hand on my shoulder stopped me.

"I will," he said around a mouthful of noodles. "I'll find someone as long as you promise me this isn't forever."

I touched his hand. "I promise. I'll see you on the other side of this war, James."

"And maybe with a little luck, we'll both be alive."

I kissed his cheek one last time and stepped back, giving myself enough space to go. This wasn't the end. If I couldn't make sure of it, then James would.

"Wait," he said again, and with a wave of his hand, his noodles vanished. "How do you intend on getting Milo back to Henry?"

I stared at him. What else was he going to come up with to get me to take him with me? Regardless of how much of a manipulative jerk he'd suddenly decided to be, however, he had a point. I'd taken for granted that Cronus would let me bring Milo to Olympus myself, or that he would send him to Olympus—but Cronus had no way of getting there, and once I landed on the island, I was positive I would never be able to leave. At least not until this war was over.

"You're infuriating," I muttered, holding out my hand. With a smug look, James took it. "I don't know how to bring you along."

"You'll figure it out," he said. "I trust you."

"Trusting me has nothing to do with what I can and can't do."

"Do exactly the same thing you did when you took me to see Milo and Cronus," he said. "Don't even think about it."

Easier said than done. The cacophony of noise around us made it difficult to concentrate, but if I didn't, then there was no telling what Cronus would do if he thought I'd backed out of our deal. So I had to. No waffling allowed.

I focused on my body, becoming aware of every inch of it, and I extended my reach to James as much as I could. It felt forced, as if I were doing nothing more than imagining it, but James knew the stakes. If he was willing to risk it, then I was willing to try.

The noise of Tokyo funneled around us, a wall of vibrations that sounded like everything and nothing at all. The roar grew louder until finally it overtook me completely, and then—

I was drowning.

Water filled my lungs as I struggled to do the human thing and breathe. I tasted salt and flailed, my hand still clasping James's, but that didn't help. He was as much of a rock as I was, and together we sank deeper and deeper into the pitch-black ocean.

We were going to die. Or at least be trapped at the bottom of the sea for the rest of eternity. Seaweed would wrap around our limbs, holding us down until the ocean was ready to pull us farther into her depths. By the time we managed to escape, time would be up, and Cronus would believe I'd abandoned him completely. Millions more would be dead, and nothing I said or did would convince Cronus to stop.

Nothing.

CHAPTER 12
DROWNING

I opened my mouth to cry out for help, but I had no more breath left in me. I couldn't see the surface. Everything blended together in a nightmare of darkness, and terror seized me so completely that I couldn't think.

This was it. This was the end.

I really should've let Ava teach me how to swim.

"Having trouble?" said a gruff voice beside me, as clear as if we were talking on the surface. I twisted around and nearly fainted with relief.

Phillip, Lord of the Oceans, floated beside us, looking as if he were walking on dry land. I didn't care that he must have known what we were doing or what I'd planned; I didn't care that if he knew, Walter must, too. As long as I didn't spend the rest of eternity at the bottom of the sea, that would all be worth it.

Help us, I mouthed, gesturing to the hand that held James's. The water was so dark that I couldn't see him anymore.

"Of course," said Phillip, and he looked in the direction

that must have been up. A strong current caught the three of us, carrying us toward the surface with formidable speed. As soon as the blue sky became visible through the water, the tide dragged us to the side, and I clawed my way toward the surface. Just a few more inches.

"Your stop, I believe," said Phillip. "Be safe."

I nodded and mouthed my thanks. I could see James through the water now, and he was grinning at his uncle and giving him a stupid wave. Figured. We'd nearly drowned, and he was smiling.

Finally we broke the surface, and I coughed up an impossible amount of seawater. Somehow my feet found the shifting sand, and I stood shakily, my knees knocking together. But we were out of the ocean and still had a few minutes left before Cronus expected me. That was the important part.

Something flashed at the edge of my vision, and I looked around wildly, my heart pounding. For a split second, I thought I saw a dark-haired figure looming on the cliffs, but I blinked, and it was gone.

Deep breaths. We were out of the ocean, and I had nothing to panic about anymore. Unless an eternal Titan hellbent on destroying everything I loved counted.

Cool waves lapped at my shins, and James stood beside me, shaking like a leaf. "All right," he rasped. "I admit that—that asking you to do that without practicing first was a—a mistake."

"No shit," I said in a voice that trembled as much as his did. We stood a few yards from the shoreline of Cronus's island, and the palace loomed above us, a giant shadow against the bright sky. "Are you okay?"

"I'll live," he said wryly. "At least until we get inside."

"How are we getting through the barrier?" I couldn't see it, but I could feel it, thrumming in my bones like a force field. If Cronus couldn't penetrate it—at least not enough to leave, even though his reach now extended as far as Cairo—then how were we supposed to?

"We walk," said James. "The barrier's meant to keep Cronus trapped, not us. Walter even insisted we didn't modify it to include Calliope. Until we realized she had you, of course."

"You mean—" I faltered. I should've tried harder to escape. Somehow I could've found a way. Phillip could've picked me up in the ocean and brought me to safety, or—

I steeled myself against the barrage of possibilities that flooded my mind. Playing what-if wouldn't change anything. I *had* tried to escape. I'd done everything I could. And right now, all I could focus on was how to make sure things finally went my way.

"I mean what?" said James, and I shook my head.

"Never mind. Let's go."

With my hand still in his and the taste of salt on my tongue, I dug my heels into the sand and pushed forward, trudging out of the ocean to meet my fate.

Unnatural silence settled over the island. The cliffs overlooking the shore stood tall and unyielding, but despite their imposing height, James spent one of the few precious minutes we had left trying to find the quickest way up.

"It's not going to work," I said, annoyed. We were wasting too much time. "Let's just go around."

"That's miles out of our way," said James.

"Then give me your arm and I'll get us there."

He snorted. "You really think I'm going to put myself through that again?"

"Do you really have a choice?" I wobbled across the beach, the sand giving way with each step I took. "Walk or reappear, James. It doesn't matter to me. I'm leaving in ten seconds with or without you."

Muttering something under his breath that I didn't quite catch, he hurried over to me. "If we wind up in the ocean again, I'm leaving."

"You're the one who insisted I had to bring you along in the first place," I said. "Besides, stop pretending you didn't like that swim. I saw you grinning."

"Yeah, sheepishly. Phillip's never going to let me live that one down."

If they were both alive at the end of this war. Taking his hand, I closed my eyes. "No water this time," I promised.

The air around us changed, the warm ocean breeze replaced with the stale scent of ancient rock. I sighed with relief. We were in the bedroom Calliope had kept me in for nine months, and there wasn't a drop of water in sight.

"Much better," whispered James.

I reached for the door. It was locked. "Dammit," I muttered, but before I could complain or suggest another trip through nothingness, James touched the handle, and I heard a faint click.

"Try again."

This time the door opened without a hitch. I raised an eyebrow, and he shrugged. "I've got a few tricks up my sleeve."

Together we sneaked out into the abandoned hallway. It wasn't nearly as decadent as the one outside the nursery, and I glanced around uneasily. I had no idea how to get there from here.

Each end of the hallway looked identical. Left or right, it didn't matter, but Ava had pulled me right when Henry had attacked the palace. Good enough place to start.

"This way," I said, creeping through the darkness, and James followed a few steps behind me. Someone had fixed the damage Henry had done to the castle, making the passageway clear.

"Are you sure?" he said dubiously.

"Aren't you supposed to always know where you're going?"

"Not in Titan territory. You're positive it isn't the other way?"

I ignored him. They had to have some way to move from floor to floor. I tried to mentally picture the parts of the palace I knew, but I couldn't remember ever seeing a staircase.

"Kate," said James with a hint of desperation in his voice. "I think you're going in the wrong—"

A crash of metal against metal ripped through the air, and a man screamed. In an instant, James yanked me back so we were both leaning flat against the wall.

"What—" I started, but he pressed his palm against my mouth. A cold giggle echoed down the hallway, and I turned my head enough to spot Calliope exiting a room at the end of the corridor.

Humming to herself, she stepped through another doorway and disappeared, quickly followed by a stooped figure that couldn't have been anyone but Ava. Where was Cronus? And who was inside that room?

"Nicholas," breathed James. "He's alive."

My conscience pulled me toward Nicholas, but I'd come here for one reason and one reason only. As much as it killed me to sneak past his cell, if I wanted any real shot at saving my son, I had to.

"We'll come back for him," I said, half a promise to myself and half a promise to James. We wouldn't have the chance to come back for Nicholas though, and we both knew it.

James led the way this time, and despite my hissed protests, he opened the door that Calliope had disappeared through. I held my breath, certain she'd be waiting for us on the other side, fully aware we were there, but instead—

"Guess there really is a stairway to heaven, after all," said James with a grin, and if I wasn't already on edge, I would've laughed at his stupid joke. We hurried up the stairs in silence. Two levels up, I nodded toward the door, and he pushed it open wide enough for one of us to fit through.

"Me first," I said. If Cronus was waiting on the other side, he wouldn't attack me. James, on the other hand, hadn't exactly been invited. Slipping through the door into the empty peacock-blue-and-gold hallway, I waited the space of three heartbeats before I flagged him to follow. "Which one is Milo's room?" I hadn't spent any time outside the nursery, but during my vision, James had left.

"Fourth one down," he said. "Kate, if anything goes wrong—"

"Hello there."

Cronus's voice, frigid and void of compassion, slid down my spine. I turned on my heel, automatically stepping in front of James to shield him, but it was an empty gesture. If Cronus wanted to kill James, he wouldn't need my permission.

"I told you I was coming," I said icily, but it was nothing compared to the way Cronus spoke. He could freeze the sun if he wanted to.

"Yes, but I do not recall consenting to a guest."

"I can't very well head back to Olympus with Milo. James is going to take him for me."

"Is that so?" said Cronus, and James nodded. His eyes were too bright and his jaw rigid, but he raised his chin and stared Cronus down.

Terror seized me. Cronus wouldn't hurt me no matter how insolent I was, not as long as he thought I would be his. But James was expendable—barely anything more to Cronus than the millions of people he had already wiped out with a single thought.

"Yes," said James. "Now, if you don't mind, I'm going to do what I came here to do."

"By all means." A strange smile twisted across Cronus's too-perfect lips, and he stepped aside with a flourish.

What was Cronus playing at? James moved forward, and I went with him. If this was some kind of trap, if Cronus had known and was only setting James up—

Cronus didn't try to stop me, though. James and I hurried toward the nursery, and my heart pounded. Was Milo still here? Had Cronus done something to him? James and I reached for the handle at the same time, but before either of us touched the metal fixture, the door burst open.

Calliope.

At first her blue eyes rounded with shock, but after a beat, she smirked. She looked like she was my mother and Sofia's age now, much more appropriate for one of the original six, but that did nothing to distract me from the fact that she cradled Milo in her arms.

"Kate," she purred. "How good of you to join us. Here I was thinking you were smart enough to stay away. Silly me."

"Kate?" said a small voice behind her, and Ava appeared in the doorway. "Oh, my god, Kate! Cronus said you were alive, but I didn't think—"

"Silence," said Calliope. Ava immediately quieted, but her cheeks flushed and her eyes danced with light. For the first time in nearly a year, she looked alive. Calliope cleared her throat and turned to James with a simpering smile. "Darling, it's been far too long."

"I'm not your darling. Give me the baby," said James, holding out his arms.

"Why would I do something like that?" she said with a sniff. "Callum is my son."

I wanted to sink my nails into that pretty little face of hers and claw her eyes out. "He's my son, not yours," I snarled. "Cronus and I made a deal. I'm here, and *Milo* leaves with James."

"Oh?" Calliope peered over my shoulder. "Why wasn't I part of this deal, Father?"

"It was not your deal to make," said Cronus. "You will do as I say and uphold my word."

"What word is that?" said Calliope venomously, her grip tightening around my son.

"The baby will be returned to Kate's family, and she will remain here with me."

Two red spots appeared on Calliope's cheeks, and she jolted strangely, as if she were fighting against some kind of compulsion. "And if I don't?"

"Then I will no longer have any use for you."

She hissed. "After everything I've done for you, after everything I've sacrificed—"

Fury rolled off of her in waves, and I had to force myself not to step away. I was so close to Milo that all I had to do was reach out and touch him. I couldn't leave him again.

"Is this your final decision?" said Cronus. "To part from our allegiance for the sake of keeping a child that is not yours?"

"He should be mine." Calliope moved back toward the nursery, but Ava blocked her way, a magenta glow emanating from her body. "Don't make me do this, Father."

A glint of metal beside Milo caught my eye. Calliope pulled the blanket back and, before any of us could react, she pressed the dagger Nicholas had forged, the only weapon that could kill an immortal, against Milo's throat.

"I will not let him go," said Calliope, calmer now as fear filled the air like poison. "You've given away something that wasn't yours to give, Father."

Behind me, Cronus sighed as if he were dealing with a petulant child. Not a murderer who had no problem killing again. "I will not ask you a second time. Turn over the child or face the wrath of the King of the Titans."

"Does the wrath of the Queen of the Gods mean nothing then?" said Calliope. Paralyzed with fear, I couldn't take my eyes from my son. I didn't care about a pissing match between them; all I wanted was for Calliope to move that blade away from Milo's neck.

"Calliope, you don't want to do that," said Ava, inching closer. Calliope wheeled around, her teeth bared as she clutched Milo to her chest.

"Don't you dare use your powers on me," she growled. Lifting the handle of the dagger, she pressed the point against Milo's chest. "What will it be, Father? Your deal or my allegiance?"

Milo let out a soft cry, and I lunged forward. But before I reached him, Cronus grabbed my shoulders and pulled me against his chest, and no matter how hard I struggled, he didn't budge.

"I will not break my word to Kate," said Cronus without emotion, and I elbowed him hard in the stomach. Nothing. "Do what you must, but make no mistake. Our allegiance hinges on that baby's life."

I thought I saw a flash of hurt on Calliope's face, but it lasted only a fraction of a second. "So you've chosen Kate over me," she said, practically spitting my name. "Then it hardly matters what I do, does it? Your allegiance will never be mine, and no longer will mine be yours."

She raised the dagger, and a scream ripped through me and

echoed through the palace. I couldn't watch, but I couldn't look away in the last seconds of Milo's short life either. I couldn't abandon him like that.

The world darkened around the edges, and for one beautiful moment I thought I was dying. My body went numb, my mind quieted into silence, and that second hung between us, frozen. I would live with this fear forever if it meant this moment never ended—if Calliope never moved the blade closer, if Milo never died, if we all stayed this way for eternity.

A flash of white light blinded me, and darkness that crackled with power engulfed us.

"Calliope," boomed an all-too-familiar voice. "Put the weapon down and give me my son."

Henry.

It shouldn't have been possible for me to be any more afraid than I already was, but now, seeing Henry float down the hallway with that black cloud around him, a choke hold of terror grabbed on to me and refused to let go.

I was going to lose both of them.

This time Calliope didn't try to hide her shock. Her mouth dropped open, but she also lowered the dagger. "Henry," she said. "What an unexpected surprise. And here Father was telling me you were dead."

She glared at Cronus, and his arms tightened around me until he was a millimeter away from crushing my bones into dust.

"You lied to me," he whispered in my ear, and his malevolence thrummed in the air around us. "After everything I did for you, this is how you repay me. With deceit and mockery."

I gulped. No more secrets now. The cards were on the table, and now all we could do was play.

"Give me my son," repeated Henry. He was less than a foot away from me now, but he didn't spare me a glance.

"And what do I get in this deal?" said Calliope, eyeing him hungrily.

"Me," said Henry quietly. "Give me my son, swear on the River Styx that you will never harm him or allow harm to come to him in any way, shape or form, and you will have me."

"Henry, no," I gasped, and Cronus clamped his hand over my mouth. No, no, no. Henry was supposed to stay with Milo and keep him safe. I couldn't, not the way he could. It had to be me. I had to be the one to stay. I tried to protest, whimpering and screaming and flailing against Cronus, but Henry ignored me completely.

"That will fulfill the terms of our bargain," said Cronus, and I stopped cold. "The baby will be raised by his family, as Kate has demanded, and I will have her."

No, that was not our deal. Not even close. Milo was supposed to be safe in Olympus with Henry and my mother and James, not down here with Calliope and Cronus. I couldn't speak though, and no one was paying attention to me. Henry nodded once, and in that second, my heart shattered.

"Very well," said Calliope, but despite the fact that she was getting everything she'd ever wanted, there was an edge in her voice, a hardness I didn't understand. She should've been celebrating. I was broken. I had nothing, and she had it all now. "I swear on the River Styx that I will not harm this baby, nor allow harm to come to him, so long as you stay with me."

"So be it." There was soft thunder in Henry's voice, and my vision blurred. There had to be a way out of this—this couldn't be what Henry had intended. He wouldn't leave me like that.

But hadn't I been willing to leave him?

"Perfect," said Calliope, and without tearing her eyes from Henry, she said to Ava, "Do it."

"But—" said Ava, her earlier courage failing.

"Do it."

Do what?

It didn't take long for me to get an answer. The magenta aura around Ava grew until it touched Henry, and like lightning, it hit Calliope. Instead of crying out, however, her smug smile only expanded.

"There," said Ava, her voice trembling. "Now let Kate and the baby go."

"You heard Father," said Calliope. "The baby stays with Henry. But if you insist, I will give him a choice. Henry, darling." She stepped toward him, and my heart pounded. "Who do you want to stay with? Me or Kate?"

Was this some kind of joke? Of course Henry wanted to stay with me, especially when we could all be a family. Henry stepped closer to Calliope though, and my eyes widened. He set his hand on her cheek in the familiar way he always touched me, and then—

His eyes fluttered shut, and he leaned down to kiss her.

What had Ava done?

Stupid question. I knew exactly what she'd done. And no matter what her reasons were, no matter what Calliope was holding over her head, no matter how many times she cradled my crying son, I would never, ever forgive her for making Henry fall in love with Calliope.

Cronus moved backward, taking me with him. Panic seized me, leaving no room for rationality, and I clawed at his hands, desperate for him to let go. I couldn't leave, not now. Not when my husband thought he was in love with someone else.

Pulling away from Henry, Calliope eyed me with distaste.

"No, do not leave yet," she said in a regal voice that would have had Cronus smiting her two minutes earlier.

"And why is that?" said Cronus.

Calliope smiled sweetly. "Because I'm not finished with her yet."

With no hand to guide it, the dagger rose in the air between us until it lined up with my throat. And in a blur of silver and steel, it flew straight toward me.

CHAPTER 13
WICKED GAMES

I didn't have time to think or breathe or worry about whether or not Milo would remember this moment. All I did was close my eyes. Time was supposed to slow down in the seconds before death—and I would really die now, with no Underworld to catch me and no Henry to save me—but nothing changed.

This was it.

A great crunch of metal against metal echoed throughout the palace, and for one horrible second I thought Henry or even James had been stupid enough to jump in front of it. My eyes flew open, but they both stood several feet away on either side of the door.

And floating in front of me, half an inch from my neck, was the dagger.

"I believe in the midst of forcing the Lord of the Underworld into your alliance, you have forgotten one important fact," said Cronus in a deadly voice that seemed to be everywhere at once. "Your fate is tied to Kate's. If she dies, so do you. Surely you are not ready to fade, my dear daughter."

Calliope's arms trembled so badly I feared she'd drop Milo. Henry gently took him from her, and for a moment I was sure she'd fight. He could disappear as soon as he touched the baby; all it would take was a blink, and Henry would be gone, safe back in Olympus with our son. But she willingly let him go.

I held my breath, waiting for Henry to leave. He stayed put though, a strange smile on his face as he gazed down at Milo. My heart sank. She had Henry now. She really, truly had him.

But the way he looked at the baby, the way his shoulders relaxed as he held him—Henry loved Milo. Ava hadn't taken that away from him, which meant a small piece of him, no matter how buried, still loved me, too.

"Here I was thinking you no longer had any interest in the little traitorous bitch," said Calliope to Cronus, her words choked with fury. "How silly of me to think you wouldn't fall prey to human emotion."

"I am King of the Titans," said Cronus coldly, and he straightened to his full height, drawing me with him so my toes barely grazed the floor. "I have fallen prey to nothing."

"Yet here you are, protecting a mere goddess, and a brand-new one at that," said Calliope. I glared at her. Not very formidable, but it was the best I could do under the circumstances. "What has she done to deserve your loyalty? Was she the one to free you? To stand by your side as the gods lined up to fight against you? All this time, she has been working for the enemy, discussing the secrets you have shared, planning a defense based on the strategies you have so willingly shown her."

Terrific. Now she was trying to get him to kill me. Calliope had it wrong though—Cronus was the one who'd fooled me for so long. He was the one who'd gotten me to spill the council's secrets by making me think he was Henry. And without realizing it, she was confirming what their arguments had already implied: Cronus didn't care about her. She was a pawn, exactly like the rest of us. Whatever his plans were, he wasn't sharing them with her.

Unlike the council, Cronus and Calliope weren't partners. They were barely allies. In Calliope's desperation to escape from Walter, she'd managed to stumble across the only being in the universe who treated her even worse than he had. And judging by the look on her face, she was finally beginning to realize it.

Cronus was quiet for a long moment, and darkness filled the hallway until I couldn't see an inch in front of me. "I have shown her and told her nothing."

"There is no other explanation," said Calliope. "The battles we have fought—they are always two steps ahead of us, circumventing my traps and plans, and they could not possibly know these things if you were not telling Kate our every move."

He wasn't though, which meant there was a traitor in Calliope's household. I glanced into the darkness where Ava was standing.

Not possible.

"Silence," said Cronus, and he dropped me. I stumbled, and his hand caught my wrist. "I will hear no more of this. If there has been any leak, it is not from me. Therefore I can only assume it is you who is the traitor, my daughter. And I do not suffer treason."

He yanked my hand until my fingertips touched another—James's. No one else was standing in that direction.

"I am finished with this pointless debate. You have what

you want, and my bargain with Kate is fulfilled. However, because I cannot ensure her safety, I cannot allow her to stay."

At last Cronus let go of my wrist, and I understood. The inky clouds, his argument with Calliope—he wanted me to leave. I couldn't though, not when Henry and Milo were in danger. I couldn't abandon them again.

The air crackled with a different kind of power, but the darkness around us muted it, and Calliope let out a frustrated cry. "You can't do this to me! She is *nothing*—"

"Then tell me," said Cronus, "if she is nothing, why do you care?"

Calliope blustered, and James gripped my hand so tightly that I thought my fingers would fall off. If I had any chance of getting him out of here alive, we had to go now. I couldn't be responsible for anything happening to him, but I couldn't leave either.

And then, in the emptiness, a midnight voice surrounded me.

Go.

Tears stung my eyes. Henry. There was nothing I could do and he knew it. If I stayed, Calliope would kill me. Like our picnic in the woods when she'd revealed herself to be the traitor, she was too emotional, too irrational for me to depend on her thinking clearly. She'd known then that she would out herself as a murderer to the entire council, and she hadn't cared. I had no guarantee she wouldn't call Cronus's bluff now.

I focused all my energy on Henry and pushed my thoughts toward him. *I love you. Don't ever forget that.*

Without giving myself a chance to change my mind, I clutched James's hand and disappeared.

We landed on an abandoned beach as the sun dipped into

the ocean. I sank onto the sand, and James gathered me up, letting me cry into his shoulder without complaint.

I'd left them. I'd sworn I would never abandon Henry, and the first chance I'd had, I'd done it anyway. If I'd talked to him before Cronus's deadline, we could have come up with a plan together. We didn't need the council's permission to act, and I'd leapt without thinking once again. This time it had cost me my family.

"I'm never going to see them again, am I?" I said. The tide washed up inches from our toes, and we didn't have more than a few minutes before we'd miss our window to return to Olympus. The thought of going back without Henry and Milo ate away at me until there was nothing left but skin and bone. Walter and Dylan were right. The entire council was right. I wasn't ready to help them, and the more I did, the worse things got.

"What happened to you?" said James.

"What do you mean?"

He pulled back enough to look at me, his eyes searching mine. "You're not the girl I met in Eden. She didn't break down into tears every time something didn't go her way."

"I'm not—" I started, but then another tear rolled down my face. "My family's gone. No one's letting me help, and every time I try, I screw things up even worse."

He threaded his fingers through mine. "Since when did you ever need anyone's permission?"

I wiped my cheeks and squinted into the sunset. "So what else am I supposed to do? I've already tried everything. My deal with Cronus fell through, and even if it hadn't, all it would've done was secure Milo's safety. It wouldn't have changed anything in the bigger picture, and the only way I'm ever going to see them again is if we win this war."

"So help us win."

I sniffed. "How?"

"Think," he said. "You know Cronus's weaknesses better than any of us. You know his strengths. You know *him*."

"Bullshit. The original six fought him for a decade. I've never so much as arm wrestled with him."

"No," agreed James, "but you're the only one who's ever stopped him in his tracks."

That moment in the Underworld, as Cronus had chased us through a desert. I'd thought I was going to die then, too. Would that have made any of this easier?

No, it wouldn't have, because the original six would've never escaped that cavern in Tartarus. They would still be there, unconscious and slowly dying while Cronus and Calliope figured a way out. Everything would've been different.

But even my one act of courage had been a supreme act of stupidity. Cronus was free because I'd walked into his cavern when Persephone had specifically told me not to, and I'd given Calliope the leverage she'd needed to get Henry to open the gate.

"Think," said James. "Why didn't Cronus kill you then?"

"Because he didn't know me. Because I—"

"Because you were kind to him when the rest of us were doing our best to keep him chained."

"Because I promised I'd open the gate."

"Yes," said James. "And he stopped because he *trusted* you."

"Look where that's gotten us," I said disdainfully.

"Yes. Look where your stubbornness and refusal to give up got us. We have a fighting chance now. It wasn't the way we imagined, but Calliope would've discovered a way to free Cronus eventually. She had damn near close to eternity, just like the rest of us."

I drew my knees to my chest. "What happens if Cronus wipes out all of humanity and you all lose your purposes?"

James hesitated, and fear sparked between us. He drew me closer. "I don't know."

"Maybe you won't fade," I said. "I mean, there's always going to be love and travel and music and gardens and—and everything. Maybe—"

"Kate." James's voice rose above the crash of the ocean, and I fell silent. "Don't worry about the worst-case scenario. Come up with a way to make sure that never happens. Focus on doing what you do best and *fight* for the people you love."

He stood, and I rose with him, my knees shaking. "No pressure or anything," I said, and despite everything, he gave me a boyish grin.

"On the contrary, you're a diamond. You shine under pressure."

I half laughed, half choked. "And you're a smelly block of cheese. Take me back before the sun sets completely."

James clasped his hand in mine, his grasp firm and unwavering. "Promise me you'll fight. No matter how bad things get, you won't break down and let Cronus and Calliope win."

I shook my head minutely. I couldn't promise that. I would fight for as long as I could, but Calliope had my family, and after two failed bargains, Cronus would undoubtedly be hell-bent on destroying humanity and everything that had ever been familiar to me. How long before my mother faded? James? The entire council?

I couldn't fight if I had nothing left to fight for.

Then do not let that happen.

Henry's voice echoed through my mind, and I looked around wildly, searching for any sign of him. Of course he wasn't there, though. He was Calliope's prisoner now—a willing prisoner who didn't know that when he kissed her, when he caressed her, he didn't really feel any of it. He didn't know it was a trick, but I did, and I couldn't leave him to suffer through an eternity of her sickening games.

I won't, I thought in return, hoping like crazy it reached him.

"Promise me, Kate," said James, and I blinked. "Promise me that you won't give up on your family."

Steel slowly wrapped around my spine. He was right. Henry needed me. Milo needed me. Whatever it took, there was no way in hell I was going to let Calliope win. "Fine, I promise. Now let's go convince Walter to stop being an egotistical bastard."

James snorted. "Your words, not mine."

We arrived in the center of the throne room. I wasn't sure what I'd been expecting, but the full council—minus Calliope, Henry and Nicholas—wasn't it.

Everyone was there, even Ella with her silver arm. Her face was pinched as if she smelled something disgusting, and she stared into the center of the throne room, where James and I stood.

"What's going on?" I said, turning to Walter. He, too, stared into the center of the circle with a stony expression, but James pulled me aside, and Walter's gaze didn't waver. He wasn't staring at us.

Instead, exactly where we'd been standing, was Ava. Or at least a version of Ava. Her form looked substantial, but only seconds before, we'd occupied the same space. She wasn't really there.

James let go of me and sat down, and I followed his lead, trying to ignore the pain in my chest when I saw Henry's empty throne. When I settled in mine, my mother took my hand.

"I'm sorry," said Ava in a choked voice, as clear as if she were really standing there. Golden light flowed from four of the thrones—the remaining original siblings, including my mother. Each ran into the center of the circle, meeting where Ava stood. The council was doing something that made her being there possible. "I want to come home."

"You cannot come home," said Walter in a painfully neutral voice. I had good reason to never want to talk to her again—and after what she'd done to Henry, that stabbing hatred at the very sight of her returned to me, and this time I was positive Calliope had nothing to do with it. Walter was her father though, and she was his favorite. Why didn't he care?

"I can't do this anymore." Ava's voice broke, and she turned to look each council member in the eye. When ours met, she winced, and I held her stare.

"Can't do what anymore?" It wasn't my place to speak, but I couldn't stop myself. "Can't assist a mass murderer in getting his way? Can't do laundry for someone who steals innocent babies?"

Her lower lip trembled, and I scraped my nails against my throne. I'd had to risk my life, my family, *everything* to earn a spot on the council, to prove I was worthy of ruling over the Underworld with Henry. Yet they were allowed to hurt as many people as they wanted so long as it meant they got their way. I was sick of it.

"Please," she begged, her hands shaking as she stepped toward me, but the golden light wouldn't hold her, and she was forced to return to the center. "Kate, I love you— Calliope made me— Please understand, I never wanted any of this—"

"There comes a point in your life when you have to make a choice," I said. "You can keep going down the easy path no matter where it takes you, everyone else be damned, or you can fight for what you believe in."

"I *am* fighting!" she exploded. "I'm doing this for Nicholas and Milo and Henry and all of you—don't you get that? Do you think I wanted to walk away from my family like this? I have a son, too, Kate. I know what it's like to love someone as much as you love Milo. Do you think if I had any other choice—"

"Enough." Walter's voice, low and anything but neutral now, echoed through the throne room. "You have said your piece, daughter, and now you must allow the council to—"

"Screw the council." Ava didn't so much as look at her father, and if she'd been more than an illusion, I had no doubt the room would have crackled with power. As it was, no one dared to speak. Even Walter looked as if she'd slapped him across the face.

"I want you to listen to me, Katherine Winters," she said. "Everything I have done, every word, every look, every betrayal, has been to help our family. Doing the right thing doesn't always mean acting like a saint. Sometimes it means getting your hands dirty and doing the thing you hate most so other people might have an easier time of it. So other people might not *die*."

"If that's your excuse, then how do you justify dragging Milo into it?" I snapped.

"He was never supposed to be part of it. He was never supposed to *exist*."

"But he does. He's here, and now Calliope has Henry, too. All because of *you*."

The council remained silent, and not even my mother reacted. So I'd been right. They all knew exactly what he'd planned to do, and none of them had stopped him.

Ava took a deep breath. "I'm sorry," she said in a measured voice, and it was such a change from seconds before that it took me a moment to understand she was sincere. Something ugly surfaced inside me. I didn't want her to apologize. I wanted her to fight. "None of this should've happened. No matter what stupid mistakes I've made...I'm sorry for those, Kate. I'm sorry to all of you for leaving you. I never wanted to, but like I said, I didn't have a choice—"

"Ava." Walter's voice reverberated through the throne room.

"You've done enough, Daddy. It's my turn to talk now," she said with inhuman quietness. "I'm sorry for everything. I love you all, and I did what I thought I had to do. But Henry's here to protect the baby now, and I can't do anything more to help Nicholas."

Around the circle, several council members glanced at Nicholas's empty copper throne. "You are willing to abandon him, knowing it may mean his death?" said Walter.

"I'm more of a danger to him if I stay and give Calliope the chance to use him to keep controlling me," said Ava. "He wants me to go, and the only way I can help save him is to return to Olympus. Cronus has decided he's going to escape the island on the winter solstice, and given what he's shown himself to be capable of, I believe him. I want to help."

In that moment, she didn't sound like the Ava I knew—the selfish, simpering goddess of love who couldn't prioritize what others needed before what she wanted. She sounded old. Haunted. Like the other members of the council did when they were so deep into planning that they let their masks slip. It was one more reminder of who and what they were—ancient. Powerful. Wiser than I could ever imagine, but shortsighted and close-minded, as well. Cut off from the real world, from the humanity they struggled to defend. Stubborn and as passionate about protecting their own interests as they were about doing their jobs.

That was Ava. Stubborn and passionate, and now lost to me as completely as our father was.

"I am sorry, daughter," said Walter, but he didn't sound very sorry at all. "We cannot pretend to know Calliope's intentions, and we must act cautiously. It is possible that Nicholas remains alive only because Calliope believes he is the key to controlling you. If you abandon her, there is no telling what she might do to him."

A murmur rose from the other members of the council, but no one objected. I didn't blame them. As much as it pained me to admit it, Walter was right.

"You will remain with Calliope until given further instructions," said Walter. "You will carry on as normal, with no sabotage or acts of ill will toward her. She must believe that your intentions are pure."

"But you haven't even discussed it!" cried Ava, and Walter raised his hand, cutting her off.

"There is no need. Two of our own are now at the mercy of Calliope and Cronus, and we cannot upset the balance until we are ready for a fight. We will heed Cronus's deadline, though we already expected it. Any further information you acquire will be useful to us, but do not give it at risk of the prisoners."

"I don't count as a prisoner?" she said, her eyes watering. "Because I don't fight the way you do, I'm not worth saving?"

For a fraction of a second, Walter's expression softened. "My dear, of course you are."

"I've done everything you asked me to," said Ava. "I've risked my life, my integrity, my friends, all for false promises. Turns out you're just as bad as Calliope is, Daddy. But at least she doesn't pretend to be something she isn't."

Stunned silence. Was she telling the truth? Had he really asked her to do all of those things? Walter paled, but he didn't argue, and that alone was an admission of guilt.

So it wasn't entirely Ava's fault, after all. She wasn't blameless, not by a long shot, but she wasn't alone in this either. Henry had been right. Walter had known I was pregnant. He'd known where I was and what was happening. He'd known, and he hadn't done a damn thing to stop it.

And the things he'd made Ava do, knowing how it would affect everything, knowing how the rest of the council would see her—how could he possibly hurt his own daughter like that?

"I'll agree to return to Calliope under your terms as long as you agree to fulfill one of mine," said Ava. "I want to talk to Kate. Alone."

A murmur rose from the other members of the council, and my eyebrows shot up.

"You know that is not possible," said Walter. "It is draining enough for us to maintain this method of communication without Calliope and Henry."

"Then she can come to me," said Ava.

"Out of the question." My mother's voice rose above the others, and they fell silent. "I will not have her risk herself again. It is a miracle she managed to get out of there in the first place."

"I know how her visions work," said Ava. "I know she can see me and hear everything I say. I don't need her to talk back to me. I just need her to listen. And I won't agree to your terms until Kate agrees to mine."

Whatever she wanted to talk to me about, she couldn't say it in front of the others. Which meant she thought she couldn't trust them—or at least couldn't trust her father.

Something about Henry? About Milo? Had she found a way to smuggle him to me somehow?

Hope surrounded me, so fragile and delicate that a single word could have shattered it into pieces. It was possible, and because it was possible, I would do it.

I nodded once, and Ava deflated, as if she'd used up everything she had to make it to that moment. "Tomorrow at sunset," she said. "In the nursery. I trust you to be there."

She had no way of knowing if I would be, but she was smart enough to know that she had me hooked, and I wouldn't miss it.

"I love you," she said, and this time it wasn't directed at any one person. Instead the words whispered through the council, touching each of us as they passed. "Goodbye for now." The golden light in the sunset floor flashed, and she was gone.

For nearly a minute, no one spoke. Not to talk about Ava, not to ask James and me what had happened on the island, nothing. Finally Ella and Theo rose. "We must return," said Theo. "Thank you for including us, Father."

Walter nodded, and confusion washed over me. They weren't here to fight? "What about the war?" I blurted. "I thought—"

"We are doing what we can on earth," said Theo. "We've made overtures to many of the minor gods, but not even Nike will support us, not without Henry."

"And the twins?" said Walter. "I thought you were making headway with them."

Ella frowned. "Lux was receptive until you turned down his terms. Now they've disappeared again, and it was hard enough tracking them down the first time around. I'm not going through that again."

James's expression grew distant. "They're in Paris."

"It doesn't matter now," said Theo. "We can't force them to help. Even the Fates have gone into hiding. Everyone's scared, and nothing we say or do can smooth things over. They're convinced if they don't help us, Cronus might spare them."

"Fools," muttered Walter. "Very well. Keep me updated as you can."

Theo and Ella nodded in unison. A split second before they disappeared, her eyes met mine, and I swore I saw pity.

"Come," said my mother, and we both stood. "You've had a long day, and I'm afraid it isn't going to get any easier. You need to rest."

"You, too," I said, taking her hand. As we walked down the hall, her shoulders slumped, and she paled with the effort it took to make it to her room. I wrapped my arm securely around her. After all she and I had been through together, after all we'd managed to survive, how long would it be before Cronus took her from me, too?

CHAPTER 14
CHAINS OF FOG

I told my mother everything that had happened in Calliope's palace, and though she didn't confirm my fears, I knew I was right. She'd known about Henry's plan—maybe she'd even helped him. And from the way she kept touching my face, it was easy to tell she was glad it was him Calliope had taken, not me.

"We'll figure it out," she murmured as we curled up on her bed together. "We've made it this far, after all."

I wasn't sure who she meant. She and I? The council? Did it even matter? This would end one way or the other, and no one, not even my mother, could reassure me that everything would be okay. Not this time.

It took me ages to fall asleep, and when I did, I dreamed of Henry whispering words I didn't understand. Dozens of questions swirled through my restless mind, but that voice offered no answers. Why had he gone through with this, knowing what it might mean? Had he done it purely to protect Milo? I'd had it handled, more or less—I hadn't anticipated Calliope interrupting, but Henry couldn't have possibly known she would either.

He should've stayed behind. He would've been much more useful as a weapon Cronus and Calliope didn't know about. He might've been the weight that tipped the balance away from them and toward the council instead, and he'd given that up to turn himself over to Calliope.

I wanted to be mad. I wanted to be furious, to rip the room apart until there was nothing left. It wouldn't accomplish anything though, and the best I could do was exactly what James had asked of me: to focus my efforts on thinking of something that the council hadn't.

Right. Wasn't pride the very thing that had nearly lost me Henry and my mother and immortality in the first place?

But the members of the council weren't exactly angels either. They could do whatever they damn well pleased, and if they could cheat, so could I. Pride it was then, along with a side of wrath for good measure. If there was a way out of this, I would find it.

After a restless night and an even more fitful day, the sun set on Greece, and at last it was time. As the council disappeared from the throne room to battle against an enemy they no longer had a prayer of defeating, I closed my eyes and slid into my vision.

Ava was waiting for me in the nursery, exactly where she'd said she would be. Milo wasn't in his crib, though. Ava's arms were empty, and Cronus wasn't standing in the shadows rocking him either. Henry must have had him then.

Peering anxiously out the door, Ava pressed her lips together, oblivious that I was waiting. I glanced over her shoulder and followed her gaze to a window in the hallway. Through it I saw half a dozen small shapes attacking an opaque fog. The evening's battle had begun.

"Kate?" said Ava, turning so suddenly that I didn't have time to move out of her way. She walked right through me. "Are you here?"

I didn't bother to reply. She wouldn't be able to hear me, so it was useless.

She stared into the empty nursery, and her shoulders sagged. "I'm sorry. I know you don't want to hear it, but it's true. I swear to you I didn't know what Calliope was planning."

This was it? Another round of apologies? I huffed and closed my eyes, ready to return to Olympus. I'd come. I'd listened. I wasn't going to waste my time with this any longer.

"I know the last thing you want to do is trust me," echoed Ava as I slipped back to Olympus. "But I need to show you something."

I snapped back into the nursery, hungry with hope. Glancing around as if she wasn't sure I was there, Ava exited the room, and I followed on her heels. She led me down the hallway and the narrow staircase I'd used the day before. We stopped on the same level that held my prison, and my stomach exploded with butterflies. Where was Ava taking me? Calliope couldn't possibly be holding Henry down here, could she?

Ava paused at a door. Nicholas's room. The clang of metal against metal ripped through the silence, mingling with his screams. I flinched, but Ava pushed the door open and stormed inside. I hurried after her.

"You swore you'd stop," she said, and it took me a moment to realize she wasn't talking to me. "I did what you told me to. Now you hold up your end of the bargain."

Calliope stood in the middle of a dank room with shelves and worktables along the edge. Discarded scraps of metal and dozens of weapons—some glowing weakly and others nothing more than lumps of steel—littered every surface.

Nicholas's forge. This was where he'd made that damn dagger.

Right beside the dying fire in the center of the room, someone had welded a metal chair to the floor with opaque fog. Nicholas slumped against it, bloody and broken in ways gods should've never been. He was half-conscious, his face slashed and purple and his body a mess of cuts and bruises.

"Your side of our deal hasn't been finished yet," said Calliope. "Kate is still alive."

Ava scowled. "That has nothing to do with—"

"I don't care." Calliope's voice sliced through the air like a scythe. "You will do what I say, or I will kill Nicholas. That is all there is to it."

He groaned, his eyeballs moving underneath his swollen lids, and Ava reached for him. Calliope stepped between them.

"I don't think so," she said with girlish delight. "You know what happens if you touch him."

"I don't care anymore." Ava darted around Calliope and knelt beside the chair. "Nicholas? I'm here. I'm so sorry, baby."

Nicholas tried to mumble something through his cracked lips and broken jaw, but it was unintelligible. To me, at least; Ava's eyes filled with tears, and she gently took his hand. When her skin touched his, a hissing sound filled the tiny prison, and Ava winced. But it wasn't until Nicholas grunted that she let go. Where she'd touched him, her palm turned scarlet, as if she'd handled hot embers.

"I will release him once I have won the war," said Calliope. "No sooner."

Ava's face twisted with barely contained rage, and she

shifted her stance as if she were about to throttle her. Calliope must've noticed, too, because in the blink of an eye, the dagger appeared in her hand, and she held it delicately to Nicholas's throat.

"I wouldn't if I were you, my dear," she purred.

It was a damn shame I was insubstantial, else I would've happily punched her lights out. Ava clenched her fists, apparently having the same idea, but she made no further move toward Calliope. "You monster," she hissed. "He's your *son*."

"We all make sacrifices. Surely you of all people must understand that."

The room trembled, and like she had the night before, Ava began to glow magenta. "No wonder Daddy never loved you. There's nothing lovable about you. All this time I thought he was in the wrong, treating you the way he did, but you deserved it. You pervert love and family until they're unrecognizable, all for your own twisted sense of satisfaction. No one, not even Cronus, deserves to burn in Tartarus more than you do."

"Is that so?" said Calliope in a dangerous voice. "It must be such a pity for you then, knowing we will win and you will never escape me."

"Oh, I will," said Ava. "First chance I get, I'm getting the hell out of here and—"

"What's going on?"

Henry stood in the doorway, cradling Milo. I moved toward them so fast that I could've sworn I created a breeze, but Henry looked straight through me, his focus on Calliope.

A knife twisted in the pit of my stomach, but he couldn't see me. He had no idea I was there. Even if he did, he'd still be looking at Calliope like she was the most beautiful thing in the world.

"Hello, darling," said Calliope. "I was just coming to see you. How's the baby?"

"He's fine." Henry gave Ava a curious look, and she averted her eyes, her hand hovering half an inch over Nicholas's. "What's going on?"

"Ava here seems to believe that despite his crimes against us, Nicholas is entitled to leave now," said Calliope, and she giggled. "As if we could afford such a risk. We can't have Nicholas rushing back with our secrets, now, can we?"

Henry eyed Nicholas the way he'd looked at Calliope after the brothers had captured her in the Underworld and tied her up in chains. My stomach lurched. The Henry I knew and loved had to be in there somewhere, but right now, this wasn't him. No matter how badly it hurt, I had to remember that. Whether it was Ava's influence or Calliope's power to cut the ties of loyalty between Henry and the rest of the council, it didn't matter. He was the enemy now.

No, not the enemy. As much of a prisoner as Nicholas and Milo.

"Of course, my dearest love," said Henry, and I gagged. "We will do what we must to ensure victory."

Crossing the room, he gave Calliope a sensuous kiss. I shielded my eyes and scowled. But despite my best efforts to ignore them, I couldn't resist a glance, and that's when I saw it.

Henry's eyes were open, and he was staring right at Ava.

In his arms, Milo stirred and reached for me. He knew I was there. Did Henry know, as well? He wasn't Cronus— Calliope would never kiss him like that if he was. But could he sense me?

To my astonishment, Ava nodded once, so slightly that at first I wasn't sure if I'd seen her right. Henry closed his eyes again, however, and I was certain. Henry and Ava were working together.

Against Calliope? For Calliope? To save Milo? Or had she told Henry that I would be here and listening in on everything that happened?

I couldn't be sure unless Ava told me, and whether or not Henry knew I was there, he was still kissing Calliope. Maybe he had to. Maybe he wanted to. I didn't have the answers, but that didn't matter. He wouldn't have been kissing her if it was up to him, and I had to hold on to that.

At last Calliope pulled away and touched her swollen lips. "Perhaps we should retire to the bedroom."

Oh, god. Were they sleeping together? Nausea overwhelmed me. Knowing he'd been with Persephone eons ago was one thing, but this was too much. He was my husband. *My* Henry, not hers.

"Yes," said Henry quietly. "Allow me to take care of the baby, and then I will join you."

With a giggle, Calliope kissed him once more and glided out of the room. For a split second, Henry deflated, his arms tightening around Milo protectively, and he met Ava's gaze again. Neither spoke. At last Henry turned and left the room, leaving Nicholas bound to the chair.

I closed my eyes. This wasn't him, and if we had any chance of getting through this without our relationship being irreparably damaged, I had to remember that. Just like I'd offered myself to Cronus in exchange for Milo's safety, Henry had done the same with Calliope. I had no right to be upset with him. With Calliope and Ava and every single member of the council who'd let him do this, yes. But not Henry.

"Kate," said Ava once he was gone. I opened my eyes. Nicholas was unconscious again, his chest rising and falling shallowly, and Ava stood beside him. "Now do you understand?"

I understood. It didn't excuse any of this, and it didn't fix our friendship. But I understood.

"Henry still loves you, you know. I didn't take that away from him. I never could."

She'd made him fall for Calliope, though. Artificial or not, it was still love, and it wouldn't erase what happened in that bedroom.

I shuddered. I had to stop thinking about that. I'd seen enough. Ava had apologized so many times that the words were meaningless now, and I had to leave before the hurt dug so deeply inside me that I could never get it out.

I was halfway gone when Ava spoke. "Cronus is going to escape on the winter solstice."

She'd already told the council that though, and she knew I'd been right there with them. I sank deeper into oblivion, already on the edge of ending this vision.

"And," said Ava, her voice so distant it was little more than a whisper, "the first place he's going to attack is New York City."

CHAPTER 15
BREAKING POINT

I snapped back to the island so quickly that the room spun around me. Dizzy, I waited for Ava to finish, but an explanation never came. She knelt beside Nicholas again, murmuring words meant only for him, and I turned away.

There was only one reason Cronus would specifically attack New York City when so many others—London, St. Petersburg, even Beijing—had to be closer. And that reason was me.

This time when I faded from Nicholas's torture chamber, I didn't reappear in Olympus. Instead, when I opened my eyes, I was in Milo's nursery again.

Cronus stood in a dark corner, as if he were waiting for me. If I hadn't been sure of some sort of connection between us before, I was now. He was keeping tabs on me. Watching me the way only a Titan could.

"You *bastard*." I shoved him as hard as I could, but of course it didn't do any good.

He peered down at me, his chin raised and eyes narrowed. "What have I done to deserve such harsh words? Have I not offered you everything, yet endured your lies again and again?"

I gritted my teeth. "You're going after my home."

"Your home is in the Underworld, and I assure you I have no intention of removing you from my path the way I will with the rest of the council. You will have eternity to remain there with the billions of souls who will die at my hand. Perhaps if you behave, I will allow you to join me on the surface for a time. Much like the arrangement you currently have with your very much alive husband."

Cold horror settled over me. "Why are you doing this? I came to you. I was going to hold up my end of the bargain. I didn't know—"

"You didn't know what?" said Cronus with that dangerous neutrality that was infinitely more frightening than anger. "That your dear Henry was alive?"

"I didn't know he followed me," I said. "I didn't know he had a plan. I'm *sorry*."

Cronus tilted his head. "No, you are not. You are sorry you have lost that which you thought you could keep hidden. You are sorry you were not the one who was allowed to sacrifice yourself for your loved ones. You are sorry you will be forced to remain alive after I have torn apart everyone you have ever cared about. You are sorry that you have lost your son. But you are not sorry you lied."

An invisible weight rested on my chest. "You're right," I said shakily. "I'm not sorry about lying. But I am sorry all of those people are going to die. And if you hadn't pushed it to this point, I would've been sorry for hurting you, too."

Cronus touched my cheek with the ghost of affection. "I thought you were different, Kate Winters. I thought you understood."

"I do. More than you've ever understood me." A lump formed in my throat, but no tears came. Begging and pleading wouldn't do me any good, but there had to be a way to fix this somehow. To make him understand. "You don't deserve this kind of pain, but then again, neither do I. Neither does the council. And neither do the billions of lives you're going to destroy. The only difference between us and humans is death. Even now, with you here, there is no difference. Can you imagine it? An ending? A moment when you cease to exist? And the people who love you, what they would go through—"

"Enough," he said. I searched his face for some flicker of emotion, but I found none. "I have made my decision. I will not show you mercy when you have shown me none. The war will continue, and I will not surrender or agree to a truce. I have tried to extend the hand of peace to the council, and they spit in my face. I confided in the one person I believed understood me, and you turned out to be the greatest liar of them all. We have nothing more to discuss."

Before I could protest, Cronus disappeared, and my hands touched nothing but air. He was gone, along with any hope I had of preserving my family.

I stared blankly into the empty space. As soon as Cronus escaped on the solstice, this would cease to be a war. It would be a bloodbath.

There had to be something I wasn't seeing, something I could do to get him to change his mind. But what could I give him now that he didn't trust me? What words could I possibly say to fix this?

A soft gurgle caught my attention, and I turned in time to see Henry wander into the nursery with Milo in his arms. He'd certainly taken his time getting up here. Had he detoured? He must have. I silently prayed it wasn't to see Calliope.

"Here we go," said Henry gently. "You're safe here."

He walked past me so slowly that he seemed to be moving through molasses. No wonder he'd taken so long. A turtle could have outpaced him. Upon spotting me, Milo waved his arms, and I managed a tearful grin.

"Hi, baby. Having fun with your daddy?"

He gurgled, and Henry smiled. "I wish I could stay here, too, but I will be back before the moon disappears from your window. In the meantime, I am sure your aunt Ava will be here soon to keep you company."

With a wave of his hand, the cradle moved a few inches, presumably into a position where Milo could see the moon. A sob caught in my throat.

Henry pressed his lips to the baby's forehead for a long moment before straightening. "Be good," he murmured, and he looked straight at me. "Your mother and I love you."

I froze. Did he know? Was it a coincidence? Another trick of Cronus's?

And I love you. Though his lips hadn't moved, his voice whispered through my mind, and I held my breath. Just like Milo, he knew I was there. Ava hadn't lied; she hadn't taken that love away from him.

I know what you're doing. I pushed the words toward him, and he turned away to stare into Milo's cradle. *And I hope you can fight what Ava's making you feel, because once this is over, I'm never letting you go again.*

It might've been my imagination, but I could've sworn he smiled.

This will end, and we will be together again. My thoughts were firm and unyielding now. *Just stay with me. Don't let Calliope convince you that you're someone you're not, and everything will be okay. I'll make sure of it.*

Without so much as a glance my way, Henry walked toward the nursery door. But as he moved by me, his hand passed through mine, and this time I knew it was no accident. *So will I.*

When I returned to Olympus, the council was waiting for me. Everyone looked exhausted and well past their breaking points, with dark smudges under their eyes and pale skin that seemed to stretch too tightly over their faces.

"Kate," said Walter. Even he looked spent. "Do you have news?"

Now they wanted to hear what I had to say? I bit back a sharp reply. They'd gone through enough that evening without having to deal with my inflated sense of injustice, as well. "Calliope really is torturing Nicholas to keep Ava in line. She has a room full of weapons I think he made—some of them look like test weapons before she finally settled on the dagger, and enough of them are infused with Cronus's powers that if we can get close enough, maybe there's a chance we could use them and—"

Walter raised a weary hand, and for once I fell silent. "If we are fortunate enough to get that far past Cronus's defenses, it means we will have already won." The note of inevitability he'd always used whenever he spoke of winning the war had disappeared.

"What happened during the battle today?" I said, and half a dozen of them looked away.

"Cronus was more...focused than usual," said my mother. "We were lucky no one was injured."

"He's fighting harder because of me," I said, and across the circle, Dylan scoffed.

"Always because of you, isn't it? Couldn't possibly be because he's getting stronger the closer we get to the winter solstice, could it?"

"Maybe," I allowed. "But I don't think it's a coincidence this happened the day after he found out I've been lying to him about Henry."

Dylan scowled, but he didn't say anything else.

"How is Henry?" said Sofia. "Did you see him?"

I nodded. What would they do if they knew Calliope had somehow convinced Henry to fight for her? Would they treat him like the enemy, too? He might still love me, but love wasn't enough to convince the council that he wouldn't fight against them if Calliope ordered him to.

"He's fighting her," I said. A half truth at best and a full-out lie at worst. "There's only so much he can do without giving himself away, but he's still in there."

"Good," said Sofia, settling back in her throne. "She doesn't know him like she knows the rest of us. Gives her less of a chance to exploit his weaknesses and use them against him."

That was exactly what she was doing, though. She knew his weaknesses—she knew he would do anything to protect me and Milo. Maybe she'd even asked Ava not to take his love for me away from him so he would remember why he was doing this. Or maybe she'd done it just so he could feel that heartbreak when he kissed her and remembered who he was really supposed to love.

Sadistic bitch.

"What did Ava want to discuss?" said Walter.

"She wanted to apologize again and try to explain." It was the truth, for the most part. "She told me that Cronus is going to attack New York City once he's escaped."

A murmur rippled through the remaining members of the

council, and James said to Dylan, "Need any more proof that he's doing this because of Kate?"

"Shut it," muttered Dylan, and James gave him a satisfied smirk. He might've liked rubbing his brother's nose in it, but I would've given damn near anything for Dylan to be right.

"Very well, we will prepare for that outcome then," said Walter, and I blinked.

"What if Ava was lying to me?" I said, and Walter shrugged tiredly.

"Then we are doomed." He stood on trembling legs. "Go rest and recuperate. We will not attack tomorrow or any other day until the winter solstice."

Dylan rose with what he must've intended to be indignation, but he looked more like an old man rising from an armchair that was too short for his legs. "We're giving up?"

"We are saving our energy and strategizing," corrected Walter. "We have exhausted our means as they are, with Cronus using the shields on the island against us. Now we must plan a different approach." He nodded to me. "Kate, I would like you to join us."

"Me?" I said, stunned, and my mother patted my hand. "I don't know the first thing about planning a war."

"But you have spent the most time in Cronus's presence since his escape, and we can no longer ignore the validity of your claims," he said. "You will collect what information you can during the day, and the council will gather each evening to receive it. Unless anyone has any other ideas," he said, looking squarely at Dylan.

Dylan shrugged and said nothing.

"Very well. Council dismissed," said Walter, and with enormous effort that showed in every step he took, he headed toward a corridor I'd never been down.

The other members of the council filtered out of the

throne room until only James, my mother and I remained. Despite looking half a second away from passing out, James crossed the circle toward us, wearing an exhausted smile.

"Seems you finally got your in," he said, slinging his arm around my shoulders. "Now's your chance to prove yourself."

"That's the problem," I said. "I don't know how."

My mother stroked my knuckles with her thumb. "You'll figure it out. Keep your eyes and ears open, and you'll come up with something."

As comforting as her reassurance should've been, she was forgetting one thing. Cronus could see me, and now that he didn't trust me, I didn't stand a chance in hell at getting any more information out of him.

Every day for the last three weeks of October, I dove into my visions with the hope of finding even the smallest of clues that could help with the council's defense. My efforts were mostly wasted, though. Calliope spent most of her time alone, staring at a holographic image of the island, and whatever strategizing she and Cronus did was a mystery to me. They were rarely in the same room together, and whenever Cronus did appear somewhere near Calliope, she was quick to find an excuse to leave.

At first I thought she was angry, with the short way she spoke to him. The more I saw them together, however, the more I noticed other things. The way her posture slipped when he was near. The way her voice and focus wavered. She wasn't angry. She was terrified of him.

I didn't blame her. Without anyone to curb his ambition and determination, Cronus grew more powerful every day until not even his human form seemed able to hold it. He crackled around the edges, and everywhere he stepped, he left black footprints in his wake. Though he saw me, he never acknowledged me. I preferred it that way.

I reported back to the council every evening until finally Dylan said exactly what I'd feared. "He's growing more powerful than we ever expected. Our barriers won't hold until the solstice."

No one in the council questioned him. They all knew we were running out of time, and without more information, they were stumbling around blind. They'd guessed the routes Cronus would take to New York, the ways he might hammer destruction onto the city that had raised me. They had a plan for each.

They were woefully outnumbered though, and nothing Ella and Theo said to the minor gods they chased across the world brought reinforcements. James often joined them, helping them find the ones hiding from Walter's wrath, leaving me alone with my mother and a handful of gods stretched to the limit. I kept to myself, and soon my visions weren't just spy missions. They were another way to avoid the council, as well.

No matter how often I saw Henry in Calliope's palace, he never again revealed he knew I was there. The more time that passed, the more I doubted that moment in the nursery; and the more time Henry spent with Calliope, the more he seemed to sink into her spell. Any hint of his defiance was gone. He did whatever she said, but Milo was always with him, and I clung to that with everything I had. He was in there somewhere, and though it would be a battle for him to break free when the time came, he stood a chance.

In the beginning of November, as Henry rocked Milo to sleep for an afternoon nap, Calliope hurried into the nursery. "Something's wrong with Cronus."

Instead of putting Milo in the cradle, Henry gathered him

up and followed Calliope. I hurried after them, and through the windows I saw a storm brewing over the island. Black clouds swirled amid the warm ocean air, blotting out the blue sky, and thunder rolled across the sea, a warning of the danger to come.

Calliope ran up the steps and through a weathered door that opened onto the roof. Henry held Milo close against the strong winds, but despite Milo's cries, he didn't go back inside.

The moment I spotted Cronus in the middle of the roof, I understood. This storm wasn't natural. His form could no longer hold him, and Cronus was now nothing more than a glowing orb of power.

Crackling with more lightning than anything natural could ever produce, Cronus's opaque fog swirled in the eye of the storm, with a black funnel expanding upward into the sky. A warning. A message. A command.

Come and fight.

I instinctively reached for Henry. Instead of mirroring the fear Calliope wore so openly, his mouth was set in a grim line, and determination furrowed his brow. Whatever was coming, he was ready for it.

"Go," he said, and he turned to look me straight in the eye. *I love you. Warn the others it has begun.*

I opened and shut my mouth twice. *What about you and Milo?*

I'll make sure he's safe. Just go.

Through the howling wind, I reached for him, my fingertips half an inch from his cheek. *I love you, too. Don't forget who you are.*

Despite the swirling black mass of death not twenty feet away, Henry managed a smile. *I should say the same to you. Be brave and do what you must.*

My eyes burned in the wind, but as I faded from the rooftop, I couldn't tear my gaze away from him. *Please don't do anything stupid.*

Before he could answer, the brewing storm melted away, replaced by my bedroom in Olympus.

I ran down the hallway, momentarily forgetting my ability to be wherever I had to be whenever I needed to be there. I needed to run. I needed to scream, but I had no voice left for anything other than the words I'd been dreading.

Bursting into the throne room, I dashed into the center of the circle, ignoring the silence of broken conversation. Whatever the council had been discussing, it didn't matter now.

"It's Cronus," I said breathlessly. "He's escaping. There's a storm around the island and—"

"We already know," said Dylan, and I shook my head. He didn't understand.

"The final battle—it's begun."

CHAPTER 16
THE LAST HOUR

Walter had to shout four times and crack a bolt of lightning before the council came to order. Everyone was on their feet, including my mother, and the energy in the room jolted between nervous and aggressive.

"We have been preparing for this moment for a year," said Walter once the din faded. "We may no longer have the allies we relied upon, but we have each other, and together we are *strong*."

No one said a word. Even Dylan couldn't muster up a battle cry. This would either be the day they finally sent Cronus back to Tartarus, or it would be the day the council fell. By this time tomorrow, I would either have a family or I'd be alone, subject to Cronus's whims and darkest pleasures.

I would've rather slit my throat with that damn dagger myself.

"We are prepared. We are together. And we will fight until we win or are no more," continued Walter. "Take an hour to do whatever you must, and we will meet back here then."

One by one, the council filtered out, some in pairs, others by themselves. At a loss, I stayed put. What was I supposed to do? It'd been hard enough watching them all go off to war the last winter solstice, but this time...

This time, it'd be the greatest battle the world had seen since the first Titan war, and my entire family would be front and center.

"I want to fight," I said once the room had emptied of everyone except my mother and James. "You said I could."

"Oh, honey." She pulled me from my seat and into a hug. "You *have* fought, in ways the rest of us couldn't. Fighting doesn't always mean going to battle with a sword and a shield. You've done more than enough, and now is the time for you to stay safe. For Milo's sake."

"Milo's exactly the reason I need to fight. I know I'm not strong enough to give you any real support, but maybe I could distract Cronus or Calliope or—or something. Anything."

Her arms tightened around me, and she buried her face in the crook of my neck, her cheek warm against my skin. I squeezed my eyes shut and tried to memorize this moment. She had to come back. And if she didn't—

No, I couldn't think like that. They'd survived the battles so far, and they'd survive this one, too. My mother would not die today. No one would.

"Come," she murmured. "We haven't got much time, and there's something I'd like to do before then. James?"

James stepped up and touched our shoulders. "This won't be fun," he said, and before I could ask where we were going, the room exploded with light as we fell to earth.

My eyes watered. Going from Olympus to the surface

wasn't anything new. Why James had felt the need to warn me, I didn't know. Until—

Until the blue sky disappeared, replaced by rock.

I would've thrown up if I could have. Even with my mother at my side, the oppressive layers of the earth pressed down on me, making my heart flutter with panic as we sped downward. I tried to force my eyes to close, but they were glued open with terror, and the best I could do was hug my mother tightly and hope like hell it would be over soon.

At last we landed in the rock cavern outside Henry's obsidian palace. My knees knocked together, and all the blood rushed from my head, making the walls spin.

"You *bastard*." I punched James in the arm as hard as I could. Not like it'd hurt him. "Why do you keep *doing* that to me?"

He grinned. "Because the look on your face is priceless. Honestly, Kate, what do you think I'm going to do? Leave you in the rock?"

I shuddered. "You wouldn't."

"I couldn't," he corrected. "Once you learn how to use the portals, you won't be able to either."

I opened my mouth to retort, but the murmur of low voices caught my attention, and I turned toward the palace. In the shadows, a crowd had formed, swarming the garden and the river on the other side of the cavern. "What's that? Who are they?"

"The dead," said James. "The lost souls, the ones who need guidance. No one's here to help, so they're stuck until you and Henry return."

I stared. There had to be thousands of them. I'd expected some, knowing that Henry wasn't down here to help, but not this.

Of course there were so many, though. With the numbers Cronus had slaughtered, I should've been surprised there weren't more. "We need to help them."

"Not right now, sweetheart," said my mother, rubbing my back. "They have eternity. We have somewhere to be."

"And where's that?" I said.

"We're going to visit your sister," she said, and all of my indignation melted away. She'd gone ages without seeing Persephone before facing her the year before. Another visit so soon could only mean one thing: she was saying her good-byes.

"Mom," I choked out, my voice cracking. "You can't leave me. You promised."

"Whoever said anything about leaving you, sweetheart?" she said, brushing my hair from my eyes. We both knew the truth, though. No matter how many pep talks Walter gave, no matter how often she reassured me that she wasn't going anywhere, she knew it was a possibility. And this time there would be no miraculous return.

I clutched her hand. "We could stay down here while the others fight. They won't miss you. And we can come up with another way to help them."

She gave me a sad smile. "Honey, you know the council needs everyone they can get right now. I have a responsibility to them, and I can't walk away."

"What about your responsibility to me?" My cheeks grew warm as my eyes burned with tears. "You promised you'd never leave me again."

"I'm not. I'm fighting for what I believe in," she said. "I've no intentions of dying today, Kate."

"But you could."

"Yes, I could," she allowed. "As Walter said, Cronus is a formidable enemy, and there's little we can do to combat him directly. However, you must remember we have thousands upon thousands of years of experience behind us, and we will put every last second of that to good use. I will do everything in my considerable power to make sure I come back to you. To make sure we all do."

She could promise me the moon, but she was choosing to forget one very important fact: Cronus wasn't beatable. Considerable power or not, there was nothing in the council's arsenal that could take him on and win. Together they had a chance, but without Henry, without Calliope, they might as well have surrendered. They'd have a longer life expectancy that way.

There had to be something. The dagger—the weapons scattered around Nicholas's torture chamber—those were advantages that could be ours, but how?

"Now come," murmured my mother. "Take us to see your sister."

I would have delayed if I thought it might work, but if my mother did die today, I couldn't live with the guilt of denying her last request to see her other daughter. And Persephone deserved the chance to say goodbye, too.

I held my free hand out for James, and he took it without a word. For all the wisecracks that came from that big mouth of his, he knew when to keep it shut, too. If he didn't make it either...

No. No one would die today. Not my mother, not James, not Henry, no one.

After one last look at the dead surrounding the palace, I closed my eyes. A warm breeze tickled my neck, and when I opened them, we were standing in the middle of a field full of flowers. Not ten feet away stood a cottage covered in vines, and even though we were in the Underworld, the sun— or at least Persephone's version of the sun—shone brightly down on us.

"Hey!" cried Persephone, and I turned in time to see her blond curls bouncing in the wind. "Get out of there!"

"What—" I started, and then I looked down. We were standing right in the middle of my sister's tulips. Oops.

My mother chuckled and took a step away from me, and I moved with her, refusing to leave her side. "I'm sorry, darling. Kate's rather new to this particular method of transportation."

Persephone stormed toward us, her feet automatically avoiding the patches of flowers as if she knew exactly where every blossom was. After spending a thousand years in this field, she probably did. "That's no excuse for trampling my tulips," she grumbled.

"I'm sorry." Despite the reason we were here, the look on her face made me smirk. Persephone wasn't my favorite person, not by a long shot, and having the chance to stick it to her was a small victory during an otherwise awful day. "Next time I'll try to aim for the path."

"You'd better." She knelt down next to the flower bed and touched the crushed tulips. "Why are you here? I go centuries without having to deal with guests, and now you decide to visit me twice in a year? Are you really that desperate for marital advice?"

I blinked. "What? No, of course not—"

"If he's going through one of his spats, just leave him alone and don't bother him until it's over," said Persephone. "He'll come to you then."

"That's not why we're here," said my mother, and she knelt beside my sister and touched the tulips. They glowed golden in the sunlight, and slowly they straightened back into perfect condition. "There. All fixed."

"I didn't need your help," muttered Persephone, sitting

back on her heels. "What I need is for you people not to step on my flowers in the first place."

I opened my mouth to tell her exactly where she could shove her flowers, but James beat me to it. "For the love of whatever you hold holy, Persephone, would you please shut up for two seconds and let us talk?"

The three of us stared at him, and he squared his shoulders, clearly doing his best to look respectful and godly. But with his mop of blond hair and ears that stuck out like a caricature, he looked about as godly as Mickey Mouse.

"Fine. What's going on?" said Persephone, and though the edge remained in her voice, her expression softened.

"Cronus is about to break free from the island," said my mother. "The battle will begin within the hour, and I hoped you might be willing to look after Kate until it is over."

My mouth and Persephone's dropped open simultaneously. "You're *leaving* me here?" I cried.

"You're making me *babysit?*" said Persephone in an equally horrified voice.

My mother focused on me first. "Kate, darling, I know you want to help, but you will help the most by remaining safe so I do not have to worry about your well-being."

"But—" I started, and though she held up her hand, I kept going. "Mom, please. You can't keep coddling me like this."

"You know you do not have the ability to fight in a way that will be helpful to the rest of us," said my mother bluntly.

"That's not my fault," I said. "You're the one who promised to train me. I could've learned."

"Not in less than two months. We were all stretched to our limits already, and even if we had, you aren't one of the original six. You simply are not powerful enough to help change the course of battle fighting head-on like that." She touched my cheek. "Please, allow us our greatest chance of success. Remain safe."

I dug my nails into the palms of my hands. "You can't make me stay here."

"I know, but I trust you to make the right decision. Milo needs a mother, and he can't have that if you're gone. When the time comes, he's going to need you. And you're going to need him."

"So you want me to just hide my head in the sand until it's over?" I said thickly. "How can you say that? You're the one who showed me how to be a fighter in the first place."

She gathered me up, and I melted into her embrace. "Sometimes fighting means surviving in the face of insurmountable odds. That's what I need you to do. Be the survivor I know you are."

I hiccupped into her shoulder, and my fingers tightened around her sleeve. "Please stay with me."

"If I could, I would. There's nowhere else I'd rather be than here with the two of you."

Holding her arm out for Persephone, she waited, and finally my sister accepted the hug. "First time you come to see me in hundreds of years, and you want me to babysit," she muttered, and my mother kissed her forehead.

"I'm sorry, darling. I'll make sure to visit more often."

That wasn't a promise she could keep if she were dead, and Persephone flinched right along with me. Was this the last time we'd be together like this?

It couldn't be. I wouldn't let it. There had to be *something*.

"I'll promise to stay here with Persephone if you promise not to risk your life," I said. It wasn't much, but until I could come up with a solid plan, it would have to do.

"Oh, Kate." My mother kissed my hair. "You might as well ask me not to go at all. I haven't let Cronus get the best of me yet, and I don't intend on starting now, that I swear to you. Have a little faith."

Easy for her to say. She was the one running off to fight. "I love you," I mumbled. How many more times would we say these endless goodbyes before it really would be the last time?

"I love you, too. Remember Milo." She pulled away and looked me straight in the eye. "Can you do that for me?"

I nodded, a heavy numbness settling over me as she turned to say goodbye to Persephone. Instead of embraces and tears, they bent their heads together and began to whisper. "Let me go with you," said Persephone. "Cronus and Calliope can't hurt me, and I could be useful."

My mother shook her head. "I need you here with Kate, to make sure she doesn't do anything stupid."

Persephone rolled her eyes. "Of course she's going to do something stupid. She's Kate."

"I'm counting on you not to let that happen."

After one quick squeeze of her hand and my mother's admonishment to be good, their goodbyes were over. Persephone's eyes were dry. How could this be so damn easy for her?

James touched my shoulder, and I spun around to hug him. "If you die, I will be *so* pissed at you," I said.

"Then let's hope that doesn't happen. If you wander into battle, I'm going to be so pissed at *you*," said James.

"Then let's hope that doesn't happen," I mimicked. "Do you need a lift to Olympus?"

He snorted. "Nice try. Your mother's got it covered." Hesitating, he pressed his lips to the corner of my mouth. An almost-kiss full of questions I couldn't answer and promises neither of us could keep. "Don't forget—I get to be your first affair, and I'm holding you to that."

"You'd better," I said, and with that, he let me go for one last hug with my mother. The knot in my throat grew unbearable, but I refused to cry. I didn't want the last moments we had to be full of blubbering sobs.

Neither she nor James said anything. They smiled, no trace of fear or anxiety on either of their ageless faces, and James offered my mother his arm. She took it wordlessly, and together they faded until there was nothing left but the breeze.

"Come on, let's get you some tea before you fall over," said Persephone. She took my elbow, and I didn't argue. If Cronus slaughtered everyone I loved, Persephone would be the only family I had left. Not exactly a satisfying consolation prize, but I didn't want to give her any reason to hate me.

As much as I wanted to reassure myself that it wouldn't come to it being just the two of us, I couldn't. It wasn't up to me, and I couldn't change the outcome of the battle through sheer willpower and thought alone. I could do something to help though, if I could only think of something that would be worth the risk.

Something Persephone had said niggled in the back of my mind, but before I could concentrate fully on it, she pushed the door open. "Adonis! What did I say about feeding the dog peanut butter?"

Adonis, Persephone's boyfriend—husband?—rose from the floor, and I gaped at the puppy at his feet.

"Pogo?" I knelt down, and the black-and-white dog Henry had given me let out a bark muffled by a mouthful of home-made peanut butter. Tripping all over himself, he scampered across the cottage and jumped into my arms. One lick on the cheek, and I could no longer hold back the floodgates.

Persephone stepped around me as I clung to Pogo and cried. She could give me all the nasty looks she wanted; she'd abandoned her family an eon ago. I'd barely started to get to know mine.

By the time my sobs ended, she had a mug of tea waiting

for me on the tiny kitchen table. She sat in the chair opposite mine, and Adonis lingered nearby, leaning against the wall and shuffling his feet. While I sipped my tea with Pogo in my lap, neither of them said anything.

Several minutes passed, and I couldn't take the silence anymore. "Aren't you afraid of what's going to happen?" I said, my voice rough after my crying fit.

Persephone shrugged. "They've been at war with the Titans before."

"But it's different this time. They don't have Calliope, and Henry—"

"What about Henry? What's wrong with him?"

With a sigh, I launched into everything that had happened since she'd left the palace after the first battle. Calliope's plot to kidnap me, the nine months I'd spent as her prisoner, Milo, my connection with Cronus, what I'd promised him and what he'd promised in return—the attacks on Athens and Egypt, Henry's fight for survival, his sacrifice to keep Milo and me safe. Everything.

"And now they're going into the biggest battle in history down two of their strongest fighters with no real hope of success." I cuddled Pogo, and he licked the crook of my arm.

Persephone drummed her fingers against the wooden table, her expression distant. "And you're going to spend the entire time here, not even trying to help them?"

"The only thing I could possibly do is distract Cronus and Calliope, and you heard Mom. She doesn't want that."

"If I were you, I'd be fighting like hell to keep every good thing I had in my life," said Persephone. "Not all of us had that chance. The relationship you have with Mother, with Henry—you two made me an *aunt,* and you're sitting here like a lump instead of doing everything you can to get them back."

"You think I want to sit here? If there was something I could do to help, I'd be doing it, but I *can't*—"

"Like hell you can't." She narrowed her eyes. "Think, Kate. Just stop and think. You're the girl who trekked across half the Underworld to reach me on the off chance I might know where to find Cronus, and you're giving up right now? I don't think so."

Were she and James conspiring to make me feel like an utter failure? I opened my mouth to protest again, but she held up her hand.

"There's always a way around a problem, and you have half an hour to figure it out before the battle begins. So you tell me, Kate—after everything you've been through and everything you've seen, are you going to sit there, or are you going to fight?"

I took a deep breath. Persephone was right; there was always a solution. There was always a way to fix something, even if it was hard. Even if it was nearly impossible.

Anything is possible if you give it a chance.

Henry's voice. Henry's words. He believed in me, even though I'd long since given up believing in myself.

Think. *Think.* The weapons. Cronus's bargain. The layout of the palace. Nicholas. Persephone.

My eyes flew open, and the pieces of the puzzle snapped into place. "I know what to do."

She grinned. "It's about damn time."

CHAPTER 17

FINAL STAND

We arrived arm in arm in the middle of Persephone's forest. The moment the ground underneath our feet shifted, she let go of me, but I didn't care. For the first time in ages, I knew exactly what I was doing.

Grabbing her hand, I dragged Persephone through the trees, toward a redheaded girl surrounded by the tamest animals I'd ever seen. A baby deer rested beside her, a singing robin settled on her shoulder, and in her lap she cuddled a litter of bunnies no bigger than my fist.

Persephone squinted. "Who is that?"

"Just let me do the talking," I said, and once we drew close enough, I called out, "Hi, Ingrid."

"Ingrid? You mean the first girl too stupid to figure out how to live?" said Persephone, and I elbowed her in the side.

"Kate!" Ingrid's squeal echoed, making the rock wall at the edge of her afterlife obvious. "You really came! I thought you were just trying to be nice, but you're really here!"

"Yeah, I'm really here." As I knelt beside her to pet the

tame fawn, Persephone's forest melted into Ingrid's meadow of candy flowers. "Unfortunately it's not for catching up."

Ingrid's face fell, but before she could get too upset, Persephone spoke up behind me. "You wouldn't happen to know how to handle a knife, would you?"

She tugged nervously on a lock of hair. "Why?"

"Because Cronus is about to destroy the world, and the council doesn't have much of a chance against him," I said. "They need help. The dead are the only people Calliope and Cronus can't hurt, and they've got a whole room full of weapons that could take them down." Or at least Calliope. If this didn't work on Cronus...

It was worth a shot. It was our *only* shot.

"And you want me to help you?" said Ingrid.

"We want all of the girls to help us," I said. "Persephone doesn't know who they are, but we were hoping you might."

Ingrid set the bunnies down and stood, brushing dirt off the white dress that must have been the height of casual fashion back in the 1920s. "As it happens, not only do I know who they are, but while Henry was trying to figure out who was behind the murders, he even let me meet them. It's a bit of a walk, but I can take you there."

At last, some luck. "We don't have time to go on foot. The battle's about to start," I said. "I've got a faster way, though."

With Ingrid's help, we gathered up eight of the other ten girls. Two of them hadn't been in the sections of the Underworld Henry had allotted for them, and we were running out of time. Eight would have to do for now.

I stood before them, shuffling my feet nervously. Because Ingrid lingered by my side, I saw the meadow in front of me, but every time one of the other girls edged closer, the background shifted into their afterlives instead. Forests, a white sand beach, an empty theme park—it was bizarre, but

I forced myself to ignore it. As long as the other girls could see me and each other, that was all that mattered.

"I'm Kate," I said. "Henry's wife."

The word felt strange on my tongue, but it got an immediate reaction from the girls. A whisper rippled through the group, and the ones in the back jostled for a better position.

"That's impossible. You actually passed the tests?" said a girl with curly auburn hair. "Like, survived and everything?"

I held my tongue. Of course they thought it was crazy. Calliope had killed each and every one of them. After a while, even Henry had thought it'd be impossible for anyone to make it. "Barely," I said. "I got lucky."

"Can't believe it was Calliope," said the same girl. "The bitch stabbed me in the back and threw me in the river. I thought it was James."

"Yeah, well, turns out you aren't so smart, after all, Anna," said a dark-haired girl on the other side of the group. The top of her head barely reached my chin.

The first girl—Anna—snorted. "Like you're any better, Emmy, insisting Ava was behind it."

"She's slept with every other god," said Emmy. "Don't see why she wouldn't go after Henry, too."

"That's enough," said Persephone. "Let Kate speak."

For the third time in an hour, I explained everything that was happening. No one interrupted me. "The battle's about to start, and our numbers are dwindling," I added at the end. "I wouldn't ask this of any of you if we weren't desperate, but we are. We need fighters."

"I don't know how to fight," said Emmy, and the other girls murmured in agreement. Anna, however, cracked her knuckles and stepped forward. The background shifted into a garden that put Versailles to shame.

"A chance for a stab at Calliope? Count me in."

One down, seven to go. "I can get us into the castle un-detected," I said. "Calliope and Cronus can't hurt you."

"Are you sure?" piped a voice from the back.

"Don't be an idiot, Bethany," said Anna. "Of course she's sure."

"I am," I said quickly. "I swear, if you do this, you won't be in danger."

"It's true," said Persephone. "I faced off against Cronus and Calliope a year ago. They tried their best, but I'm still here. Not a scratch on me."

Another murmur rippled through the group. "You're sure the weapons will work, too?" said Emmy.

I hesitated. No, I wasn't sure. Even if one of us managed to take out Calliope, I had no idea if this would work on Cronus. And what if they weren't corporeal on the surface? What if they were ghosts, like I was in my visions?

"We have to try," I said. "If nothing else, we need to dis-tract them long enough to get Henry out of there. We need him on our side. The council is heavily outgunned, and if we don't find a way to help, they will fall. Maybe not today, maybe not tomorrow, but eventually Cronus *will* get the best of them. Of us," I added. "And Henry will die with them."

Silence. I shifted my focus from one face to the next, searching for any sign that they would agree, but none of them met my eye. Before I could give convincing them one last shot, however, Bethany called from the back, "Count me in."

"Me, too," said Emmy, and one by one, the others also volunteered.

"Thank you," I said. "I can't tell you what this means to—"

Crash.

The earth around us trembled, and several of the girls

shrieked. Ingrid clutched my arm, and we all looked up at the sky above us. Most souls had no idea where they were and thought their afterlife was the real thing, but Henry's girls knew the difference. They knew that the sun's warmth was an illusion, and beyond the fluffy clouds was the ceiling of an enormous cavern. And that was why they were the only ones who could help us.

The trembling subsided, but it didn't matter. The battle raged above us, and we didn't have any time to waste. "I need a whiteboard and a marker," I said, and several of them stared at me blankly. "A blackboard and a piece of chalk then."

Nine of them appeared around me. Illusion or not, being dead had its advantages.

I sketched the layout of Calliope's castle as best I could, marking each important location—Nicholas's cell, the nursery, Calliope's room—as accurately as I could. In three minutes, we had a plan. Whether it worked or not, at least it would give the others a chance.

Getting them up to the surface would be tricky, but the gaping hole in the cavern where Cronus had escaped the first time was still there. He was trapped on the island, but I tested the exit twice. I could get in and out without any trouble.

"You first," I said to Persephone. She looked at my offered hand like it was made of acid.

"How can I possibly be sure you know how to control it? You trampled my tulips."

I rolled my eyes and grabbed her wrist. The Underworld dissolved, replaced by the stark white walls of my room in Calliope's castle. "Happy now? Stay here."

Persephone glared at me, but I disappeared before she could insult me further.

I took two girls at once, and within a minute, we all clustered together in the room. The girls fidgeted, and more than a few pairs of eyes widened in terror as a tidal wave crashed against the cliffs protecting the castle.

"Just stick to the plan," I said. "And whatever you do, don't forget that no one can hurt you. Not Calliope, not Cronus, no one."

"Can they hurt you?" piped Emmy's voice.

"If we do this, I'll be fine," I lied. No one could promise anyone anything, but they needed to hear it, and it wasn't my job to tell them the truth right now. "We don't have any more time. Trust me. Trust yourselves."

I pushed the door open and sneaked into the hallway, followed by several pairs of hesitant footsteps. I didn't look back to make sure everyone was following us. They had come; the best I could hope for now was that their courage didn't fail them.

The hallway between my room and Nicholas's was suspiciously empty. Did Calliope believe that no one could break into the castle, or did she foolishly not care? I crept forward, prepared for any sort of traps she or Cronus might have set, but we made it to Nicholas's room without interruption. The door, however, was locked. "I have to go in there and get the weapons myself," I said, but Emmy elbowed her way through the group of girls.

"Let me."

Pulling a pin from her hair, she knelt beside the doorknob. I listened for any sign someone was coming, but five seconds later, the lock clicked open.

"Piece of cake," said Emmy with a grin, and I shot her a grateful smile. Pushing the door open, I burst into the room, fully expecting Calliope to be waiting for me. Instead Nicholas sat chained to the chair, surrounded by his workshop of weapons.

"Kate?" he said, squinting through two black eyes. Blood

dripped down the side of his face from a nasty gash on his forehead. Calliope must've been here recently. "Persephone?"

"Hello to you, too, brother," said Persephone. Behind her, the others poured into the workshop, their eyes widening at the sight of Nicholas and the array of weapons.

I knelt beside his chair and inspected the glowing chains. "I can't touch them," I said apologetically.

"I know," he said. "Don't worry about me. Go on and get Cronus."

"I'm not leaving you behind. Emmy, can you undo this lock?"

Emmy separated from the others and joined me, Persephone hot on her heels. "That's more complicated," she said. "But I think I can do it."

"Try."

"She'll get it," said Persephone. "Go ahead without us. We'll get Nicholas out of here."

"Thanks," I said, and Persephone waved off my gratitude. "They're my family, too. Now go."

A clash of metal against metal shook the very air around us, and the other girls quieted. I took a deep breath. Time to be a leader. "You all know what you're supposed to do," I said with as much confidence as I could muster. "Grab a weapon infused with fog, and go give them hell."

Anna let out a whoop and, clutching a mace, she streaked out of the room and up the narrow staircase that led to the rest of the castle. One by one, the other girls followed, clutching swords and staffs and other weapons I couldn't identify. I waited by the door until their cries diminished. The chances of them succeeding were slim, but as long as their distraction gave me enough time to rescue Milo and Henry, then at least our efforts wouldn't be wasted.

"Seems like they're enjoying themselves," said Nicholas

heavily. He grinned. Several of his teeth were missing. "Get that lock undone. I want to join them."

"Yeah, right," I said, and I swiped a glowing knife with wicked hooked teeth from the remaining weapons. "You're lucky to be alive."

Persephone gave me a look. "He has a right to fight for his family, just like you do. Now stop dictating and go get your son."

Biting back a response, I nodded, and a second later Milo's nursery replaced the workshop around me. Thunder echoed through the air. The council had to be close.

"Milo," I gasped, rushing toward the cradle. It was empty. Of course Henry wouldn't let him out of his sight during the battle, but something inside me withered. I'd hoped to get Milo out of there and safe with Adonis before finding Henry, but that clearly wasn't going to happen.

I turned to leave on foot, but instead I crashed face-first into a warm body and stumbled to the ground. My heart damn near stopped. Had Calliope expected this? Was she lying here in wait while Cronus distracted everyone else? I gripped the knife with hooked teeth, fully prepared to use it.

"Kate?"

Not Calliope. Ava. "Where is he?" I said, scrambling to my feet. She blocked my way out, her cheeks pale and her eyes round. Clearly she hadn't expected me. Good. That meant Calliope likely didn't either.

"Milo?" she said. "He's with Henry."

"And where exactly is that?"

Ava bit her lip. "I can't tell you. Calliope will kill you."

"Not if I get them away from her before she knows I'm there," I said. "Unless you decide to tell her."

"What? Of course I wouldn't," she said, stunned. "I'm on your side."

"Then tell me where Henry and Milo are."

She swallowed, her eyes red and shining with tears. "She'll kill all of us. Me, you, Henry, Milo, Nicholas—"

"Persephone and Emmy are getting him out of there as we speak," I said. "He'll be fine."

"Emmy? You mean Henry's—"

"It's a long story."

Ava hesitated, and at last her expression hardened. "Come on. I'll take you there."

Alarm bells went off in the back of my mind. "Why should I trust you?"

"Because we were friends once," she said. "And because I'd want someone to help me protect my son if our positions were reversed."

Right. She'd mentioned her son before, and while I believed her, it seemed awfully convenient that she'd bring him up now. "You never told me about him."

"Eternity's a long time to cover between classes," she said. "His name's Eros—Eric now, I suppose. Are you coming?"

Searching the entire castle room by room would take too long, and for all I knew Henry and Milo were bunkered down in a place I'd never be able to find on my own. So before I gave myself time to consider it, I nodded.

We ran through the hallways, and I tried to ignore the rolling black clouds through the windows and the bone-shattering crash of water against rock. The council was getting closer. Maybe we'd have a chance, after all.

"Where are they?" I shouted over the roar, and Ava dashed up the staircase, pulling me along with her. The hooked knife nearly slipped from my grip, but I hugged it to my chest. I couldn't lose it.

"On the roof with Calliope and Cronus," said Ava.

My heart sank. Persephone was supposed to cover that

area, but she was undoubtedly still with Nicholas. If none of the other girls had made it up there yet after clearing their sections of the castle, we would be on our own.

It didn't matter. Milo and Henry were on that roof, and I would've gone up there as naked and mortal as the day I was born if it meant having a chance to save them.

I followed Ava without question. She could have been leading me straight to my death, but I desperately wanted to believe that the Ava I knew and loved was in there somewhere, willing to give her all and risk her life for the greater good. She wouldn't have led me astray, and I had to believe that this Ava wouldn't either.

The door to the roof appeared, and I took a breath. I would know soon enough, one way or the other.

CHAPTER 18
BLOODSHED

We burst into the open air, the afternoon sky blacker than night. The cyclone that had been Cronus was gone, spread across the sky and struggling against pinpricks of light that looked like stars. The council. I ducked my head. If my mother saw me and got distracted—

That had to be a risk I was willing to take. My mother was strong. She wouldn't let Cronus get the best of her. If I had any chance of getting through this, I couldn't doubt her. I couldn't doubt myself.

Calliope stood at the edge of the roof, her hair whipping in the wind and her head tilted upward toward the heart of the battle. Henry stood at her side, his arms shielding a bundle of white blankets from grains of sand that cut through the air like bullets. What was he doing, bringing Milo up here?

I shoved aside my protests. Milo was immortal, and there was nowhere safer for him than with Henry. I couldn't get distracted.

"Calliope," I cried. My voice was nearly lost to the wind, but she faced me, her eyebrows raised in surprise.

"So you really are as stupid as I thought you were," she said as she walked toward me, leaving Henry and Milo behind. "Come to die?"

"Not quite." I gripped the hooked knife. It had to be as good as her dagger. "Let Henry and Milo go. This is between you and me."

Calliope's eyes widened innocently. "Henry's free to leave whenever he wants. It's not my fault he chose me over you."

My blood boiled. "How does it feel to know that your reality is nothing more than a fantasy you've concocted and blackmailed your way into? Nobody loves you. Not your husband, not your children, not your brothers or your sisters—no one."

The air around her crackled angrily. "Do you think I care? I win, Kate. I have everything you've ever wanted, and soon everyone else you love is going to be dead. You're going to spend eternity alone, and no one's going to be there to save you anymore."

"It isn't *about* winning." I took a step toward her. "Even if you never let Henry go, somewhere inside him, he's always going to love me—because he wants to, because we're good together. Not because Ava forced him into it. And no matter how alone I am, I'll always have the comfort of knowing that at least someone in the world loves me because they want to. But you—you're nothing but a heinous, lonely, unloved bitch, and that's all you're ever going to be."

Calliope screeched and barreled toward me. In the few seconds we had, Ava tried to push me behind her, but I sidestepped her and sprinted toward Calliope, clutching the hooked knife. I had one chance, and I was damn well going to take it.

We collided, immortal against immortal, and the force of it nearly sent me flying. Her nails scratched my face, her shrieks of rage rang in my ears, but her hands were empty. Mine weren't.

"I'm going to beat your pretty face to a pulp," growled Calliope. "Once I'm done, I'm going to make your son watch as I scoop out your eyes and peel your skin from your body. And maybe, once you're nothing more than a lump of quivering flesh, I might let you—"

Her eyes widened, her words cut short as I sank the hooked knife into her side. "You might what?" I said. "You might let me die?"

Calliope fell off of me, her brow furrowed in confusion. She stared at the knife sticking out of her side. "How did you—"

"The weapons Nicholas forged," I said. "You're not the only one with brains, you know."

She tugged on the knife, wincing as the hook ripped her skin apart, doing more damage going out than it'd done going in. Blood soaked through her pale blue dress, and she dropped the blade on the ground with a clatter. "But..."

Her eyes went blank, and without another word, she collapsed.

I stared at her body, and the way my hands shook had nothing to do with the bitter wind. After two and a half years of struggling to stay alive in her wake, that was it. I'd done it.

It felt too easy. I kicked her body to be sure, and when she flopped like a dead fish, I staggered backward. I'd killed her. I'd really, truly killed her.

I was a murderer. It was justified, but she hadn't had her dagger. I could've given her a choice, and instead I'd killed her in cold blood. How did that make me better than her?

I wasn't, not anymore.

Clenching my jaw, I turned away. I'd have time to hate myself later. Calliope might've been dead, but the whirling cloud of doom overhead hadn't stopped.

"Henry!" I cried. Abandoning Calliope's body, I dashed toward him through the violent gusts. "You need to take Milo and get out of here."

He stared up at the sky, and at first I thought he hadn't heard me. As I opened my mouth to repeat myself, however, he turned toward me, his moonlight eyes glowing. For a moment I thought I saw a flicker of something behind them, but it vanished. "Leave, Kate," he said, his voice sounding like a thousand gods speaking all at the same time.

I gaped at him in horror. "Are you—are you *helping* Cronus?"

"You weren't supposed to come."

"Yeah? When has that ever stopped me?" I reached for Milo. "If you won't take him to safety, then I will."

He snatched the baby away from me, and a knot formed in my throat. This couldn't be happening. Henry should have been in there somewhere, waiting for this, waiting for the moment he could finally break free. But I only saw the blank face of a powerful deity. Not Henry. Not my family.

"Ava! Whatever you're doing to Henry, stop it!" I shouted over the deafening roar. No response. I looked over my shoulder. Ava stared at me, her mouth hanging slack-jawed and her eyes wide with fear, and it took me a moment to figure out why.

Calliope's body was gone.

A girlish giggle echoed through the storm, mingling with the screeching wind and the crash of waves rising higher and higher. I froze. How was it possible? I'd watched her die.

"Funny thing about those weapons," said Calliope, and I whirled around again. She stood beside Henry, his arm wrapped around her shoulders the way he always held me. Her dagger floated in the space between us. "They were discarded because they didn't work."

Behind me, someone screamed, and the glowing blade hurtled toward me. I scrambled backward pivoting in hopes it would fly past me, but it followed my movements without missing a beat.

My back hit something solid. The edge of the roof. The dagger pressed against my throat, and I leaned back as far as I could without falling. "Henry," I choked. "Please."

"Don't listen to her, Henry," said Calliope in a sickly sweet voice. "She's the enemy, remember? You're loyal to me."

"Only because she's using her powers against you." I gulped in the gritty air. "Come on, Henry, you're stronger than this."

"Yeah, Henry," called out a voice from the other end of the roof. Persephone. Out of the corner of my eye, I watched as the other girls joined her. "I thought you were better than this."

"Persephone?" Henry frowned. "What are you—"

"Don't listen to her," said Calliope. "You've got me now."

Henry shook her off, and he stepped toward Persephone and the gang of girls. "What are you all doing here?"

"Rescuing your sorry ass," said Anna, swinging her mace. "And taking down this bitch."

She let out a war cry, and the girls took off across the roof, heading straight for Calliope and Henry—and Milo.

"Stop!" I shrieked. My cries fell on deaf ears though, and they only sped up. "Henry, get out of here! Take Milo and *go!*"

He ignored me and stared at the girls as if he'd never seen anything so strange in his life. Beside him, Calliope waved her hand, and the dagger flew from my neck to settle directly above my heart. The tip of the blade dug into my skin, and I winced as a drop of blood soaked into my shirt.

"Please," I begged. "Just go."

The sound of twisting metal drowned out my pleas, and half a dozen bewildered voices rose above the commotion. Though he was fighting a battle far above us, the fog that was Cronus had created a barrier in front of Calliope, protecting her. Persephone and the other girls pushed against it, roaring with outrage. Their weapons struck the fog again and again to no avail.

"Around," commanded Persephone, and the others scattered. No matter where they moved though, they couldn't get any closer.

Calliope smirked. "Here's the deal, Henry." She set her hand on his arm, and he flinched away. Was he back now? Had he come to his senses? "You're going to send all of these pretty little nuisances back where they came from, and maybe I won't kill Kate."

The blade dug into my chest, widening the wound, and I gasped as the fire of a Titan spread through me. Henry tensed, but as soon as it had come, his fear was replaced with the mask of impassiveness he wore when he was hurting the most. He was there. Did Calliope know? Had she let him go on purpose?

"What will it be, Henry?" she said. "I wouldn't linger too long on the options if I were you."

Deeper now, through cartilage and bone until it was half a millimeter away from piercing my heart. Light exploded in front of me, and sweat poured down my face as the fog spread through me, securing a choke hold on what remained of my life.

I'm sorry. Henry waved his hand, and Persephone and

the others disappeared, their useless weapons falling to the ground in a clatter.

Blood trickled down my chest now, and I couldn't look away from Henry. It didn't matter that Calliope had severed his loyalty to me; she hadn't severed mine.

"Do it," I snarled, summoning up the last of my strength. Martyr complex or not, maybe this would be enough for Henry to bring Milo to safety. "I dare you."

A shriek pierced the howling wind. Nicholas came through the roof door, and Ava pounced on him, kissing his purple cheeks and capturing him in an embrace. Even if no other part of my plan had worked, at least we'd freed Nicholas. At least we gave Ava a reason to fight with us.

"How cute," said Calliope. "A reunion before Cronus sends you all into oblivion."

Nicholas straightened and held Ava protectively. "You're never going to win," he said. "Cronus could kill us all, and you would still only be second."

Calliope growled, and immediately I saw the effect his words had on her. Her fists tightened, her jaw clenched, and her cheeks flushed. In her distraction, the dagger slipped from my chest. Eyeing the blade, I shifted slowly to the side, hoping against hope she wouldn't notice.

"Being my son will only buy you so much lenience," she said. "Is this how you want to spend it?"

"Lenience? Is that what you call what you did to him?" Ava shrugged off Nicholas's arm and stormed toward Calliope. Without her, Nicholas sagged and collapsed against the wall, his legs shaking so badly that it was a wonder he could stand at all.

Calliope met her in the middle of the roof, nose to nose. "You're in this as deep as I am. Forget what you did to Kate—you've been betraying the council from the beginning.

You think they'll be so willing to forgive you for that?" she said, a malicious glint in her eyes. "You're dead either way."

Ava smirked. "I'm here because Daddy asked me to come. He's known everything this whole time. And as for why I helped you with Kate—" Her smile faded, and she glanced at me. "It's because Daddy knew we couldn't win the war without Henry. Even your own husband is against you."

Calliope hissed, the golden aura around her nearly blinding now. "Do you think I care why you did it? It happened. It's over. Because of you, I win. Henry loves *me,* not her. Not anymore."

"That's the best part," said Ava. "Henry doesn't love you, you fool. He never has. He's been pretending the whole time."

I inhaled sharply, and Calliope spun around to face him. "Is this true?" she demanded. Henry's lips formed a thin line, and he gave Ava a reprimanding look. That was all the confirmation I needed.

Calliope hadn't stolen him from me, after all. He was still my Henry.

Go. I pushed the thought as hard as I could in his direction. *If you don't now, she's going to kill Milo. I'll be okay.*

He hesitated. Calliope was screaming at him, but her words became nothing but background noise as his voice surrounded me. *You need to come with us.*

I can't.

Yes, you can. The moment I leave, Calliope is going to try to kill you. I will not leave until I know you are safe.

I glanced around the roof. Ava was still here. Nicholas still leaned helplessly against the wall, barely conscious and beaten within an inch of his life. I couldn't leave them, but Henry was right—there was nothing keeping Calliope from killing me now, not with Cronus tied up in battle. *Okay.*

Henry exhaled. *Meet me in the bedroom in Olympus.*
I will.

A pause. *Ava's telling the truth.*

The words wrapped around me, a salve against all of the pain Cronus and Calliope had caused me. Had caused us both. *I know. We have to go.*

You first.

I closed my eyes, and a second later, that familiar sensation ran through me. When I opened them, I stood in the sunset bedroom I'd shared with Henry, and I held my breath. He had to come. He wouldn't break his promise like that, not with Milo's safety at—

An ugly screech echoed through the heavens. Calliope. Panic seized me, but before it had time to set in, Henry and Milo appeared. I threw my arms around them, nearly sobbing with relief. "You're safe."

"As are you." Henry pressed his lips to my forehead, but our reunion didn't last more than a few seconds. "I must go back."

"You—what?"

Henry held Milo out for me, and I froze. The baby's blue eyes were wide open, and he waved his little fists, watching me. Waiting for me to finally take him. I ached to hold him, but the moment I touched him, I knew I would never be able to leave him again. And we had a war to win.

"Go on," said Henry quietly, and I shook my head, clasping my hands behind my back. "He needs you."

"So do you," I said thickly. Refusing my son was the hardest thing I'd ever done, but I had to. "I'm not taking him, Henry."

We held each other's gaze, and I refused to back down. Whether or not he wanted to admit it, he knew how this was going to end. And we didn't have time to argue. At last

Henry sighed, and a cradle appeared between us. Without looking away from me, he gently set the baby inside, tucking his blanket around him.

Once Henry straightened, I snatched his hand, holding it with a crushing grip. "I'm going with you."

Henry winced. The deafening clash of the battle raged below us, and every second he wasn't there was another second we might lose. "Kate, I must."

"If you go, I go."

"I cannot risk you."

"And I can't risk you. We're a team. We work together. From here on out, no one gets left behind, and no one does something stupid without consulting the other first."

A muscle in his jaw twitched. "If you go back, Calliope will do everything in her power to kill you."

"I know." I squared my shoulders and summoned every last shred of bravery I had left. "I was born mortal. I always knew I was going to die, and I'm not afraid of it. But I am afraid of losing you. I am *terrified* of eternity without you."

"And I you," he said quietly. "Milo—"

"If something happens to me, then you'll come back to take care of him," I said firmly. "And if something happens to you, I'll do the same. I promise. He won't be alone."

Henry hesitated, and the sounds of the battle grew louder. We didn't have time for this.

"Henry, I love you. I'm not asking your permission. I'm asking you to tell me what I can do to help."

He opened his mouth, but before he could say a word, I cut him off again.

"Besides staying here."

He managed a faint smile at that. "We're a team, you say?"

"A team." I touched his cheek. "From now until the end.

Whether that's today or in a million years, we're in this together."

A long moment passed. His eyes locked on mine, and the
air seemed to still around us. In his cradle, Milo made another soft sound, and Henry deflated. "There is one thing
you could do to help."

"Anything."

He set his hand over mine, and I released my grip on his
wrist before threading my fingers through his. "Did you
see the way Cronus faltered when the girls attacked him?"

I shook my head. "I can't tell what he's doing in that fog."

"He was distracted. Enough for us to edge in closer." He
squeezed my hand. "I need you to fetch the girls from the
nursery and do everything you can to divert his attention to
the roof. If you do that, we might have a chance."

A smile spread across my face. "You didn't send them back
to the Underworld?"

"Of course not. It was a brilliant idea." He bent down
to brush his lips against mine. "Now let's go win this war."

I kissed him back. "Together."

"Together."

I arrived alone in the peacock-and-gold hallway outside
the nursery. Henry presumably appeared on the roof, but
even though I strained my ears, I didn't hear any signs that
the tide of battle had shifted.

"It's about damn time," said Persephone as I opened the
nursery door. The other girls milled behind her.

"I'm sorry," I said. "We need to—"

"We know," said Ingrid, tapping her temple. "Henry already filled us in."

Right. "Then let's go play chicken with a Titan."

We raced to the roof, and I took the stairs two at a time,

every bone in my body drawn to Henry as if we were magnets. As we burst through the doors, however, I skidded to a stop.

Ava and Calliope stood in the center, only inches apart. Ava glowed magenta, Calliope gold, and Cronus swirled behind them, a massive funnel of pure power. Henry wasn't there.

Had he stayed in Olympus? No, I wasn't that lucky. I glanced upward. The streaks of light were dimmer than before. The council was losing. But another appeared, brighter than the others, and the fog seemed to part to make way for it. Henry had joined the battle.

"Go!" I cried, and the girls hurtled forward, picking up their weapons as they reached them. They might not have been deadly, but wherever they connected with the fog, it shimmered, and a shower of sparks burst through the darkness.

"I will kill you." Calliope's voice seemed magnified, louder than thunder. "Once I've won, I will skin you alive and watch you bleed."

Ava's wind chime laughter filtered through the air. "You won't ever win. You deserve worse than fading. You deserve to have your name erased from history, and I'm going to make sure that happens. You're pathetic now, but just wait— once I'm done, you'll be *nothing*."

With everyone distracted, I skirted around the glowing goddesses, searching for the dagger. It wasn't in Calliope's hands, which meant it had to be around here somewhere. Maybe she was hiding it in a pocket, but with the way she and Ava were going at it, she would've taken a stab at her by now if she'd had it nearby.

Come on, come on, it had to be around here somewhere—

There. I spotted the glinting dagger lying on the ground

near the edge of the roof, where I'd stood only minutes before. Swiping it off the ground, I turned toward Calliope. It was now or never.

I raced across the roof, holding the dagger like an ice pick. Calliope was so wrapped up in her argument with Ava that she didn't see me coming, and I slammed into her. The golden glow disappeared as she crumpled underneath me, hitting the ground hard.

I pinned her in place with my knees. For one everlasting moment, we stared at each other, my grim satisfaction reflecting as horror in her eyes. I raised the dagger. This time, I wouldn't hesitate.

"Father!" she screamed the instant I thrust the weapon toward her neck. Even as the word was still leaving her lips, a wisp of fog appeared, and time seemed to slow around us. The closer I got, the harder it was to move, and the dagger stopped completely half an inch from her throat. No matter how hard I tried, it wouldn't budge.

"Nice try, Kate," said Calliope with a sneer. "Pity that's all you're ever capable of."

A gust of wind hit me, ripping the blade from my hand. With a shriek, I flew through the air and landed hard on my back, cracking the stone roof beneath me. The fog sliced through the wound in my chest, and I groaned.

"So this is how it ends," said Calliope, and she scooped up the dagger. "I'd say something witty, but you're just not worth it."

I squeezed my eyes shut, and an enraged scream filled the air, mingling with the crash of the ocean until I could no longer tell one from the other. This was it. This was the end.

One second. Two seconds.

The pain never came.

A collective gasp echoed across the roof and through the

sky, as if the entire world had drawn its breath at the same time. Finally I had to look. Calliope stood near me, but her hand was empty; the knife was gone.

And between us crouched Ava, the handle of the dagger buried directly above her heart.

CHAPTER 19
LIGHT

Behind me, Nicholas cried out, and his grief rose above the wind. The pinpricks of light in the unnaturally black sky echoed his pain, and at last I understood.

"Ava?" As she sank to the ground, I crawled to her side. My hand hovered over the wound. It was deep—too deep not to be fatal, unless I got the dagger out before the fog could penetrate her heart. Could I without making it worse? Wasn't much of a choice. If I didn't, she would die for sure. I gripped the handle. "This is going to hurt."

Slowly I pulled it out, and her screams shattered the clamor of battle. As soon as the blade was free from her chest, I pressed my hand against the wound, willing the blood to stop flowing. She couldn't die. Not after all of this.

"I'm sorry," she wheezed, her eyes rimmed with red. "I thought—I thought it was for the best, I thought—"

"You did nothing wrong." Her face swam in front of me, and I blinked rapidly. "Thank you. I'm so sorry I ever doubted you."

"You—forgive me?" she whispered.

"Of course." I pressed my lips to her forehead. "I love you."

A trickle of blood escaped the corner of her mouth. "Finish this," she said, barely audible. For one horrible moment I thought she wanted me to kill her, but she wrapped her cold fingers over my fist, the one that held the dagger, and I understood.

I glanced over my shoulder. Calliope stared at Ava, and despite all her posturing, undeniable shock spread across her face. Why? Wasn't this exactly what she'd meant to do?

No, this was an accident. She hadn't been aiming for Ava. She'd been aiming for me. Either way, I couldn't afford to give her the chance to build her defenses. Lashing out, I went for her ankle, and grim satisfaction filled me as the blade sliced through skin and bone.

Collapsing to the ground, she screamed, a horrible, gut-wrenching sound that resonated through every cell of my body. With inhuman strength, she clawed at my hand, fighting to dislodge the dagger. "It's over, Kate. Let it *go*."

As she tried to take the blade from me, it cut her palms to ribbons, and her blood flowed freely down my arm. Her fingers dug underneath mine, and she began to pry the dagger loose from my hand.

"You really don't know when to quit, do you?" she said in that girlish voice. Just a few seconds more, and she would have it. I cried out as the handle began to slip from my bloody grip, and tears of frustration streaked down my face. "I'm going to get Henry back, and Callum will be mine. He's my son, not yours, and there's nothing you can do about it. I'll make sure whenever he hears your name, he knows you abandoned him. I'll make sure he knows you never loved him. I'll make sure he hates you more than he hates any-one in the—"

I roared, half blind with rage. My hand slipped past her, and between us, something made a sickening wet sound. She doubled over and went rigid, her eyes round with shock.

Breathing heavily, I tried to shove her off me, my fist still wrapped around the handle of the dagger. Something was wrong though—when I tried to pull back, the dagger resisted, and Calliope folded her body around my arm.

Her cries turned to gurgles, and she tore at my elbow with what little strength she had left. The weapon slipped from my grip, and she fell away, clawing at her chest.

I scrambled back. The silver handle stuck out of her chest at a sideways angle, through her sternum and pointing directly to her heart. Blood poured from the wound, and she convulsed, the golden aura around her fading until there was nothing left.

"You—" she managed, but the rest of her words died along with her. Her body stilled and her eyes stared at me, empty and unseeing.

"No," I whispered. "You did this to yourself."

All at once, the sky exploded, and white light blasted through the darkness. The din of war gave way to a chorus of the most beautiful voices I'd ever heard, and underneath me, Calliope's body began to glow again. I hurried back to Ava's side and took her hand. Nicholas joined us, and despite the fat tears rolling down his cheeks, he was smiling.

The black clouds reformed into a funnel, and it grew smaller and more concentrated until the darkness formed a man. Cronus.

"Rhea!" he boomed, his voice everywhere at once. The white light took form as well, and Rhea descended from the sky. She still wore the form of the little girl she'd been in Africa, but despite her stature, she radiated power.

Moving past Cronus as if he wasn't even there, Rhea knelt beside Calliope's empty body. "My daughter," she whispered. At her touch, the blood disappeared, and the knife fell to the ground, dull and void of Titan power. "What has happened to you?"

I wiped my eyes, smearing blood across my face. The overwhelming weight of what I'd done hit me, and my body sagged under the pressure. I'd killed her child. Everything I'd feared Calliope doing to Milo, I'd done to Rhea. I really was a murderer.

I hadn't meant to do it though—I'd only been protecting myself. Calliope was the one who hadn't given up. She was the one who'd gone after me. She was the one who'd started this all.

If I'd had the chance to do it again though, I would have. "I'm sorry," I said thickly. "I had no choice."

A silver tear rolled down Rhea's cheek. "No, I suppose you did not."

One by one, the other gods joined us on the roof, no longer hindered by Cronus. They didn't go to Calliope and Rhea, though; instead they appeared in a circle around Ava, Nicholas and me.

Walter arrived first, and he sat on the cracked roof beside me, drawing her head into his lap. He petted her hair, whispering words I couldn't hear, and Ava smiled weakly. A strange light emanated from his hands, and I knew without asking that somehow he was keeping her alive.

"Please, Mother," said Walter, his voice choked. I'd never seen him cry before. "You cannot save your daughter, but you can save mine."

Rhea grew still. "What's done is done. My daughter chose this path, and so did yours."

The world around me narrowed until all I could feel was Ava's hand in mine, growing colder by the second. No. *No.* It was completely within Rhea's power to save Ava. She had to.

"You can't just let her die." I struggled to stand, but someone set their hands on my shoulders, holding me down. Henry. "All she was trying to do was stop Cronus. She was doing what you wouldn't."

Rhea said nothing. Cronus knelt beside her, and though his expression was emotionless, he touched Calliope's face.

"Please, Cronus," I begged. "Ava doesn't have to die."

He looked at me, and in that moment, I allowed myself to hope. Maybe after all this time, he'd gained an ounce of humanity. Without a word, he gestured toward us, and a wave of pleasant numbness passed through my body. The fire inside me cooled. He'd healed me. He understood, after all.

I clasped Ava's hand and looked down at her, but instead of stopping, blood flowed from her chest with every weakened beat of her heart. "But..." I looked up, and Walter bowed his head.

"She does not have to die, but she will," said Cronus. "Consider us even."

The edges of my vision darkened, and the sunset sky seemed to spin until everything was a blur. "Even?" I whispered, and as if every drop of grief and despair and guilt rushed out of me at the same time, I screamed, "You're letting her die so we'll be *even?*"

I struggled against Henry's grip, but he wrapped his arms around me so tightly I could barely move. "Kate, calm down," he said, his breath warm against my ear, but it was pointless.

"He's killing her!" I shrieked, and James knelt beside

Henry. My outrage smothered the relief that came with knowing he was all right. "It's not my fault—you can't make this my fault!"

It's okay, whispered Ava's voice, and her fingers tightened around mine. *You're right. It isn't your fault.*

I clung to her hand. *I'm sorry. I'm so sorry. It shouldn't be like this.*

But it is. I'm ready.

A loud, hiccupping sob escaped me. *We'll find a way around this, I promise. I'll find a way to fix you.*

A faint smile appeared on Ava's bloodstained lips. *Not this time, Kate. I love you. We all do, even if some of us aren't very good at showing it sometimes.* Her blue eyes, fast draining of life, turned toward Henry. *Don't forget that. Or me, okay? I won't ever fade completely as long as someone's here to remember me.*

I couldn't breathe. Sob after sob ripped through me, and it was all I could do to speak. "I won't."

One by one, the members of the council joined Ava to silently say their goodbyes. Everyone, even Dylan, cried wordlessly. As destroyed as I was, it had to be nothing compared to what they were all going through, and I forced myself into silence. But even though it was selfish, I couldn't let go of her hand. Walter didn't stop stroking her hair either, his fingers glowing with the only thing keeping her alive. In those precious few minutes, he aged a thousand years.

At last, as the sun dipped below the horizon, the light in Walter's hands died. And just like that, Ava was gone.

The world went silent. Even the ocean grew still, and the violet shades of dusk hung in the sky far longer than they should have. No one spoke. No one moved. No one took that step from before into after, and we all lingered together in that eternal moment.

It should've never ended, but the council couldn't deny

time forever. Eventually Henry set his hand on my back, and though he was gentle, he pried my fingers from Ava's cold ones. The separation cut through me, but there was nothing I could do. She was dead.

Walter cleared his throat and set her head down on the rooftop. Standing on shaking legs, he struggled to draw himself to his full height, clearly weakened. "An eye for an eye," he said. "Let it not happen again. Will you go peacefully, Father?"

"No," said Cronus, and before fury could overtake what little sense of self-preservation I had left, Henry rubbed my back, his touch soothing the fire out of me.

"You will," said Rhea. "It is over. I will not allow you to continue this cycle of destruction. They have taken one of ours, and we have taken one of theirs. That is the end."

Cronus's form began to blur into black fog, but as soon as it started, white light encased him, and he growled. "Let me go, Rhea."

"I will not," she said with quiet resolve. "Neither will the council. This is their world now, and you have proven you have no place in it. I will only repeat our son once—will you go peacefully?"

Silence.

"Then you leave me with no choice," said Rhea, and the light around Cronus grew blindingly bright. I looked away, and Cronus cried out, the first real sound of pain I'd ever heard from him.

Good. He deserved it.

"Stop! I will—go peacefully," he managed to say, and the light lessened.

"Very well. My son?" said Rhea, and Henry released me.

"I will return shortly," he said, kissing my hair. "James, take care of her."

As he stood, James's arms replaced Henry's, and for the first time, I took a good look at the council. Everyone was there, even Ella and Theo. Everyone except—

"Where's my mother?" All the blood drained from my face as the world once again began to spin. "James, where is she?"

"She's fine," he said quickly. "I promise. She's with Milo."

"I want to see her," I said, and he nodded, running his fingers through my hair like Walter had done for Ava. Maybe he thought it would help, but the hollowness inside me didn't lessen. I wasn't sure it ever would.

Rhea touched Cronus's elbow, and Henry took her hand. My eyes met his, and he nodded once before the three of them disappeared, undoubtedly back into Tartarus. The last thing I wanted was to let him out of my sight, and familiar dread pooled in my stomach. What if something went wrong and I never saw him again?

Before my fear could work itself into anything substantial, James gathered me up and helped me to my feet. His cheek glistened, and I brushed the pad of my thumb against his wet skin. "I'm sorry." I couldn't say it enough.

James shook his head, his lips moving as he fought to find his voice. I hugged him, and he clung to me, needing me as much as I needed him.

"Come on," I said. "Let's go home."

My mother was waiting for us in Olympus, rocking Milo's cradle as he slept. Relieved, I staggered toward her, barely able to see straight.

"Oh, my darling, you're all right," she cried, throwing her arms around me. For a moment I couldn't breathe, but I didn't care. She was all right, Milo was all right, Henry was all right—

But Ava wasn't.

All at once, what was left of my inner strength crumbled. "Ava's dead," I whispered, choking on the words.

My mother tensed, and from the doorway, James cleared his throat. "Calliope, as well," he said roughly. "Rhea and Henry are escorting Cronus back to Tartarus now."

"A small victory," my mother said as her eyes filled with tears. "At least…at least…"

She didn't finish. For the first time in my life, my mother shattered. Her knees gave out, and she eased down onto the edge of her bed. Though I desperately wanted to go to Milo, I curled up with her, struggling to hold it together while she cried. She'd spent years pouring her strength into me and hiding her hurt so mine wouldn't worsen. Now it was my turn.

"The way we treated her this past year…" My mother created a handkerchief and dabbed her eyes. "She shouldn't have been there. We should've let her come back when she asked."

"It's not your fault," I said. Walter had been the one to make that decision. "She tried to tell me why she was doing it so many times, and I never listened. Cronus—" My voice broke. "He wouldn't save her. He healed me, and he could've healed her, too, but because of me—because of me, he refused."

My mother leaned her head against mine and drew me into her arms. "It is not your fault either," she croaked, but there was conviction in her voice. "Cronus would have never saved her, even if you'd been by his side and fulfilled your promises to him. Honor means nothing to him. He is defined by the power he has, and all you did was bruise his ego. You did not change who he is or who he chooses to be."

I hiccupped. "I hated her so much. I thought—I blamed her for everything, and all she was trying to do was help me or—look after Milo or—or save Nicholas's life. And Walter—"

"Walter did what he had to do in order to win the war." My mother tucked a lock of hair behind my ear. "He has his own demons to face now."

My chin trembled. "I should've done something. I should've listened or—or fought for her or forgiven her or—anything."

"You did," said James. "You did all of those things. Your mother's right. It isn't your fault, it isn't her fault, it isn't—it isn't Ava's fault. It's Calliope's. And she's gone now. There's nothing more we can do but remember Ava and keep on loving her."

I nodded tightly. I could give her that, and I would. We all would.

In the cradle, Milo let out a soft cry. "It seems like someone's eager to see you again," said my mother. Despite her red-rimmed eyes, she managed a smile as she scooped him up. "Do you want to hold him?"

More than anything in the world. As I reached for him, however, I hesitated. A few more inches, and I would feel him. He was really there. An invisible barrier full of questions and doubts held me back, and I lowered my hands into my lap. "What if I can't do this? What if I can't be his mother?"

"You already are," she said, and I shook my head.

"I'm not as good at this or—or as strong as you are."

She rested her head against mine again, and her hair tickled my neck. "Yes, you are. In so many ways, you're stronger than I've ever been. Sadness doesn't equal weakness, sweetheart. If anything, it shows the love you have inside you, and nothing stronger in this world exists. Ava knew that better than all of us."

A shadow moved in the doorway. "Your mother's right,

you know," said Henry. "The best way we can honor Ava is by loving the people in our lives as much as we can. That's all she would have wanted." Sitting on the mattress beside me, he gave my mother a smile. "I see you've met my son."

"He's beautiful," said my mother, and Milo let out another soft wail. "He wants you, Kate."

Wiping my cheeks with my bloody sleeves, I nodded. My mother placed Milo in my arms, and he settled against me, a perfect fit. He was warmer than I'd expected, and heavier, as well. Turning his head toward me, he nuzzled my chest, and my heart nearly burst.

"Just like this," murmured my mother, adjusting my elbow so I was supporting his head. "There you go."

"Look at that," said James. "You're a natural."

As Milo calmed, he stared up at me with his big blue eyes. Whatever connection we'd managed to forge before intensified, and in that moment, my world shifted. He was so beautiful and innocent, and I would spend eternity making sure he had the chance to stay that way. He would never know war or hatred or the agony of loss. He would never spend his days counting down to a loved one's last. He would never feel alone or unworthy or unloved. He would know happiness. He would know peace. He would know family. And he would always have me and Henry.

A tear dripped down my chin, falling and hitting Milo on the nose. He made a face, and Henry chuckled.

My mother stood. "I'll leave you three be," she said, and though she was smiling, the grief hadn't left her voice. I wasn't sure it ever would completely. Together she and James exited the room, closing the door behind them.

"He looks so much like you," murmured Henry. "Every time I held him, all I could see was your face. I missed you, Kate."

I brushed my knuckles gently against Milo's cheek. He may have had my eyes, but he had Henry's dark hair. And his ears. "Whatever happened on the island between you and Calliope..."

He tensed. "Kate, I—"

"It doesn't matter." I looked at him. "You did what you had to do to protect Milo. I know that."

His hand slid up my back, and he squeezed my shoulder. "Nothing happened. Ava never used her powers on me. I was pretending the entire time."

I leaned forward and kissed him. His lips were sweet against mine, and I didn't let him go until Milo whimpered between us. We both knew pretending meant he'd somehow had to convince her he loved her. Part of me burned with the need to hear everything, but none of it mattered, and I wasn't about to let Calliope hurt us from the grave. Whatever Henry had endured, we would get through it together. One day, if he wanted to talk about it, I would listen. But until then, I would pretend I believed him. To protect and love him the way he protected and loved me.

We were a family, and no one, not Calliope, not Cronus, not even death itself, could take that from us.

CHAPTER 20
ETERNAL

Sometime during the night, I untangled myself from Henry and slipped out of bed. He slept soundly, clearly exhausted after the battle, but no matter how hard I tried, I couldn't fall asleep.

Reaching into the cradle, I touched Milo's forehead to make sure he was still there. Reassured by the rise and fall of his chest, I padded out of the room, closing the door behind me. Even in the dead of night, the ceiling glowed brilliant blue, and the magnificent sunset swirled underneath me.

I didn't consciously decide where to go. One minute I stood in the hallway, and the next my feet carried me into the throne room in search of someone else. After the evening we'd all had, chances were slim anyone else would be awake, but it was worth a shot.

In the entranceway, I stopped cold. The sky wasn't blue here; instead the ceiling was dark as night, and the stars twinkled above us. The thrones were gone, and in their place a glass coffin rested on a raised platform. Inside, dressed in a white gown with roses in her hair, lay Ava.

Without thinking, I crossed the room and pressed my palm against the glass. Her lips were the color of cherries, and in the dim light, I could almost see her smile.

A lump formed in my throat. I opened my mouth to say something—to apologize, to promise I'd never forget her, to forgive her again and again until the universe had no choice but to believe me—but I couldn't force out the words. She couldn't hear them anyway, and I'd said it all in her last moments. She already knew.

"She isn't really there."

I scowled. "Leave me alone."

A rustle of fabric, soft footsteps, and Walter stood by my side, looking every bit as aged as he had on the rooftop. "It's a reflection of sorts, but more realistic than a simple picture."

I pulled my hand from the glass and shifted half a step away from him. "Where's her body?"

"Gone," he said. "Back into the universe."

"Then why is this—this hologram here?" The empty throne, the empty bedroom, the empty hole in our lives where she'd once been—as if all of that wasn't enough to remind us she was gone.

Walter inhaled deeply, and as he exhaled, faint thunder rumbled through the throne room. "She lived a very long time, and her life touched many others. Those who wish to say their goodbyes will have the opportunity to do so."

"Yet you aren't doing the same for Calliope."

He winced. "My wife chose her path. She chose to separate herself from the council. Ava did not."

"No, she didn't," I said. "You chose it for her. You're the reason she died."

Walter stared into the coffin. "I have made many mistakes—"

"Mistakes?" My snarl echoed from one end of the room to the other. "Ava's dead, and all you can say is that you made some *mistakes?*"

Walter faltered. Though he tried to draw himself up to his full height, tears spilled down his face, defeating any intention he had of intimidating me. "It is not your place to say—you could not possibly know the circumstances—"

"I know Ava's dead. I know she only joined Calliope because you told her to."

"For Nicholas," he said. "For the greater good."

"Is this worth the greater good?" I gestured to the coffin. "Is this worth knowing that if it hadn't been for you, Ava would still be alive?"

"She would not be alive," he said hoarsely. "None of us would be. Henry would have never joined the fight, and Cronus would have won. It is as simple as that."

"Rhea won the war, not Henry. He wasn't even fighting on our side for most of the battle."

"Yes, he was," said Walter. "On the rooftop, he was countering Calliope's abilities. A difficult thing for any of us to do, even more difficult without being discovered, but he managed. When he came to us with your plans to surrender to Cronus, we knew what he intended to do, and with Ava aware that Calliope wanted to take Henry as well, we set up the ruse. All along, he was feeding us information about her and Cronus's tactics. We would have never stood a fighting chance without his help. Or without Ava's help. She is the reason—*you* are the reason he agreed to fight at all."

"There had to be another way to keep Ava out of it. There's *always* another way."

"If there was, do you think I would have risked her?" said Walter. "Do you truly believe if there had been any feasible alternative to draw Henry into the war without her—"

"You could have asked. You could have given him time. You didn't have to play Calliope's games and risk everyone's lives." At last I faced him. "We're not pieces on a chessboard, but that's how you treated us, and now you're paying for it. We all are. So I hope whatever lies you've told yourself keep you warm at night, because no one in their right mind is going to bother with you once everyone knows what you did."

He touched the casket, and all the fight drained out of him, leaving a husk of a man where the King of the Gods had stood only moments before. "I know what I deserve. I do not need anyone, you or the Fates or the universe itself, to detail the mistakes I have made. I am paying for it now, and I will pay for it throughout the rest of my eternal existence. If that is not the hell you wish for me, then I do not know how much more I could possibly hurt to satisfy your desire for vengeance, daughter."

"I am *not* your daughter."

Walter bowed his head. Every instinct I had screamed for me to leave before he retaliated somehow—emotionally, physically, it didn't matter—but my feet refused to move. This was the longest conversation I'd ever had with the man who was supposedly my father, and this was what it'd come to.

"You are my daughter, as surely as Ava was," he said quietly. "She was the only one of my children who ever bothered to see me for who I really am. The others only ever saw power. Calliope only ever saw a philanderer. But Ava understood the love I have for you all. She understood that a man can feel things he does not express, and that lack of expression does not deplete that love."

"I know that." She'd been the one to insist Henry loved

me no matter what. "You realize if you'd never cheated, none of this would've ever happened?"

"If I'd never cheated, you would have never been born." He looked at me with lightning in his eyes, and I held his stare. "James would have never been born. Ella and Theo, Irene, Persephone—I loved my wife. My misdeeds are not her fault. But I will not apologize, to her or to any other, for bringing my children into this world. Including you."

"Then you're no better than she is. Love doesn't give you a free pass to hurt your family. You do remember what family is, right?"

He tilted his head. "And what do you mean by that?"

"You never came to see me." I dug my nails into my palms. If I could draw blood, then maybe the fury trying to claw its way out of me would have some release. "You knew what I was going through after Mom was diagnosed, but you didn't care."

"I have many mortal children," he said slowly. "There was no guarantee you would pass the test, and I did not want to risk forging a connection with you in case you did not."

"Why, because you were worried about your precious secret being revealed?"

"Because after everything your mother told me about you, I knew that if I came to see you, I would love you instantly. The pain of losing children I have never known is hard enough. But to lose one I love..." He stroked the edge of the glass coffin.

My shoulders shook with silent sobs. "I needed you. I needed someone to tell me it would be okay. I needed to know I wasn't alone, and you couldn't bother with me because you were too afraid to love me?"

"The council has watched over you from the beginning, playing bit parts in your life. Loving and protecting you as we did in Eden. You were never alone, Kate, even in your darkest of days."

"But I didn't *know,*" I burst. "It doesn't make any difference if I never knew."

"I am sorry." His voice broke. "I am sorry for never being the father you needed. I am sorry for not being the king my people deserve. And I am so sorry for letting my daughter make the ultimate sacrifice. I do not expect you or anyone else in this world to forgive me now that she is gone, but I hope one day, for Ava's sake, you will allow me to be your family. To be your father, as I should have been when you were growing up. It is what Ava would have wanted for us both."

I wanted to spit in his face, to tell him to go screw himself and find another daughter who was willing to love such a manipulative creep, but the truth of what he was saying froze me in place. He was right. This was what Ava would have wanted. Not only because I needed a father, but because Walter needed a daughter who loved him despite his flaws, who understood him and gave him a chance. I'd done my best to show everyone, even Calliope and Cronus, that compassion and understanding. Ava would've wanted me to do the same for him. To not fail Walter like I'd failed her.

"You're asking for more than I know how to give," I said quietly, and all of the fight drained out of me. I focused on the image of Ava's face again. "You hurt me. You hurt my mother, and you hurt our family."

He set a tentative hand on my shoulder. "I know. And I will spend eternity doing what I can to make it up to you. I cannot promise much, but I do promise that you will always have me—you will always have all of us. As it should have been from the beginning."

Pressing my swollen lips together, I nodded. After all the

pain he'd caused, I couldn't forgive him as we stood there side by side, but someday I would try. For Ava.

The glass coffin remained in the throne room for three days, and the image of Ava was never alone. At first only the council members came to see her, each of us wanting to be alone with her. After we'd all had our turn, Walter opened up the portal to Olympus, allowing others to come through without assistance.

As the hours passed and news of her death spread, gods I'd never seen before appeared in Olympus to pay their respects. Some of the names were familiar, but nothing prepared me for the sheer number Ava had touched in her life. The throne room was always full in those three days of mourning, and the veil of sadness only grew heavier with each new face.

A boy with blond curls kept vigil by the coffin, never speaking a word. Both Nicholas and Dylan joined him at different times, and while he sat stiffly at Dylan's side, the boy seemed to relax in Nicholas's presence.

"Eros. Eric now," said Henry as we lingered near the hall-way and watched. "Her oldest son."

My vision blurred, and I had to excuse myself. I knew how deeply Ava had touched the rest of the council, but seeing the paths her long life had forged, the family she'd formed in the millennia she'd lived—it only reopened wounds I was sure would never fully heal.

On the third day, dawn crept across the starry ceiling. Walter called us all together, and we stood in a circle with the other gods, watching as the glass coffin filled with light. At last, as the sunrise blended away the last vestiges of night, the casket disappeared.

While the rest of the earthbound gods left one by one, Eros remained. The thrones returned, circling the spot where Ava's reflection had stood only moments before, and we each settled into our proper place. I cradled Milo, who slept soundly, and tried to ignore the empty seats on either side of Walter. Nicholas, the worse for wear but healing, set his hand on the armrest of the seashell throne that had been Ava's. As he brushed the tears from his cheeks, I looked away.

"Brothers and sisters, sons and daughters," said Walter into the silence. "While we will forever mourn the loss of our own, the time has come to acknowledge that their positions among us must be filled."

I glanced at my mother. Replacing Calliope made sense—like Henry couldn't rule the Underworld alone, surely the same was true for Walter and his realm. But Ava?

She patted my hand. *All in due time.*

"I will handle the replacement of my queen," said Walter. "In the meantime, I ask that Diana take the role temporarily and assist me as needed."

"Of course," said my mother. "Whatever I can do to help."

Walter inclined his head. "Thank you. As for Ava's place, we must once again scour the world to find one who is worthy. It will not be an easy task. Ava was…" He paused. "She was irreplaceable. We cannot pretend otherwise, but we must continue on. Kate."

"Yeah?" I said, and my mother's hand tightened around mine.

"I think it appropriate that you take Ava's place. Temporarily," he added. "Until we find someone capable of filling her role."

"What of her duties in the Underworld?" said Henry before I could protest. "I need her by my side, especially now, with the kingdom left unattended for so long."

"I am not asking for a great commitment on her part," said Walter. "Only enough to tide us over until we have found a new goddess. She can handle it during her summer months away."

I shook my head. "I'm staying in the Underworld during the summer now. I don't want to leave Milo." Or Henry, but that wasn't the sort of excuse Walter would understand.

"It would be no great thing for you to focus on helping us with Ava's duties in the meantime," said Walter. "Of us all, you are best suited for the role, at least for a short period of time."

A short period of time to Walter could have easily been a hundred years. "I can't," I said. "I'm sorry, but I can't replace her, and I can't leave my family."

"I'll do it," said Eros—Eric. Even though his voice was high and boyish, he'd featured prominently in a few of the myths I'd learned, which meant he couldn't be that young, after all. "It's what my mother would have wanted."

"As generous an offer as it is," said Walter, "you are not a member of the council. You do not have the ability."

Eric's face fell, and seeing his disappointment on top of his grief was a punch to the gut. "I'll help him," I blurted. "He can report to me, and I'll make sure everything goes according to plan. Just as long as I don't have to leave the Underworld for extended periods of time."

Walter turned to Henry, who nodded once. "That is acceptable to me, so long as Kate is not forced into any position she does not feel she is ready for."

"Very well," said Walter. "In addition, I ask that Kate and Eric be in charge of finding a suitable candidate for a more permanent role."

A goddess. He wanted us to find another goddess. Or a mortal to take the test and earn immortality the way I had. "How?"

He shrugged. "I do not particularly care how you handle

it, only that it is done. Henry is familiar with the process. He can help you."

Henry murmured his agreement, and just like that, it was up to me and Ava's son to find someone who could take over her role on the council—someone who couldn't possibly exist.

Then again, Henry must've thought the same when he began his search for a new queen. If he could overcome his fears and hesitations, I could do the same. "Okay," I said softly. "I'll try."

"I know you will," said Walter. "And you will do wonderfully."

That may have been stretching it, but I would do Ava justice. She deserved that much. Across the circle, James smiled at me, and I managed a small one in return. Even if I wasn't up to the task, he would be there every step of the way. They would all be.

The council wasn't perfect, not by a long shot. Dylan would probably never like me. They would always give each other knowing looks I would never understand. Walter and I would probably spend most of forever butting heads, and it would be a long time before he saw me as an equal. But despite the fights, despite the lies, despite the frustration and secrets and eons of history I would never catch up on, they were my family now. And I wasn't letting them go for anything.

Henry, Milo and I returned to the Underworld the next morning. Despite the gloominess of the caverns, there was nowhere else I would've rather been. We were home.

As we entered our red-and-gold bedroom, I stopped in the doorway and gazed around, swallowing the lump in my throat. Ava had decorated it before I'd arrived the year before. How long would it be before everything stopped reminding me of her?

Never, I hoped. I'd keep my promise to remember her always even if the guilt and pain killed me.

Henry bowed his head until his face was only inches from mine. "It will get easier."

"Promise?" I said.

"Yes." He pressed his lips to my forehead. "I cannot tell you it will ever go away, but that pain is part of you now. It is part of all of us. And because we know it, because we have had to survive it, we will do what we must to make sure we never have to experience it again."

I exhaled. "I miss her. I don't know how Walter expects us to just replace her like that."

"I never thought I would find a replacement for Persephone either," he said quietly. "And as it happens, I did not. I found something even better. I found you."

My hand rested over his heart, and I didn't speak. Words couldn't have possibly described how much I loved him in that moment. Burying his nose in my hair, Henry held me as we swayed back and forth to a silent rhythm.

"You will never find someone to replace Ava because that person does not exist," he murmured. "But you will find someone who understands love as Ava did. Who embodies it. Who has, without question, inherited the passion and devotion that defined her. And one day, perhaps in a few years, perhaps many centuries from now, you will stop in the middle of whatever you are doing and look around, and you will realize that things are okay again. Perhaps never completely whole, because nothing can fill that gap of loss. But the parts around it will grow. You will love. You will be happy. You will laugh again. And that day will be better than today. I promise."

With the baby between us, I hugged him, burying my nose in the crook of his neck. "I love you," I whispered. "Thank you for choosing me. Thank you for letting me in."

"I am the one who should be thanking you." His lips brushed against my hair, and his fingers tangled in the ends as he splayed his hand across my back. "And I will, for the rest of eternity. You saved my life, Kate. You gave me everything. There is nothing I would rather do than be with you forever."

"You will be," I mumbled into his chest. "I'm never letting you go again."

He pulled away enough to touch his lips to mine. "Good."

I captured him in another kiss, deeper this time and full of everything I couldn't say. How much I loved him, how thankful I was not just for him, but for the family we had together—all of it. I may have saved his life, but he'd saved mine, as well. Neither of us would ever have to go through that dark loneliness again.

Between us, Milo made a small sound, and I broke the kiss to gaze down at him. He gurgled and waved his tiny fists. "Yes, all right, a kiss for you, too," I said, grinning, and I dropped one on his forehead. "Such a demanding little boy."

"The staff put together a nursery for Milo in the room next to ours," said Henry. "He has everything he needs."

"Yes, he does." I looked up at Henry once more. "Can you do me a favor?"

"Of course," he said. I hesitated, and a moment later I launched into the most difficult question I'd ever asked him.

To Henry's credit, he didn't argue. He didn't like it, but neither did I. That didn't change anything. And it was the right thing to do. He took my hand, and slowly the bedroom around us faded, replaced by black rock and a monstrous cavern.

The entrance to Tartarus.

"I sealed off the pathway in the wall," said Henry. "Only we can reach it now."

I nodded. No need to take any chances. Wordlessly I kissed Milo again and handed him to Henry. My arms felt empty without him, but he'd been in enough danger to last him an eternal lifetime. He would be safe with Henry no matter what happened.

Slowly I made my way to the gate. The bars, once carved out of the black rock itself, now glowed with white light. Rhea. I stood up as straight as I could. "Cronus, I want to talk to you."

For several seconds, nothing happened. Not that I expected him to come running the moment I called, but he didn't have to make this difficult.

"Please," I said, the word sour on my tongue. "I won't wait forever."

At last an opaque fog slithered across the ground, but it stopped short of the bars. Unlike before, when he'd had enough of a reach to wreak havoc in the Underworld, Cronus was completely trapped now.

The fog solidified into the silhouette of a man, and Cronus stepped toward the gate, as tall and proud as ever. "Kate, my darling, I knew you'd come back for me."

"I'm not here to release you," I said. "I'm here to be with you."

"Oh?" said Cronus, eyebrow raised. He focused on something behind me, and I scowled. He had no right to look at Henry and Milo after everything he'd done. "In what manner?"

"As your friend. And if not that, then to keep you company." Even if I would've rather burned in a lake of fire. "No one should be alone like this for eternity."

Cronus's expression grew thoughtful. "I did not realize you cared."

"I don't," I said coolly. "I hate you for what you did to my family. I hate you for not healing Ava. I hate you for being a megalomaniac who can't see past your own desires. But you saved my son's life the day he was born, and I will never forget that." I paused. "I know what it feels like to stare into a black future with no one left in your life, and no one deserves that. So I'm going to come see you. Not every day, but enough to make sure someone's watching you. Enough to make sure you're not alone."

He narrowed his eyes. "And if I do not wish for you to come?"

"Too damn bad. This is how it's going to be whether you like it or not, so you might as well get used to it."

A long moment passed, and at last Cronus nodded. "Very well. Until then."

He disappeared into the fog, and the tendrils drifted backward until the darkness swallowed them completely. I took a shaky breath, trying to calm my racing heart, and Henry placed his hand on my back.

"I love you," he murmured. Those three words would never lose their magic. "Even if you are frustratingly good sometimes."

I brushed my fingers against Milo's cheek, reassuring myself for the hundredth time that he was still there. "Someone on the council needs to be," I said, and Henry chuckled.

"Yes, I suppose you are right. Now come." He took my hand, his touch a reminder of everything about this world that I loved. "Let's go home."

The black rock around us faded, leaving only lingering remnants of the war and heartache we'd battled. Henry was right—it would get better in time, as all things did. As much as loss had defined us, so did our capacity for hope.

And from here on out, no matter what the future had in store for us, we would face it together. Always.

★ ★ ★ ★ ★

GUIDE OF GODS

And so the GODDESS TEST
series concludes—
for now.

But Aimée Carter is
about to begin
a new series.

Turn the page for a glimpse into a new world
where a test decides your future but one girl will take destiny
into her own hands.

Available late 2013

1

UNLUCKY

Risking my life to steal an orange was a stupid thing to do, but today of all days, I didn't care about the consequences. If I were lucky, the Shields would throw me to the ground and put a bullet in my brain.

Dead at seventeen. It would be a relief.

I touched the back of my neck and tried not to wince as I hurried through the crowded market. That morning, my skin had been pale and smooth, with only a freckle below my hairline. Now that noon had come and the test was over, it was marred with black ink that would never come off and ridges that would never smooth over.

III. At least it wasn't a II, but that wasn't much of a bright side.

"Kitty," called Benjy, my boyfriend. He tucked his long red hair behind his ears as he sauntered toward me, taller than most of the others in the marketplace. Many of the women glanced at him as he passed, and my frown deepened.

I couldn't tell whether Benjy was oblivious or simply immune to my bad mood, but either way, he gave me a quick kiss. "I have a birthday present for you."

Guilt washed over me. He didn't see the orange in my hand or understand I was committing a crime. I should've never dragged him into this, but he'd insisted on coming, and I had to do this. I'd had one chance to prove that I could be worthwhile to society, and I'd failed. Now I was condemned to spend the rest of my life as something *less* than everyone in that market, all because of the tattoo on the back of my neck. Stealing a piece of fruit meant only for the IVs and successful Vs wouldn't make the rest of my life any easier, but that small gesture of resistance would be worth it, even if they arrested me. Even if they really did kill me, after all.

The orange felt like wax underneath my fingers, and I held it gently, careful not to squeeze it. This was the first and likely last time I would get to taste an orange, and I wasn't about to turn it into pulp.

Benjy opened his hand and revealed a tiny purple blossom no bigger than my thumbnail nestled in his palm, and for an irrational moment I wondered if he had stolen it, too. Nothing like that was sold in the market. Unlike me, however, Benjy would never take that risk.

"It's a violet," he said. "They're a perennial flower."

"I don't know what that means." I glanced around, and next to a booth selling pictures of the Valentine family was one boasting perfumes. Tiny purple flowers covered the table. They were only decorations, not a good. Not something that could get him killed or arrested and sent Elsewhere, like my orange. The seller must have let him take one.

"Perennial means that once they're planted, they keep growing year after year." He placed the flower in my palm and gave me a kiss on the cheek. "They never give up, like someone I happen to know."

I managed a smile. "Thank you." I sniffed the violet, but if it had a scent, it was lost in the smells surrounding us.

Despite the cool autumn day, it was sweltering inside the market. People were packed together, creating a stench that mingled with the sizzling meats, fresh fruit and hundreds of other things the vendors tried to sell. I usually didn't mind, but today it made my stomach turn.

"We need to go," I said, cupping my fingers around the flower to keep it safe. The orange in my other hand seemed to grow heavier with every second that passed, and it wouldn't be long before someone noticed us. Benjy stood out in a crowd.

His eyes flickered toward the orange, but he was silent as he followed me toward the exit, slinging his arm around my shoulders. I tensed at his touch, waiting for him to brush my hair away and spot my tattoo. He hadn't asked yet, but that courtesy wouldn't last forever.

I'd seen the posters and heard the speeches. Everyone had. We all had our rightful place in society, and it was up to us to decide what that was. Study hard, earn good grades, learn everything we could and prove we were special. And when we turned seventeen and took the test, we would be rewarded with a good job, a nice place to live and satisfaction that we contributed to our society—everything we would ever need to lead a meaningful life.

That was all I'd ever wanted: to prove myself, to prove that I was better than the Extra I really was. I deserved to exist, even though I was a second child, and the Valentines hadn't made a mistake not sending me Elsewhere.

Now my chance was over, and I couldn't even earn an average IV. Instead of living that meaningful life I'd been promised since before I could remember, I'd managed a III. There was nothing special about me—I was just another Extra who, according to the government, should have never been born in the first place.

I was a waste.

Worst of all, as much as I wanted to hate them for my III, it wasn't the government's fault. Everyone had an equal shot, and I'd blown mine. Now I had to live with the shame of having a permanent record of my failure tattooed onto the back of my neck for everyone to see, and I wasn't so sure I could do it.

Benjy and I had nearly reached the exit when a weedy man dressed in a Shield uniform stepped in front of me, his arm outstretched as he silently demanded my loot. The pistol holstered to his side left me no choice.

"I found it on the ground," I lied as I forked over the orange. "I was about to return it to the merchant."

"Of course you were," said the Shield, and he rotated his finger, a clear sign he wanted me to turn around. Benjy dropped his arm, and panic spread through me, white-hot and urging me to run.

But if I took off, he might blame Benjy, and all I could hope for now was that my stupid decision didn't affect him, too. Benjy had a month to go before he turned seventeen, and until then, he wouldn't be held responsible for his actions. Until that morning, I hadn't been either.

The stares of the crowd made my cheeks burn as I turned and gathered my dirty-blond hair away from the nape of my neck. Even if I wanted to, I couldn't hide the mark or the angry red blotch that surrounded it, still painful from the needle that had etched my rank into my skin.

Benjy stiffened at the sight of my III. I stared straight ahead, unable to look him in the eye.

The man brushed his fingertips against the mark, feeling the three ridges underneath that proved it wasn't altered. Satisfied, he dropped his hand. "Is she telling the truth?" he said, and Benjy nodded, not missing a beat.

"Yes, sir. We were on our way to the stall now." Benjy twisted around to give him a glimpse of his bare neck. "We're only here to look around."

The Shield grunted, and he tossed the orange in the air and caught it. I scowled. Was he going to let me go or force me to my knees and shoot me? Less than five feet away, browned blood from another thief still stained the ground. I forced myself not to look.

Maybe he'd send me Elsewhere instead, but I doubted it. The bastard looked trigger-happy.

"I see," he said. He leaned in closer to me, and I wrinkled my nose at his sour breath. "Did you know your eyes are the same shade as Lila Valentine's?"

Lila Valentine, the niece of the Prime Minister, was so wildly popular that hardly a week went by when someone didn't mention that the bizarre blue shade of my eyes matched hers.

"No," I said through gritted teeth. "Never heard that before in my life."

The Shield straightened. "What's your name?"

"Kitty Doe," I said, trying to keep the snarl out of my voice. No one with an ounce of self-preservation talked to a Shield like that, but after what had happened this morning, I didn't have it in me to kiss anyone's ass.

Out of the corner of my eye, I noticed Benjy frown, and I could almost hear his silent question. *What do you think you're doing?*

Stupidly risking my life, that's what.

The Shield stroked his pistol. "Stay put. Move, and I'll kill you, got it?"

I nodded mutely. Not like I could tell him no, after all.

The man turned his back, slipping through the crowd and putting several people between us. Benjy touched my elbow, and our eyes met. No need for words. I knew exactly what he was thinking.

Without hesitating, we bolted.

ACKNOWLEDGMENTS

Writing the conclusion to Kate Winters' story is one of the hardest and most rewarding things I've ever done, but it would have never been possible without the enthusiasm and support of readers.

So first and foremost, thank you—yes, you—for reading this series. I could have never done this without you.

In addition, I'd like to acknowledge and thank the following people:

As always, I would be nowhere without my magical agent, Rosemary Stimola, and her endless knowledge and support.

The entire Harlequin TEEN team, especially my incredible editor, Mary-Theresa Hussey, senior editor Natashya Wilson, and PR extraordinaire Lisa Wray. Thank you all for taking a chance on these books.

Caitlin Straw, for putting up with me every step of the way.

The ever-growing community of YA bloggers, especially those who supported this series from the beginning.

All of my writer friends, especially Courtney Allison Moulton, Carrie Harris, Lauren DeStefano, Sarah J. Maas, and Melissa Anelli.

All of the people in my life who have ever listened to me ramble about writing, especially Nick Navarre, Ally Hess, Kendall Basore, and Kristine Kempl.

The mother council, including Karla Olson-Bellfi, Barb Zdan, Mary Sweet, Lisa Rutledge, Mary Robert, and Sue Edwards-Haesler.

But most of all, I want to thank my father, Richard Carter, for all of his sacrifice, support, and corny jokes. You're the best dad I could ever ask for. Love you most.

Be sure to read the first three books in
THE GODDESS TEST NOVELS

Available wherever books are sold!

A modern saga inspired by the Persephone myth.

Kate Winters's life hasn't been easy. She's battling with the upcoming death of her mother, and only a mysterious stranger called Henry is giving her hope. But he must be crazy, right? Because there is no way the god of the Underworld—Hades himself—is going to choose Kate to take the seven tests that might make her an immortal...and his wife. And even if she passes the tests, is there any hope for happiness with a war brewing between the gods?

Also available:
The Goddess Hunt, a digital-only novella.

 **HARLEQUIN®**TEEN
™ www.HarlequinTEEN.com

HTGTSTR

From *New York Times* bestselling author

RACHEL VINCENT

SOUL SCREAMERS

The last thing you hear before you die

*Contains the first two books and ebook prequel in one!

*Contains the second and third book and the ebook novella *Reaper*.

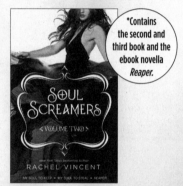

Coming April 2013

HARLEQUIN®TEEN
www.HarlequinTEEN.com

HTRVSSTR

From *New York Times* bestselling author
of The Iron Fey series
JULIE KAGAWA

BLOOD OF EDEN

Includes an exclusive excerpt from the next Iron Fey novel.

AVAILABLE NOW   COMING MAY 2013!

IN A FUTURE WORLD, VAMPIRES REIGN.

HUMANS ARE BLOOD CATTLE.

AND ONE GIRL WILL SEARCH FOR THE KEY
TO SAVE HUMANITY.

www.BloodofEden.com

HTBOETR

The Clann

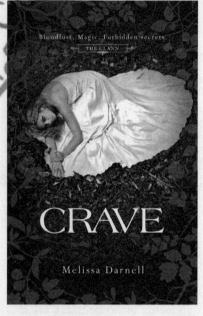

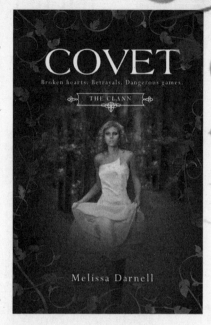

The powerful magic users of the Clann have always feared and mistrusted vampires. But when Clann golden boy Tristan Coleman falls for Savannah Colbert—the banished half Clann, half vampire girl who is just coming into her powers—a fuse is lit that may explode into war. Forbidden love, dangerous secrets and bloodlust combine in a deadly hurricane that some will not survive.

AVAILABLE WHEREVER BOOKS ARE SOLD!

Be sure to look for CONSUME
coming September 2013!

www.HarlequinTEEN.com

HTCRTR5

THE LEGACY TRILOGY

"I recommend you get this book in your hands as soon as possible."
—*Teen Trend* magazine on *Legacy*

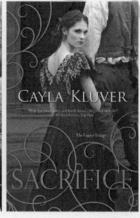

On the eve of her seventeenth birthday, Princess Alera of Hytanica faces an engagement to a man she cannot love. But she could never have imagined falling for her kingdom's sworn enemy. Amid court intrigue and looming war, Alera must fight the longings of her heart and take the crown she is destined to wear. But as magic, prophecy and danger swirl together, it will take more than courage to lead a kingdom.

AVAILABLE WHEREVER BOOKS ARE SOLD!

HARLEQUIN®TEEN
™ www.HarlequinTEEN.com

HTLEGTR6

"Michele Vail has brought Egyptian mythology into the modern world—and given it some reaper attitude! Zombies, high school, magic, and romance—what's not to love about *Undeadly?*"

—Richelle Mead

The day I turned sixteen, my boyfriend-to-be died. I brought him back to life. Then things got a little weird…

On her sixteenth birthday, Molly Bartolucci is chosen by Anubis to become a living reaper. It seems cool, until her hot new boyfriend, Rick, dies at her party—and Molly brings him back to life. That's when things get a little weird…

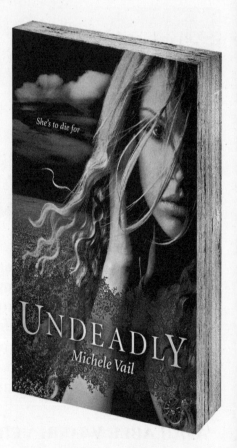

She's to die for

UNDEADLY

Michele Vail

Available wherever books are sold.

HARLEQUIN®TEEN

www.HarlequinTEEN.com

HTUTR

"A riveting and emotional ride!"

—New York Times bestselling author Simone Elkeles

No one knows what happened the night Echo Emerson got the scars on her arms. Not even Echo. Seeking the truth, Echo should know better than to get involved with Noah Hutchins, the smoking-hot loner with the bad attitude. Yet the crazy attraction between them defies all rules. Now Echo and Noah must decide how far they'll push the limits to find answers, redemption and possibly love.

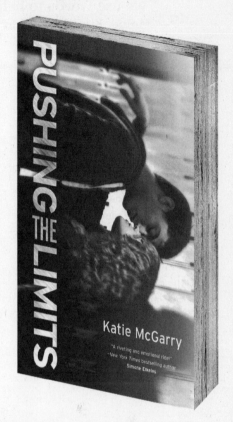

"McGarry details the sexy highs, the devastating lows and the real work it takes to build true love."

—Jennifer Echols, author of Love Story

Available wherever books are sold!

Be sure to look for *DARE YOU TO* coming June 2013!

www.HarlequinTEEN.com

HTPTLTR3

"Speechless reminds us that love is louder when we use words to help, not hurt."

—Courtney Knowles, Founder of *Love Is Louder*

Everyone knows that Chelsea Knot can't keep a secret.

Until now, because the last secret she shared turned her into a social outcast—and nearly got someone killed. Now Chelsea has taken a vow of silence—to learn to keep her mouth shut, and to stop hurting anyone else. But there's strength in silence, and in the new friends who are, shockingly, coming her way. People she never noticed before. A boy she might even fall for. If only her new friends can forgive what she's done. If only she can forgive herself.

Also available from Hannah Harrington

Saving June

Available wherever books are sold.

 **HARLEQUIN**®TEEN
™ www.HarlequinTEEN.com

HTSTR2